messy

a novel

by heather cocks &
jessica morgan

poppy

Little, Brown and Company
New York   Boston

Also by Heather Cocks & Jessica Morgan

spoiled

Authors' Note

This is a work of fiction. Characters, places, and events are the product of the authors' imaginations and are not to be construed as real. Any resemblance to actual events or persons (living or dead) is purely coincidental. Although some celebrities' names and real entities and places are mentioned, they are all used fictitiously.

Poppy

Hachette Book Group
237 Park Avenue, New York, NY 10017
Visit our website at www.lb-teens.com

Poppy is an imprint of Little, Brown and Company.
The Poppy name and logo are trademarks of Hachette Book Group, Inc.

The publisher is not responsible for websites (or their content)
that are not owned by the publisher.

First Paperback Edition: July 2013
First published in hardcover in June 2012 by Little, Brown and Company

Library of Congress Cataloging-in-Publication Data

Cocks, Heather.
Messy : a novel/by Heather Cocks and Jessica Morgan.—1st ed.
p. cm.
Summary: Brooke wants to start a blog revealing the inner workings
of Hollywood in order to be in the spotlight but has no time to
write one, so she enlists the help of a ghost-writer, seventeen-year-old
Max McCormack, who needs the money but not the hassles when
the adorable actor Brady Swift comes between them.
ISBN 978-0-316-09829-8 (hc)—ISBN 978-0-316-09828-1 (pb)
[1. Interpersonal relations—Fiction. 2. Blogs—Fiction. 3. Celebrities—
Fiction. 4. Actors and actresses—Fiction. 5. Los Angeles
(Calif.)—Fiction.] I. Morgan, Jessica, 1975– II. Title.
PZ7.C6473Mes 2012   [Fic]—dc23   2011026948

10 9 8 7 6 5 4 3 2 1
RRD-C
Printed in the United States of America

For our dads, whom we love very much

one

"YOU WERE *SO* GOOD in that movie. Talking dogs are my *favorite*."

Max McCormack felt a snicker bubbling up, like a secret, and willed it to die. Famous people—or in this case, a famous person's groupie wearing a top so small it would embarrass a bikini—were so reliably, deliciously dim.

"What was your line again?" the blonde asked, scooting so close to the guy that she was practically in his lap.

"Bow-wow-*wowza*," he boomed.

Molly Dix's foot found Max's underneath the table and began applying pressure, trying to shatter her focus. Max barely blinked. *Molly, you amateur.* They'd been friends for six months now; she should know Max's boots would be steel-toed.

Max refocused her eyes on an empty space across the L.A. eatery's sprawling patio and took a steadying breath. The rules of the game were simple: First to break paid the breakfast check. Max never broke—which was convenient, since she *was* broke—and she certainly wasn't going to start now. She assumed an expression of supremely blithe indifference and saw Molly's shoulders start to shake. *Victory is mine*, she thought triumphantly.

"Hahahaha! That's, like, the best catchphrase!" gushed the girl. "It's better than, like... what's that one part from that thing with the guy?"

"'You talkin' to me?'" the guy crowed in a terrible Robert De Niro impression.

"Right!" the girl trilled. "You're totally the Al Pacino of dogs!"

Molly's laugh caught in her throat, but she managed to turn it into an outrageous coughing fit. The lovebirds in question shot them both a dirty look, then moved a whopping one table away, as if to say, *Stop watching. Except, please don't.*

Max sat back in her chair and grinned at Molly. "Still undefeated," she said in a low voice. "Too bad for you that you're the only person I know who gets up early enough to eat with me."

Molly shook her head, amazed, and propped a Nike-clad foot on the chair to her left. "That one was impossible. I don't know how you didn't lose it."

"Years of practice," Max said. "Have you *noticed* the people at our school?"

That Max wholeheartedly approved of gawking at the rich and famous would have surprised her classmates at posh Colby-Randall Preparatory School, the majority of whom were children of celebrities, celebrities' agents, or celebrities' agents' cousins (or, at the very least, deludinoids who thought they were one miniskirt at the supermarket away from being discovered). Most of them knew Max only as the snarky green-haired girl who lived in their peripheral vision. But to Max, people-watching was the city's best free entertainment, and giving L.A.'s celebrities what they clearly wanted—attention—was a deliciously perverse way of paying it forward: Be careful what you wish for, fools.

Curling herself into a little ball on the chair—at five-two, this wasn't hard—Max mused to Molly, "I figured that living with a guy as famous as Brick Berlin would give you an ironclad poker face."

"Yeah, but my dad doesn't usually woo people at the breakfast table. Thank God," Molly said, pulling her hair into a ponytail. "But I'm still totally awkward whenever somebody famous comes for dinner. You saw me after Robert Downey Jr. brought over that *Iron Man* Bundt cake. I went catatonic."

Complicating Max's pro-gawking worldview was the fact that Molly, Max's best friend since the fall, was the until-recently secret daughter of the world's biggest movie star (both professionally and physically: Brick's biceps were like pythons). But Molly was different. She hadn't even known about Brick until last summer, right before she moved to California from Indiana; even then, she never courted notoriety, and so—other than a few accidental incidents after she'd arrived—for the most part, it didn't court her. Whereas people like the Pacino of Pooches over there went begging. It was a clear distinction.

"We might have to make this harder—like, force you to keep a straight face while standing on your head or something," Molly said, watching the couple take photos of themselves sipping from the same latte. "What is this, fifteen straight wins?"

"Sixteen," Max corrected her. "If this were an Olympic sport, I'd be on a Wheaties box."

"Yes! You'd be the Michael Phelps of eavesdropping."

"The endorsement deals would definitely solve some of my problems." Max sighed.

Sometimes Max thought Molly had invented this game as a way of springing for breakfast without getting Max up in arms about accepting charity. Max appreciated the gesture too much to fight it. Plus, Molly's Brick Berlin–funded black Amex was easily up to the task of weekly eleven-dollar coffee-and-pastry jaunts, whereas Max's bank account contained a whopping $86 and change. L.A. was not the best city to live in with parents who believed in self-sufficiency and the value of menial labor.

But what Max never told Molly was that their game

mostly functioned for her as a small daily affirmation. It was exhausting, and a tad demoralizing, living in a place where every third person thought he or she was the next big talent, and thus ignored you if you didn't look like you could buy a screenplay, buy *their* screenplay, and/or make them a star. (Nobody ever confused Max McCormack, with her neon bob and wardrobe occasionally held together by safety pins, for a Somebody.) So these eavesdropping sessions were a pleasant reminder that no matter how bored or poor Max was—or how much she dreaded going to school and hearing her classmates weep that life without the latest Louis Vuitton simply wasn't worth living—things could always be worse: She could be *that* girl, writhing on some guy's lap just because he had three platinum records. Seeing the stereotype in action was so unappealing that Max felt like the universe was validating her efforts to remain as disengaged from her schoolmates and surroundings as possible.

The prospect of an entire summer away from the ridiculousness of Los Angeles was the only thing keeping Max sane. *NYU, NYU, NYU,* she repeated to herself, like a mantra.

"You're going to shred that thing before you even fill it out," Molly said, interrupting her train of thought. Max looked down at the notebook propped up on her lap. The corner of a loose page was poking out, and she'd been absentmindedly fiddling with it so intently that it had practically disintegrated.

"*If* I ever fill it out," Max said, sighing. "My writing sample is currently a three-word essay that says, 'NYU Writing Sample.'"

"Give it time," Molly said, looking sympathetic. "Writer's block can't last forever, right?"

"I guess we'll find out." Max fished around in her bag for a pen, then wrote

McCORMACK, MAXINE E.

"There. If this were the SATs I'd be halfway to a passing grade."

Molly chuckled and checked her watch. "We need to jet," she said. "You're going to be late, and I have a meet in half an hour in Santa Monica."

"Ugh. I would seriously rather run twenty miles with your cross-country team than deal with Dennis today," Max said, quickly shoving her notebook into her bag. "I think he invented something new last night. The kitchen smelled like evil."

Max sometimes wished she could borrow Molly's old life in Indiana, where everyone had part-time jobs at nice, normal places like Barnes & Noble or Baskin-Robbins. Instead, she was working for a man whose vocation, as he loftily called it, was making artisanal meat substitutes, which he believed would save the world's animal population and win him a Nobel Prize (Max caught him practicing an acceptance speech in the employee lounge—aka the utility closet he'd outfitted with a futon and a sink). When his restaurant, Fu'd, first opened a few months ago,

Dennis's "tofu arts" were confined to basic tofurkey and veggie patties, but after some success with something he called Fauxrk Chops, he'd morphed into a mad fake-meat scientist. The smell associated with his calling was less intoxicating than simply toxic; Max was pretty sure it was only a matter of time before Dennis's fifteen minutes of fame ran out and the FDA quarantined the place.

"Good luck," Molly said. "I'll be thinking of you when Coach Petit is screaming at me to feel the burn."

Max gave Molly a half-salute farewell and jaywalked across the street, bursting through the front door just as her boss was slinking out of the back to give his speech about the day's specials.

"Thank you for joining us," Dennis sneered, rolling up his stained white sleeves over an arm tattoo that read FERGALI-CIOUS in cursive. His three-inch-tall bleached Mohawk looked limp and sticky. "So the soup today is Hearty of Lentil with Faux-cetta, and we have a new sandwich that I want you to push-push-push. It's a croque-monsieur." He paused for what he thought was dramatic effect, but which actually was just irritating. "And it's made with *real* toe ham."

All of Dennis's nonmeats had asinine mashed-up names. But even though Max's head knew he'd said *toham*, her ears (and churning stomach) heard only *toe ham*, and the stuff Dennis was waving around certainly smelled like his feet had something to do with its origins.

Dennis narrowed his beady brown eyes. "I take it from your face that you have *thoughts*, Max?" he said.

You need the money. NYU. NYU. NYU.

"Um, no. No thoughts. Just daydreams, sir," she finally said. "I was, uh, imagining whether the toham croque would be more divine with veganeddar or notzarella."

Dennis snorted. "Cute. Watch the attitude," he said, flipping the slice of toham at her. It landed with a smack against her bare forearm. "It scares the customers. Now get this place ready to go—we open in five."

The meat slithered off Max and onto the floor with a squish, like reptilian bologna. Max's skin crawled so fast she thought it might escape.

"Right, like *you're* the scary one," whispered her coworker Pete as they watched Dennis storm back out behind the café's counter.

"Don't speak too soon," Max said, swiping the toham off the floor and dangling it in front of Pete's nose. "I'm holding weaponized lunch meat, and now I know how to use it."

Pete fiddled nervously with the ring on his pointer finger. "At least you don't have to make the sandwiches." He made a mournful sound. "This is not what I moved to L.A. for. I am *totally* wasting my face back here."

He disappeared into the kitchen with a sigh. Max took her post behind the sandwich counter, rested her chin on her fist, and gazed at the café's black-and-white checkered floor, the charming wicker chairs parked at gleaming glass tables, and the painted script above the door that read ALL FU'D IS GOOD FOOD. This isn't what Hell had looked like in her imagination. In fact, when she'd read on Eater LA that a new meatless restaurant was opening up on trendy Third Street, it had sounded like an excellent place to make a few bucks. Max had been a vegetarian most of her life, and apart from being one of the only places hiring, Fu'd was conveniently just far enough south of Colby-Randall to feel removed from its social orbit. But within three weeks of being hired, two things happened to dampen her outlook: Dennis made her eat "twicken"—a tofu-wheat chicken substitute that tasted even worse than it sounded— and two actresses from the new *90210* got photographed snacking on the bacon-flavored yam jerky (which, admittedly, was delicious; Dennis was way better with vegetables). Within days, Fu'd was on the map, full of both celebs who wanted to look socially conscious and their pseudostalkers with very nosy cell-phone cameras. But the café's newfound notoriety also piqued the interest of Max's trend-obsessed classmates, most of whom regarded her with a blend of confusion and horror—to them, "having a job" was slang for getting their noses done.

"Yo!"

Great. Here they come now.

Chaz Kelly and four of his burly Colby-Randall football teammates loped up to the counter, the chains clipped to their low-riding jeans rattling like spooked snakes.

"What up, Kermit! Got any steak up in here?" Chaz boomed.

Max placed her palms flat on the mint-green Formica,

as if summoning whatever Zen it might possess. "Brilliant, Chaz," she said, tipping up her head so that she could see his face, which was a good six feet, five inches off the ground, as round as a soccer ball and about as empty. "Your wit is matched only by your literacy."

Chaz frowned. "You're so queer, Kermit," he said, flicking her hair. "Gimme a Coke. And don't get any of your head mold in it."

Chaz's football buddies all started chortling and punching his extensive biceps, onto which were tattooed smaller replicas of those exact biceps. Max gritted her teeth and turned to face the guy who stepped ahead of them in line. Her amber-flecked eyes met a warm pair of deep blue ones. Max's breath caught in her throat a little bit, just like it did every day, just like it had when she was in eighth grade and Jake Donovan had glanced at her while giving a book report on *Twenty Thousand Leagues Under the Sea*. She'd been so hypnotized by his beauty that she barely heard him saying how bummed he was to learn the title didn't refer to a bunch of underwater sports teams.

"Sorry about Chaz," Jake said. "He's my best offensive lineman, but he's kind of..."

"Offensive?" Max finished for him. "No kidding. It's a miracle that he's mentally capable of recognizing the color green."

Jake seemed apologetic. "His helmet breaks a lot," he said. "Don't worry. We're not going to be here very long.

Chaz is obsessed with Selena Gomez, and he read that she eats here sometimes, so he's scoping it out."

"How romantic," Max said, peering around at Chaz trying to use his car key to slice a hole in the knee of his two-hundred-dollar True Religions. "What should I get for them? We only serve locally sourced organic teas and tisanes."

"What's a tisane?" Jake asked.

"I have no idea," Max confessed.

"I'll just tell Chaz it's organic Gatorade," he said, slapping some bills onto the counter. "Keep the change."

As Jake headed off to join his teammates, Max allowed herself a tiny smile. Despite the fact that she'd been crushing on him for years, Jake hadn't even learned her name until after she'd given him a pep talk before last fall's school production of *My Fair Lady*. Now, if they weren't quite friends, they were definitely friends-*adjacent*. Which made Max feel slightly less pathetic. There was nothing more *obvious* than the spunky, unpopular girl having the hots for the quarterback. But secretly liking one of your friends (adjacent)? Way less like the plot of an old Freddie Prinze Jr. movie.

Max rang Jake's purchase through the register and put his change in the tip jar. She let her hand linger a second, wishing she could stuff the generous twelve-dollar surplus in her pocket. Despite working nearly every day after school and every Saturday for the last four months, she was still well short of what she needed for NYU. But everyone at Fu'd split tips—well, unless you were Dennis. Last week, when that bony girl from *Frigid Valley* had come in, Max sold her a plate of carrots and then watched as the girl did nothing but stare at it for ten minutes before slapping a Benjamin on the table and announcing that she was stuffed. Dennis had swiped the bill without a word. Two hours later, Max was at the In-N-Out drive-thru sinking her teeth into her first cheeseburger in six years. It was delicious. It tasted like spite.

"Kermit!" Chaz yelled. "What's taking so long? It's just a Coke, dude."

Dennis burst out of the kitchen and poked Max hard in the back.

"What did you do?" he demanded. "Never mind—I don't want to hear it. Just go clean out the grease traps in the tofunnator. *Now*."

Chaz made the "Oooooh" sound universal to high school boys who liked getting people in trouble. Max wanted to protest, but fighting with Dennis was always a losing battle. With a deep breath, she shoved her way into the kitchen. The smell of body odor, stale tofu, and lemon Pine-Sol hit her in the face so hard she broke into a coughing fit.

NYU. NYU. NYU.

It wasn't working.

two

The warm gun lay next to her body. Blood streaked toward the front door, which was locked from the inside. As Ileana struggled to sit up, she realized two things: She hadn't shot the gun, and she wasn't bleeding. And she was in a story I don't know how to finish. So, three things.

Max smacked the delete key and leaned back in her chair, picking at the stud in her upper ear.

"Ooooh, I like this one. It's for a 'bookeeper' with great communication skills," said Molly with a snicker from across the room. (After the day's disastrous shift, Max had called her over for an emergency job-hunting session.) "What this woman actually needs is a proofreader, although I love the idea of you running around locking up all her old boyfriends."

Max grunted.

> Mack Duncan stared at the spleen on the floor. It looked like a giant slug and smelled like it had been cooking in the heavy South Florida heat for about a week and oh my God this was on *CSI: Miami* last week and it ended with him saying "a murder most ob-spleen" aaaaaaaaaaargh

The application wasn't due until May—the program's founder was a Colby-Randall alum who mandated that a spot be held each year for a student of his alma mater's choosing—but Max had been trying for weeks now to churn out a good writing sample. *Applicants for New York University's creative writing apprenticeship program will submit an original work or essay of no fewer than three thousand words, demonstrating the ability to develop compelling characters, plot, and tone,* the instructions read. So far, Max had started, and erased, about thirteen stories whose characters, plot, and tone made her want to puke all over her keyboard. It was so much easier writing stuff for school or scribbling bits and pieces in her spiral-bound notebooks, piles of which were shoved under her bed for posterity (or to give everyone something really amusing to do at her funeral, when she was too dead to be mortified). But this was the first thing she'd ever written that actually counted for something, beyond a letter grade scrawled on the corner of the page next to another one of Ms. Perkins's stains of dubious origin. The last one smelled like Thai curry.

"I don't suppose you're secretly a registered nurse," Molly said. "You could make fifty bucks an hour at Botox parties if you're willing to stab people's faces with needles."

> The keg rolled into Digger Bond's leg, nudging him awake and forcing him to confront the fact that [insert event here] had not gone as planned. His first clue: [something hilarious]. His second clue: He sucks and I'm going to be a waitress forever.

Delete delete delete . . .

"Or you could get paid a hundred bucks an hour to shoot video of your feet stepping on milk cartons."

Max jerked up her head. "What?"

Her friend grinned. "Finally. My next step was selling your eggs just to get your attention."

"Sorry," Max said. "I'm kind of distracted. I think getting assaulted by fake meat sucked out my writing mojo."

"All the more reason to stop banging on that thing and get over here and look at craigslist with me," Molly said good-naturedly. "I'm not sure I can do this by myself anymore. I had no idea how many people wanted to invest in other people's ovaries."

"Oh, you haven't even gotten to the good ones," Max

said, pushing herself away from the old iMac on her desk and plopping down on her bed's torn quilt next to Molly and her laptop. "Last month I almost applied to be some old lady's 'bird manicurist' just because I wanted to see the inside of her house. You know that place was full of those creepy collectible babies you can buy off the back of *Soap Opera Digest*."

"So you're saying I should return the one I got you for your birthday?"

Max laughed. When Molly had moved to Los Angeles from the tiny Indiana town of West Cairo, she and Max had clicked into the kind of rapport Max rarely had with people. Maybe it was because Molly hadn't known Max was the headmistress's daughter the first time they'd talked, or maybe Molly was too nice to care about being socially associated with the offspring of an authority figure (unlike everyone else at any school Max had ever attended). Either way, Max appreciated feeling like she had an ally against all those Colby-Randall Stepford teens. And when Molly—after a brief stress-induced detour back to the Midwest—decided to return to L.A. for good to make it work with her crazy family, she'd made Max promise to keep her sane and calm now that she lived in a house with stone lions in the driveway and its own climbing wall. Perfect social symbiosis.

"Okay, seriously, though, how about being an English tutor?" Molly now said. "You're into writing. That might be fun."

"Nah, it says here you have to send in a completed script, no rights reserved," Max said. "Sounds fishy. And it's five bucks an hour. I make more than that scrubbing Dennis's grease traps." She frowned at the screen. "Which, thank God, is not a euphemism, unlike the listing here that says it wants a girl who can work a feather duster."

"Gross!" Molly squirmed. Then she rummaged for her phone. "What time is it?"

Max pointed to the computer's clock. "Six forty-three. Why, are you and Teddy heading out?"

Molly tried to tuck her russet bangs behind her ear, but they weren't grown out enough yet, so they just flopped back into her face. "He's taking me for Indian food after practice. It was my mom's favorite. It would've been her birthday today. Or...I mean, technically I guess it's still her birthday."

Molly's mother had died the previous summer, after blurting out Molly's parentage secret on her deathbed. Even after years of watching *Lust for Life*—whose stories ranged from dramatic confessions to face transplants to, according to Internet spoilers, the love story between an AWOL Air Force nurse and the handsome circus ring-master she recently recapitated—Max never imagined she'd know someone to whom anything that soapy actually happened.

Max smacked her forehead. "Oh, my God. I am a *jackhole*," she announced. "You mentioned that last week and I totally forgot. I'm sorry, Molly."

But Molly smiled.

"It's okay," she said. "Actually, I'm kind of glad you forgot. I'm sick of being Dead Mom Girl. The other day Brooke asked if it would be cathartic to watch *Beaches*."

Max snorted. "Yes, Brooke Berlin is so sensitive to people's pain," she said. Molly's half sister, whom Max had disliked since the eighth grade (the duration of which Brooke spent calling her "little boy"), was something of a tornado of self-involvement. When Molly arrived in Southern California, the sisters had gotten off to what could be described charitably as a rocky start. "It must have really soothed your wounds when she tried to make the whole country think you were some scabby alcoholic hussy."

"Well, that was by accident," Molly defended Brooke. At Max's expression, she amended, "Okay, some of it was an accident. But in a weird way, all of that drama with leaking stuff to *Hey!* turned out to be the best thing that could've happened. I think I kind of needed a nuclear moment to realize how much I wanted to fight to make things work here."

"Brooke Berlin *is* a nuclear moment, that is true."

"All right, all right, no more Brooke bashing," Molly said. "We've been getting along pretty well since I decided to stay in L.A. The mink slippers she got me for Christmas are really comfortable."

"She also got you a *wig*."

Molly giggled. "She thought I might want to wear it while I grew out these bangs."

"I guess that *is* kind of funny," Max said grudgingly.

"See? Even you have to admit that she's been a lot better since we made up."

"A bit better," Max allowed. "In a very Brooke way. And mostly only to you. But look, I'm happy about that. You deserve a break."

"Thanks," Molly said, picking at a stray thread on Max's quilt. "You and Teddy have been awesome. I'd probably be in a mental hospital if you hadn't decided to eat lunch with me that first week."

"That's true. I am a hero," Max said with a nod. "How are things going with Teddy, anyway?" She paused. "Wait, hang on. I should warn you that I both care and am completely grossed out discussing my brother's love life. Okay. Please continue."

"I will spare you the juiciest details," Molly said, grinning. "But things are good. Really good. It's kind of awkward at school sometimes, though. The other day Chaz Kelly saw us hugging and yelled at us to save it for prom night, and your mom was standing *right there*."

"I heard about that," Max said. "But I also heard him ask Jake whether he should get his left fist tattooed onto his right fist, so I would go ahead and assume even my mother knows Chaz is an asswagon."

"Please promise me you'll never use that word in front of Bone," said a voice from the vicinity of the doorway, followed by the form of Max's brother, Teddy, shuffling into the room. "He's looking for an insult that rhymes with *dragon*."

"Sounds like band practice was…educational," Molly said.

"I don't know why you put up with Bone Johnson's lame-ass lyrics," Max scoffed. "I swear, I've never heard anything more tragic than the song where he rhymed *shrubbery* with *secret hot-tubbery*."

"Yes, but the ladies love his wounded soul, or something," Teddy said, plopping down into the overstuffed armchair in the corner of Max's room after brushing away three socks, two folded crosswords, and a plate with a two-day-old sandwich crust on it. "Maybe I should invite him over here. Show him what real tragedy looks like." He sniffed the air. "Is that topheasant?"

Max threw a pillow at him. "Shut up. I have to get out of that smellhole and I only have two more minutes of Molly's help before she clocks out," she said. "Or else I might get desperate and reply to this ad for…" Max paused. "Wait. I could make *twenty-five grand* as a surrogate mother? For that money I could be Juno, no problem."

Teddy nodded very seriously. "You *do* own a lot of hoodies."

"Hey, how about this one: 'Wanted: same-age Official Blogographer for teen actress/It Girl's social media empire. Competitive pay, social and lifestyle perks, complimentary Diet Coke,'" Molly read. "Actually, that's kind of perfect."

"Are you cracked out?" Max retorted. "I would never in a million years work for one of those nutjobs. Also, in this town, 'lifestyle perks' usually means 'colonics.'"

"I actually like this idea," Teddy said, rubbing his hands together. "My sister, the professional hanger-on."

"Because I *so* want to fetch dry cleaning and, like, be forced to buy this girl meth in a bathroom stall," Max countered.

"Just think, in four months you could be dating a Jonas brother."

"Or dumping a drink on him."

"Will you still talk to us when you're wrangling her gown at the Oscars?" Teddy pretended to fret.

"Give her a break, Teddy," Molly said, laughing. "Seriously, Max, maybe you should think about it. You want to write. This is a writing job. You could probably do it at home half the time. And aren't you even a little bit curious?"

"Oh, no, not Maxine," Teddy said. "She doesn't believe in how the other half lives."

"What is wrong with thinking it's ridiculous, for example, to pay a facialist to exfoliate you with diamond dust?" Max said hotly. "And it doesn't even help. Jennifer Parker *still* looks like she fell asleep on a pizza."

"Maybe this *is* Jennifer," Molly mused. "I heard her saying the other day that she's working on adding a message board to JenniferParker.com, because she's applying to be on *Celebrity Roller Derby.*"

" 'Celebrity'? Please. *Cancún Barracuda Swarm* was two years ago, and I think it might've even gotten yanked *while* it was airing."

"Yeah, but not before the scene where one of them ate her face," Teddy said. "It was so moving, Molly. Max made me watch it with her because Jake tweeted—"

"Aren't you guys late for something?" Max said frostily.

Molly closed her laptop and stood up, squeezing Max's shoulder. "Look, I know it seems bleak, but I promise you are not going to be making toham sandwiches for the rest of your life."

Teddy joined her near the door. "That blog thing could be a pretty painless gig," he said. "Maybe writing about something else every day will cure your writer's block."

"Who says I have writer's block?" Max said, shooting a poisonous look at Molly.

"Your delete key," Teddy said. "I can hear it crying all the way up in my room. You have a signature deletion pattern, sometimes mixed in with just bashing the keyboard with your palms, like it's a drum—"

"Go away now."

"Maybe if you tried writing a romance novel? I hear they're timeless, and full of artsy synonyms for—"

"OUT."

Max saw Molly smack Teddy lightly as he closed the door while reaching for her hand with his other arm. Max sighed. She really *was* happy for the two of them—they'd spent most of Molly's first six weeks in Los Angeles not admitting they were into each other, and all the unsubtle yearning was more annoying than the hand-holding. But having your best friend date your brother meant you had

22

to share custody, and Max hadn't felt done with Molly yet today. She still needed a job. Or a writing topic. Both.

She flopped back down into her desk chair.

> Matilda swept her fiery bangs out of her eyes and glared at the muscled laird standing before her, his kilt leaving little to the imagination as he mounted his steed and said, "asdfjkl'asdfjk; agkhltkjhk."

She stopped her hand on its way to the delete key, then highlighted it all and clicked Cut instead. *Take that, Teddy.*

Since she obviously wasn't getting anywhere with her submission, Max opened up a new browser window and headed back to craigslist. There it was again: *official blogographer.* It was terrible word. A nonexistent mash-up. Weren't *real* words good enough anymore?

On the other hand, *blogographer* had nothing on — and nothing to do with — *toham.*

Max leaned back in her rickety wooden chair and took stock of things. At this rate, she wouldn't get into the NYU program, because she couldn't make her brain operate above a fourth-grade level, probably because she spent every day inhaling lethal meat-substitute fumes. Dennis was pickling her brain. And then stealing her tips.

Her eyes drifted around her room, past the giant heap where her hamper had exploded, across the posters of classic Keanu Reeves movies (Max had decided in middle school that his rampant awfulness came back around to making him amazing), finally settling on the gray-and-red paisley wallpaper that was peeling in several places. Her dad had promised her room would be next to be renovated, but then he'd lost his job at Cal Tech and she'd overheard her parents having a tortured conversation about how they'd make ends meet on her mother's salary. Max had marched right in on them and announced how much she loved paisley.

So even though CRAPS—Max's favorite nickname for Colby-Randall Preparatory School—paid Mrs. McCormack enough that they weren't poverty-stricken, they definitely weren't rolling in spare cash. Max knew she had to fend for herself if NYU was going to happen, and that might require drastic measures. Casting a furtive sidelong glance at the door, Max clicked the "Reply to" link.

Relax, she scolded herself. Probably nothing would come of it, anyway, and it could just be her dirty secret. But Molly and Teddy were at least a little bit right. If writing was the end game, a job doing *any* writing had to be better than where she was now. Whoever Teen Actress/It Girl was, she couldn't possibly be any worse than assault with a deadly sandwich meat.

three

"...AND SO I WAS, like, Mom, of *course* the Chloé bag is fine, but it's not like it's *Chanel*."

With a shrill laugh that echoed sharply in the school's high-ceilinged hallway, Jennifer Parker and three of her cronies brushed past Max—bumping roughly into her arm without acknowledging it, as if Max's limb were merely very thick air—toward Mr. Kemp's classroom. Max cursed her predictable bad luck. Of *course* Jennifer was on the Colby-Randall Spring Carnival Planning Committee. Far be it from Max to make it through one semester without being forced to hear Jake Donovan's girlfriend drone on about how she was one audition away from getting a *final* audition to read for the part of Third Cheerleader on the Left in one of the straight-to-DVD *Bring It On* sequels.

"*So* tremendous to see you, too," Max groused at their backs. But none of them answered. In Max's experience, nobody ever had much to say to a headmistress's kid except "You're not going to tell on us, are you?" Her mother would say this was because Max tried to push everyone away, with her caustic tongue and her neon coif. Teddy—to whom this problem did not apply, because he was in a rock band, which was so Hollywood—would say it was because of her habit of preemptively thinking everyone sucked. But Max knew better: Everyone *did* suck. They always had. Following her mom to three different L.A.-area schools had taught Max that much, from being kicked in the face in fourth-grade gym by a future Olympian who told her to "get out of the way of greatness"; to getting stuck at a table in sixth-grade art with Carla Callahan, the kid from the *E.T.* sequel *E.E.T.*, who did nothing but make dots on paper with her Hello Kitty pencil while yapping about how Spielberg thought she was the next Anna Paquin (and yet still got an A for her "brave minimalist approach"); to Jennifer Parker, whose credentials for social greatness included one long-dead sitcom and a string of execrable made-for-TV movies, most recently *The Pied Viper*, about a murderous flute player. Max had nothing to say to these people. If she was destined to be a pariah, better to do it on her own terms.

Max hung back from following them into the classroom. She felt jittery and weird. Not at the prospect of spending more time marinating in her and her classmates' mutual hostility—sometimes that could be invigorating—but because after this, she had a meeting with YourNewItGirl@gmail.com. At It Girl's suggestion, they were meeting for dinner at Mel's Drive-In on Sunset to see if they had "a copacetic rapport." Max focused her nervous energy on retying her Doc Marten boots and trying to brush the fine film of chalk dust off her black skirt. It had never recovered from this morning's blackboard race in calculus. Nobody else had come out of class looking like a powdered doughnut. Maybe designer pants repelled dirt in a way H&M's one-ply cotton could not.

Swatting at her skirt was just making the situation worse, so Max gave up and leaned against the wall to watch other kids trickling into the meeting—prim student-government types, a couple of overeager freshmen, and Magnus Mitchell and some other athletes who were clearly there for their college transcripts or under parental duress. Max could relate to that. Mrs. McCormack tried to force school spirit into Max by prescribing extracurriculars as punishments, in the hope that one of them would stick (the carnival planning committee was for routinely ditching her last two classes to drive down to Irvine to go to concerts). It was a cunning plan, in theory; alas, if only the esteemed Headmistress Eileen McCormack had known that the motherly and teacherly pushing made Max *less* interested, and in fact made her want to drop out of high school altogether in favor of being one of those stoner trustafarians who panhandled in front of

The Grove. Except without the trust fund. Or the drugs. So, basically, a loiterer.

"Are you coming in, Max?" asked Mavis Moore as she passed by.

"I guess," Max said, shouldering her book bag. She glanced down at the tangled gray lump under Mavis's arm, which had long skinny needles poking out of it. "Your colon is looking good."

Mavis, a fellow junior described most diplomatically as "quirky," had been knitting her way through the human body since spring of sophomore year.

"Thanks," Mavis said proudly, holding up what looked like a soft, squishy sausage. "I'm almost done. Just a few major organs left. I've got the spleen going at home."

Max grinned. "You know, if you could mass-produce those, you'd probably be a millionaire. It's either a great study aid or something doctors could safely throw at the TV screen whenever *Grey's Anatomy* makes up something idiotic."

Mavis blinked several times rapidly. "I would never sell my innards," she said, wandering into the classroom.

"I love that girl," Max said under her breath. For every ten Jennifer Parkers with their competitive Chanel and razor-sharp elbows, there was at least a Mavis to keep things fresh.

Mr. Kemp's room had been chosen for the meeting, ostensibly because the tall, arching windows got fabulous natural light, but Max spoke CRAPS fluently enough to know that translated to "Because there is a perfect view of lacrosse practice." As if anyone needed such a hormonal excuse to like that room—in fact, all the rooms at Colby-Randall were beautiful. The school was a rambling old estate that had, over the years, annexed surrounding properties and either converted or rebuilt them. The result was a lot of newfangled outbuildings (like the Brick Berlin Theater for Serious Emotional Artistry that rose like a white shark fin from the ground by the man-made lake) surrounding the majestic old main house, with its lead-paned windows, dark wood paneling, creaky old floors, and closets that were surely as full of juicy secrets as they were of upperclassmen making out. It would be perfect for a horror film. Half of Max's classmates were Jennifer-flavored zombies, anyway; she could just turn a camera on and let it roll.

As soon as Max headed in, she saw Jake Donovan sitting next to Jen in the back row. "Over here, dude," he called out.

Max felt a wave of pride, then quickly squashed it. She didn't want to be the kind of girl who trembled every time a popular kid acknowledged her existence.

"Ugh, you can't sit here," Jennifer whined, throwing a pained look at Max's clothes. "I'm allergic to dust."

"Then how come you auditioned for that horse movie?" Jake asked, befuddled.

"Sweetie, movie sawdust is hypoallergenic," Jennifer said, as if addressing a very small child. "It's make-believe. Like Fox News."

"Did you get the part?" Max asked. "Or did they give it to an actual horse?"

Jake snorted gleefully. Max turned to face front, but not before she saw Jennifer whip out her cell phone and start typing. No doubt this would make for a frosty Twitter update. Jake and Jen were constantly sniping at each other through the Internet. As much as Max liked Jake's congenial doofyness—and his hot, hot face—she couldn't figure out why he and Jennifer were still dating. Did the universe give Jake six-pack abs in exchange for common sense?

"Okay, everybody," Max heard a familiar, commanding voice say. "Let's bring to order the first meeting of the Colby-Randall Spring Carnival Planning Committee."

A hush fell over the room as Molly's half sister Brooke Berlin walked into it, immediately owning the space with her imposing height and, of course, even *more* imposing paternal pedigree. Brooke was alternately adored and feared by everyone in the school. Until last fall she was mostly feared, thanks to her tendency toward bossy, imperious behavior; however, after her nemesis Shelby Kendall broadcast some very personal letters of Brooke's on the school news station, everyone developed sympathetic amnesia about the many ways Brooke had terrorized them. Now she was seen as more of a benevolent dictator, less Kim Jong Il than a very bronzed Simon Cowell. Max tried to tolerate Brooke for Molly's sake, but after years of being treated like a piffling underling, she privately would've enjoyed it if Brooke seared off every last blonde hair in a tragic tanning-booth accident.

Brooke took a central position behind Mr. Kemp's desk, flanked by her sophomore assistant (legal name: Martha; painfully trendy Brooke Berlin–created pseudonym: Brie, bestowed on her like a charitable donation) and a couple of fidgety juniors and seniors. One of them was Anna Fury, whose mother, the infamous Judge Fury, had the country's number one syndicated courtroom show. Anna whipped out a gavel from her purse and rapped it so vigorously on the desk that she almost conked Brooke in the chin.

"Anna!" Brooke barked. "This is not Mommy's courtroom. Put it away."

Anna shrank back toward the blackboard. It was hard to pull a power trip based on your mom's daytime TV show in front of Brooke Berlin, whose father's face was on no fewer than four billboards within a half-mile radius of the school.

Brooke cleared her throat and shook her long blonde curls away from her shoulders. "As you know, this year is the twenty-fifth anniversary of the carnival, and as such, I fully intend for it to kick serious ass," she began. "Not that it will be so hard to beat last year's. I don't know what Keely Harris was smoking when she went with the Tribute to Ryan Seacrest theme. Anyway, I'm sure I'll come up with the perfect idea myself eventually, but first let's be democratic about it."

Jennifer's hand shot up. "The movies of Brick Berlin!"

31

she practically panted. *"Amendment to Hell* has that whole Ferris wheel chase scene!"

Even Brooke, who counted Jennifer among her best friends, rolled her eyes. "No."

"How about an Ode to Shopping?" suggested Justine McGrath, whom Max recognized as being on the cross-country team with Molly. "Each ride could be, like, themed by a different brand. The Christian Loveboatin tunnel, a Jimmy Choo-choo..."

"...a Silence of the L.A.M.B. funhouse, with real kidney snacks," Max piped up.

Justine scowled.

"Anybody else? Anybody *serious*, who actually *cares* about things other than sarcasm?" Brooke said, glaring at Max. "Come on, people. We are the highly educated leaders of tomorrow. And also, I don't have all day. Barneys won't hold those new Brian Atwoods for me past six."

"How about a courtroom theme?" Anna suggested hopefully.

"No, do vampires!" called out Emily Matsuhisa. "My dad's restaurant just catered the birthday of one of the *Twilight* special-effects guys, so I bet we could get a deal on fake blood."

"The music of Katy Perry!" Magnus shouted. "My mom once dated her manager!"

"What if we made it like a mini-Disneyland?" said Jennifer. "I once did a Disney TV series, as you all know, so I have major pull."

Max couldn't help snorting.

Jennifer raised her hand. "Brooke, can I move to eject anybody who isn't willing to be a positive creative force in this room?"

"Why *are* you here, Max?" Brooke asked. "Don't you hate anything fun?"

Max smiled innocently. "I don't see any of that here, so we're good."

Brooke crossed her arms. "I'm sure your mother would be very upset to hear that you're not giving this carnival your all. I'd just be devastated if you got grounded and missed the three days your clothes came back into style."

"Fine," said Max. "How about Justin Bieber? Or '*The Crucible*: A Celebration,' or why not just build a replica of the Taj Mahal, *that* seems totally rational and affordable...."

"Oh, Max," Brooke said, shaking her head sadly. "Bollywood is *so* last year."

The room exploded as people volleyed suggestions left and right. Max sank back in her chair and stared up at the clock hanging over the chalkboard. Four ten. Just another ninety minutes or so and she'd be due at Mel's to meet her random actress. If only she'd blown off this committee meeting, she'd have had time to drive home and change. Today she felt extra conscious of living in a Fendi world on a Forever 21 budget. Especially since she just noticed that her shirt had a hole in the sleeve.

There was a barely audible thud as a triangle of paper

landed near her feet. Pretending to pick lint off her tights, Max swiped the clumsily folded note off the floor and opened it in her lap.

IF I START SNORING PLEASE KICK ME BEFORE JENNIFER THINKS IT'S MY THEME SUGGESTION.

Max grabbed her pen and wrote:

A nap-themed carnival might be better than whatever Justine just said about Betty White.

When Jake read it, he laughed under his breath. Max noticed Jennifer doing that thing where she was pretending to gaze out the window but was in fact actually watching Jake. After a respectable amount of time had lapsed, Max fished her phone out of her pocket and pulled up Facebook. Jennifer's status update read *Lacrosse players soooooo much hotter than football players, fyi.* Social media really was a godsend when it came to spying on people who had no filter. If only Max were up for a gig writing the blogography of the Jake and Jennifer relationship. She was already an expert.

✦ ✦ ✦

"Max, wait up!"

Max stopped on her way across the school's front lawn and saw Molly jogging toward her. "I just wanted to wish you luck at your meeting with Miley Cyrus," she panted, wiping the sweat off her face with the hem of her CRAPS Track and Field Invitational T-shirt.

"If it is Miley Cyrus, I may lobotomize myself with a milk shake spoon."

"I think this is the part where I tell you to keep an open mind," Molly said, pulling her right foot into a stretch behind her back. "Charmaine thinks it's Heidi Montag. She wants to know how freaky Heidi looks in person."

"I find it suspicious that some random girl in Indiana knows all my secrets," Max said.

"Not any of the important ones," Molly said lightly. "Oh, but she did tell me to say that you should stop reading Jennifer's Twitter."

"Not a chance," Max said. "The last hour of the meeting she tweeted six things about how quarterbacks have weak calves."

Molly snorted. "Okay, I'm off. Teddy and I are supposed to go see *The Hangover 3D*, and I stink from practice. Have fun with the chick from *Jonas L.A.*"

"You won't be laughing when it turns out to be Dakota Fanning," Max called out as Molly sped off.

Dragging her backpack carelessly behind her, Max walked the short distance to her car. Unlike Teddy's 4Runner, which he had paid for by selling his comic book collection, Max's yellow Chevy wagon was an inheritance from their aged neighbor who'd had his license revoked due to glaucoma. The tailpipe was hanging by an intricate duct-tape braid, and the back right window had gotten smashed by the kid across the street during his BB-gun phase, so it was covered in Saran Wrap and taped along the sides.

Calling this car a hunk of junk was exceedingly tactful. People at CRAPS were so terrified of it, they refused to park near her. So some days, like today, Max parallel parked across three front spots, just to do it.

She unlocked the door, pushed the button on the handle, and yanked upward. It opened with a loud groan. Dakota Fanning was going to *love* that. Max putt-putted out of the lot, pointing her car down the canyon road toward Sunset, then turning right and cruising the short distance to Mel's, a Hollywood landmark of a greasy spoon. It was an odd choice for a meeting, which maybe was precisely why It Girl picked it. Maybe it was a test. Or maybe she wasn't as scene-obsessed as all the wannabes at Colby-Randall.

Max parked at Mel's and pulled out a wrinkled red cardigan from behind the driver's seat. That and her *Bachelor*-branded notebook were the two hallmarks she'd given to It Girl so she'd recognize her. These were, in Max's way, *also* a test. Because if this girl didn't understand the secret comic genius of that train wreck of a show, or offered to pay for her dry cleaning, then she wasn't Max's platonic work soul mate at all.

She slid into a booth and ordered a chocolate malt, putting her notebook right at the edge of the table. Her heart thumped. Max realized this felt uncomfortably like a blind date, and worse, she was actually *nervous*. Maybe she'd been counting on this gig more than she'd thought.

"You have *got* to be kidding me. WordNerd94 is *you*?"

Max felt a cold, creeping sensation spread slowly across her chest. She looked up at the golden curls framing a face she knew all too well, a face that wore an expression of disbelief tinged with amusement. Her heart sank.

"Well, well, well, Maxine. So you want to be my employee?"

four

BROOKE BERLIN ALWAYS EXPECTED things to go her way. *Eventually.* History backed her up: The events of six months ago, when her father's secret love child moved in with them and temporarily ruined her life, could have gone *much* more horrifyingly than they did. Sure, she and Molly had gone through a rough patch that ended in Brooke accidentally chasing her back to Indiana, but they were past that now, thanks in part to her and Brick taking a nightmarishly rustic road trip to West Cairo to win Molly back. When they'd arrived, after three days without hair product and sweating oil from eating mostly Sonic Tater Tots, Molly swore she'd already decided to come back—but Brooke figured her and Brick's disheveled patheticness lent their pleas a sincerity that helped the cause. (Even so, as soon as Molly's intentions were clear, Brooke wasted no time in making Brick sell his god-forsaken RV and fly them home on a private jet, like civilized people. Even sincerity had its limits.) Now, several months hence, she and Molly had slowly settled into a sisterly routine. Molly was as well adjusted as anyone could ask, which Brooke attributed to her own recent efforts to look past her sister's ill-conceived bangs and humble hayseed beginnings and find the kindred spirit within. They were, if not terribly alike, very bonded. Score another one for Brooke Berlin.

So Brooke assumed her blogographer ad would be a hit. Surely any rational, breathing human would leap at the chance to get in on a budding showbiz empire, especially once they realized she was the daughter of the man who coined the phrase "*Sayonara*, scumsucker." But getting a response after just five minutes exceeded even *her* imagination. Of course, that response had been from a guy sending her a picture of his feet, but it had started the ball rolling: In quick succession she got two e-mails from people asking if she knew Taylor Lautner, one from a girl who wanted to know if they'd be in *Seventeen* together, and then a reply from WordNerd94. It was sparse—just a brief mention of writing aspirations—but also spelled correctly. Way more promising than the one that followed, from a thirty-six-year-old man wanting to write a piece called "Dear Jake Gyllenhaal, I'd Like to Buy Your Vowel."

Max finally closed her gaping mouth. "Brooke."

"Max."

"Brooke."

"Max," Brooke said again, impatiently. "Can we move on to some other words?"

"Sorry," Max said. "It's just that the ad said 'teen actress/ It Girl,' so I was expecting some sort of, you know...teen actress/It Girl."

"And *I* was expecting someone who isn't the social equivalent of menstrual cramps," Brooke retorted. "Tough day all around."

This depressing turn of events was the opposite of what Brooke had pictured. Obviously, she wanted her blog strategy to work. She *needed* it to work. But she'd envisioned it involving a bookish beauty who would be eternally grateful to Brooke for changing her life, beginning with a makeover that blossomed her into a spunky mini-Brooke, and continuing through highly nurturing shopping and social adventures. Instead, Brooke's best candidate was her high school's resident pale, acid-tongued loner whose gold-tinged eyes and green hair made her look like a refugee from some nerdy movie about elves.

A model-esque beauty in trendy glasses appeared behind Brooke's shoulder. "Max McCormack? Surely you jest."

"We covered that part already," Brooke told Arugula, relieved that her best friend had arrived to diffuse some of the awkwardness. "We're already up to the bit where I say, 'But aren't you some kind of antiestablishment shut-in?'"

Max stood up. "I have a sudden urge to go behead all my old Barbies."

"Oh, please. Don't be so melodramatic." Arugula scooted into the booth. "Maybe this is destiny. Maybe the hand of fate is trying to give you a massage."

Max glared stonily at Arugula. Brooke stifled a snicker. She and Ari had been best friends for ages, long before anyone—including Arugula—figured out Ari was the class genius. Brooke liked basking in the reflected glory of her friend's intelligence, but sometimes it was hard to keep a straight face.

"Whether fate is getting handsy or not, Arugula does have a point," Brooke opined. "Obviously you answered my ad for a reason."

Max smacked the table. "God, that ad. I am going to kill Molly for not telling me it was you."

"I don't run everything I do past Molly," Brooke said, offended. "We may be sisters, Max, but we are our own people."

"Sure. Whatever."

Brooke studied Max. There was nothing to indicate that she'd be a particularly successful writer. But then again, Brooke had always assumed from their previous interactions that Max didn't have any ambition to be anything except sarcastic, and that she would live out her days as a cranky drugstore cashier, staring pointedly at all the weird things people had in their baskets and trying to make the kids buying condoms feel really uncomfortable. The fact that she'd confided career aspirations in an e-mail to someone she thought was a total stranger made Brooke wonder if Max had hidden depths.

"Okay. I can't afford to waste the time I've carved out in my schedule," Brooke said, feeling decisive. "And since I skipped Yogilates, we might as well do this."

"Oh, no," Max said. "I'm not staying. I need an actual job."

"This *is* an actual job, and technically, you have already stayed," Brooke said. "Obviously you're not my first choice, but maybe you'll be good practice for interviewing *real* applicants."

She pulled a clipboard out of her giant leather bag and brightly clicked open a pen that said *Avalanche!* on the side.

"That's your dad's latest, right?" Max said. "The one he's shooting in Florida?"

"Yes," Brooke said, pleased as she always was when people were abreast of her father's career. "Would you like me to get you a pen?"

"It is my life's ambition to advertise such an impressive feat of cinema verité."

Brooke shook back her curls and leveled Max with a smile that said, *Nice try, but you can't provoke me.* "Let's start at the beginning," she said. "What do you think of my shoes?"

Max shook her head and rose. "They're blue. That's what I think. And since that is totally not a real question, I'm going to go home to catch the *Lust for Life* prime-time special. Julianna is supposed to find out that her recapitation surgery is illegal and that Pip's head might get reclaimed."

Brooke put down her pen and affixed Max with a very serious look. "God invented the DVR for a reason," she said. "Sit down and respect the process."

Max appeared to be wrestling with something, perhaps a very muscular inner demon, and then plonked back down. Brooke mentally patted herself on the back. She knew she had a way of making it hard for people to wriggle out of things. She'd inherited it from Brick. It was how she kept managing to wrangle Molly into driving her places (at last count, Brooke had flunked her written driver's test six times, although it wasn't her fault—that stupid rectangular manual was ergonomically nightmarish to read).

"My shoes?" she prompted.

"They look like you left your feet outside a Siberian tree farm for three weeks."

Wrong, but at least it was creative. Brooke silently ticked the box on her form that read *Pithy Turn of Phrase.* "Favorite outfit of mine?"

"Are you ser—"

"Respect the process."

"I like whatever it is you're wearing when I'm not around you."

Brooke nodded and made another mark, this time next to *Sass Factor.* The waitress slammed Max's chocolate malt onto the table.

"Interesting," Arugula murmured, reaching over to check a box with a flourish. This one read *Can I Sneak Fattening Snacks?*

"You Tyra Banks?" the waitress asked, flicking her thumb at Arugula's head.

"Yes," Arugula deadpanned. "*Top Model* auditions are in two days at 4100 Bar in Silver Lake. Seven AM sharp. Bring your bikini waxer."

The waitress skipped away, looking exponentially more cheerful.

"You sent her to Silver Lake?" Brooke whispered. "There are *hipsters* there."

"It will be character-building," Ari said primly. "Now, Max, who is your celebrity role model?"

"Brooke Berlin."

Arugula's lip twitched. "Present company excluded."

"Courtney Love, obviously."

"Style motto?" Brooke asked.

" 'I shop to avoid nudity.' "

"How noble," Arugula muttered.

"Best *American Idol* winner?"

"Duh, Kelly Clarkson. I can't even joke about that," Max said.

"How many of Daddy's four Dirk Venom movies have you seen?" Brooke continued.

"Three," Max replied. "I skipped the second one because I don't believe in Kate Hudson."

Brooke looked up, surprised. "That's actually my ideal correct answer."

"Some truths are too powerful to ignore."

Brooke regarded Max curiously. "Let me just confer with my associate for a minute." She turned to Arugula. "So what do you think?"

"Well, she dresses like one of the orphans in *Annie*."

"Mmm. And she eats dairy."

"And I think her hairdresser also did my parents' hedge maze."

From across the table, Max cleared her throat exaggeratedly. "I'm *right here*."

Brooke looked at her. "Yes, you are. Tell me, why *is* that?"

"Me? Why are *you* here?" Max countered. "If you were really an It Girl, wouldn't you already have, like, *people*?"

"I am an It Girl. Unfortunately, the world just doesn't know it yet," Brooke hedged. "You saw me in the play last fall. I was a triumph. The *Los Angeles Times* wrote, 'Brooke Berlin is *on*!'"

Max frowned. "They were just listing the play in the events calendar. The rest of that sentence was, like, 'Brooke Berlin is on*stage* at Colby-Randall Preparatory School's nonmusical fall production of *My Fair Lady*,' or something."

"Details," Brooke said, waving an immaculately manicured hand. It was a favorite sentiment of hers. "The point is, my star is on the rise."

"My mother is sending Brooke's headshots around town," Arugula added.

"I'm sure that has nothing to do with her also being Brick's agent," Max cracked.

"There are two kinds of actors in this town," Ari said. "Nepotists and the unemployed."

"But I want to *get* the parts on my own," Brooke insisted. "So I need something that makes me stand out from all the other boring nepotists. Why not let people get to know me online? All the celebrities these days are pouring out their hearts on the Internet. Just look at what it's done for Kanye."

"I *did* spend a week wondering whether he ever got that cherub rug," Max admitted.

Brooke made a check mark next to the box reading *Comprehends the Magnitude of Celebrity Social Media Interaction vis-à-vis the Minutiae of Everyday Life.* (Arugula had written that one.) "Exactly," she said. "If I play this right, in a month, it could be *my* cherub rug people are worried about."

"I'm sure some lobotomized fan will find this job very fulfilling."

"That lobotomized fan could be you!" Brooke pointed out, waggling her pen in the direction of Max's face. "But you never told me why you applied."

Max gritted her teeth. "Because my job at Fu'd is making me consider taking my own life by diving into the tofu liquefier, but I still need cash for...stuff."

Arugula stared at Max intently. "It's not drugs, is it? I've always thought Teddy had a tweaker look about him."

"Was that before or after he rejected you?"

"Seriously, why do you need the money?" Brooke said, holding up a silencing hand to the side of Arugula's outraged-looking face. Her need for dish outweighed her need to defend Ari's honor. Plus, it *was* after he rejected her. "This job pays very well. Not that it's yours. I'm just saying."

Max was quiet again, staring at the countertop and tracing invisible things with her finger. Just in case, Brooke checked to make sure they weren't satanic symbols. One never knew. Being under the sway of Dark Forces might explain why Max had done that to her hair.

"I want to go to NYU's summer writing program," Max eventually admitted. "But it's really expensive."

"So it's true that you actually *want* to be a writer," Brooke said thoughtfully.

"Yeah, a writer. Not a tweeter."

"This *is* a writing job," Brooke said. "If it were tweeting, I'd have called it tweetographer. Brooke Berlin's essence is bigger than a hundred and forty characters, so I'm going old-school. I need someone to expose what a witty, enlightened asset to humanity I am, by writing blog entries as if they're me."

"You don't see the contradiction in that statement?"

"The entries will all be rooted in fact," Arugula said. "Brooke simply won't have the time. She'll be too busy going to auditions and assiduously maintaining her public persona."

"Also, I don't like to type," Brooke confided. "I inherited my mother's groundbreaking modeling hands, and everyone knows typing warps them."

"So, you already have an assistant. Dictate them to Martha."

"Her name is Brie now," Brooke scolded. "People are so callous not to respect that."

"Again with the contradictions," Max muttered into her malt. Brooke winced; every sip was, like, fifty crunches. "Can't *Brie* do this?"

Brooke shook her head. "She's terrible at keeping secrets. Last Thanksgiving, as a test, I asked her what she was getting me for Christmas and she actually told me. I need someone who will be anonymous."

"Well, good luck with that," said Max. "I'm sure pathetic minions are a dime a dozen in this town."

But her tone lacked its usual bite. Brooke tapped her pen on her clipboard a few times, deep in thought. She hadn't expected honesty from Max, who was now sitting there looking a little bit nauseated and—was she imagining it?—kind of bummed. Maybe the little troll doll needed this more than Brooke realized.

"I know we're not exactly friends, but if Molly likes you there must be *something* redeeming about you," Brooke allowed. "And you *do* share my controversial stance on Kate Hudson."

"Thanks...?"

"Look, I know what you think of me," Brooke said. "And if I were you, I might think it, too. But there's a lot riding on this for me. I'm taking it very seriously. Maybe you should consider doing the same."

Brooke slid out of the booth, ripped off a piece of paper from her clipboard, and scribbled the job's very generous salary on it. She handed it to Max. "That's my cell number, and *that* is the amount I'm willing to pay my blogographer. If you decide you're interested, and if the dozens of other applicants fail the Hudson test, maybe we can work something out."

Max took the paper and gazed at it, mutely. Ari reached around Brooke and slid a five-dollar bill onto the table.

"For the milk shake," she said. "Not *drugs*."

Max's face was full of contempt. "Right, like I would do drugs that cheap," she breezed, standing up and leaving the bill on the table for the waitress. She made a big show of dropping Brooke's piece of paper in the trash on her way out.

Well, I tried, Brooke thought, watching Max leave. Then she quickly snatched the paper out of the bin before any potential stalkers could do it. An It Girl had to be vigilant.

✦ ✦ ✦

Max left the diner worrying that it was only a matter of time before Brooke told the whole school that tacky, tragic misfit Max McCormack had *feelings* and *aspirations* and was so pathetic that she was answering ads on craigslist. Brooke was the queen bee. And in Max's experience, stinging people was what queen bees did. She therefore avoided Brooke like the plague for the rest of the week, even attempting to *feign* the plague to get out of a carnival planning meeting.

But as the week passed and Brooke said nothing about her at all, the job snuck back into the forefront of Max's mind. When she saw the salary, she'd barely kept her eyes from vacating her skull. That amount made no sense. For a second Max thought it was still part of Brooke's phone number. Like an extension. A really, really long extension. But no, it seemed that Brooke Berlin was in fact nutty enough—or rich enough; probably both—to pay someone handily to pretend to be her. NYU might be a reality.

Why did it have to be Brooke Berlin? Why couldn't it have been someone totally removed from her school life? Why *hadn't* it been Dakota Fanning? And why had her subconscious decided that being some girl's ghost-blogger sounded kind of fun, in the *exact* instant the job became so obviously untenable? It was an awfully rotten joke for her brain to play on her.

Max was still bummed when she showed up for her double shift Saturday morning and saw that the line outside Fu'd—which wasn't even open yet—wrapped around the building, despite the brisk early March air. Max had to claw her way to the door past two teens who screamed that she was cheating, and one fortysomething mom who was weeping onto a sign that said GIVE PIECE A CHANCE.

Max slammed the door behind her and pressed her body against it to keep it closed while she flipped the lock. An apron promptly smacked her in the head. "What the hell?"

"Hurry, put that on," Pete whispered, tugging nervously on one of the three earrings in his right lobe. "He's been on a rampage."

"What's the line for?" Max hissed back.

"Didn't you get the e-mail?" asked Pete, helping her tie the apron. "He got Dime Piece to do a signing today."

Dime Piece was a ten-year-old cross between Lil' Wayne and Eminem who made headlines by announcing he was going to rob a bank when his album dropped and then, unbelievably, actually attempting to do it.

"I thought he was in juvenile hall," Max said.

"His lawyer got him off," Dennis said, by way of announcing his arrival. "A legal masterstroke. Now he's decided to embrace the meatless life, at least for today, and for a reasonable appearance fee." He reached over and flicked Max's left ear with his finger, hard. "Don't think I didn't notice you were late."

"My shift doesn't even start for another five minutes," Max protested, clasping a hand to her stinging lobe. This gig was getting more Dickensian by the minute.

"I prefer you here fifteen minutes beforehand, which makes you ten minutes late," Dennis said smugly. "And that means you mop the bathrooms. Congratulations. I hope your tardiness was worth it. Now, doors open in four minutes. Be fast, be polite, and push the veganami."

The first five hours of Max's shift passed in a blur of shrieking, sobbing, and sweat. Dime Piece turned out to be a garden-variety brat who just wanted to trip up all the servers, ordered his bottled water decanted into an empty Sprite can before being poured over ice in a glass, and actually tried to tie Max's shoelaces together while she was taking orders from the thirteen adults in his posse, whose chief concern was encouraging his repellent behavior. Fans alternately mobbed him and the counter; by the time Dime signed his last CD and left, half the chairs in the place were upturned, Fu'd was out of veganami, and the cops had come to escort away a grown woman who slapped a nine-year-old girl she thought had cut in line.

Unbelievably, it went downhill from there: On their break, Dennis made them all learn how to brew a protein shake that had the texture of cake frosting and the taste of chicken teriyaki, which Max knew would lead to her bingeing on a giant Chipotle burrito full of revenge meat on her way home. And then, before she could even retie the kerchief keeping her sweaty, matted green hair off her face, Max had to work the afternoon rush, which was predictably full of people she didn't want to see.

"Kermit, you look like a wet lawn," Chaz Kelly boomed. "Gimme a bratwurst with sauerkraut and a Dr Pepper."

He threw some money at Max's face before plodding over to a table with his friends.

"Okay, so what are you going to give him this time?" Jake Donovan asked.

Max could hear the smile in his voice, but as she lifted her head to return it, she saw him standing next to a stone-faced Jennifer Parker. It was all Max could do not to groan in her face.

"Notwurst with toham shavings and a Colon-Eze Tea latte," she said instead. "You should probably stop coming here with him. It's only going to get worse."

"Good advice. I'll take one of those notwursts, though, but just with ketchup.",

"No, Jake, they're too greasy," Jennifer said, shoving in front of him.

Jake looked annoyed. "I can order what I want, Jen."

"Not if you enjoy my company," she said.

Jake seemed right on the verge of giving the sarcastic answer Max had already formulated for him in her head, but instead he just muttered, "Fine." Max watched him slink to a table next to Chaz and fish his phone out of his pocket. This Twitter fight would be epic.

"Um, *hello*, I'm still here," Jennifer said, snapping her fingers in front of Max's eyes. "Get him a baked sweet potato, and give me a fakon-lettuce-tomato sandwich on wheat, minus the wheat, hold the fakon, and absolutely no tofunnaise because I've got a really important audition in an hour and that stuff makes people's breath smell like cardboard."

Max ignored that. "So basically you want a piece of

lettuce and a slice of tomato on a plate? Maybe just order a salad."

Jennifer narrowed her eyes. "Jake only talks to you because he feels sorry for you, you know. We all do. Because you're so..." Jen cast her eyes up and down Max. "*You* know."

Max drummed her fingers on the counter and tried to keep calm. "Will that be all, Jennifer?" she asked. "That's nineteen dollars and sixty-eight cents. It's 'Buy Two, Get One Public Emasculation of Your Boyfriend Free' day."

Jennifer handed her some cash with a sneer. "No tip for you, *Kermit*," she said.

"I have one for you, though," Max said. "Don't blame the tofunnaise for your breath."

Jennifer turned purple. "I want to speak to the manager!"

Dennis burst out of the kitchen, ready for battle. Jennifer started yelping about Max's insubordination, and the whole room seemed to slow down as Dennis alternated between trying to appease Jen and yelling at Max, jabbing his finger violently in the vicinity of her nose.

"...and you will apologize to this lovely young customer, and then I swear to God, McCormack, you will spend the rest of the day regrouting the urinals," Dennis was ranting. "And you won't be getting paid a cent."

Something inside Max snapped. She gazed at Jennifer's smug face, then back at Dennis's frothing visage, and broke into a beatific smile.

"That's illegal, Dennis, you sycophantic slime," Max said.

This stunned Dennis into silence.

"And another thing," Max continued. "You can take this job and shove it up your tofunnator. I'll expect my last paycheck in the mail, or else I will report to the food safety inspectors that you only clean your liquefiers once every two weeks."

Max ripped her apron off, balled it up, and threw it square at Dennis's face before sailing out the door to a round of applause from half the restaurant. As she unlocked her canary Chevy, she dug out her cell phone. If her dignity had to have a price, it might as well be a high one.

"Molly?" she said when her friend answered. "Is Brooke with you? I need to talk to her about something."

five

"ARE YOU SURE ABOUT THIS?"

"Of course not," Max said, leaning over to peer at the nude patent-leather pumps on her feet. "These shoes are like three sizes too big for me. If I wear them tonight I will crack my skull."

"You know I'm not talking about the shoes," Molly said, sliding off her luxe king-size bed. It was so tall, she had to hop the last inch or two to the floor. "Are you really okay with working for Brooke? You can be honest, I won't be offended. I *have* met her."

Max had been asking herself the same question. She'd spent the last few years trying to avoid people like Brooke, and now she was supposed to *become* Brooke. Already their partnership was a roller coaster. When Max finally reached her the other day, Brooke had spent way too many of Max's precious, limited cell minutes explaining that she'd already interviewed several better candidates who understood the power of a four-inch heel. Max got in only one word before Brooke swerved and announced that having a blogographer she already knew and trusted—or, Brooke then clarified, whom *she* knew and *Molly* trusted—would involve a much more gentle learning curve. They hung up, and five minutes later Brooke called back and asked Max if she would consider a "quieter" hair color; ten minutes after *that* she'd phoned to tell Max her first assignment would be Saturday night, following Brooke through the eighteenth birthday party of a mega-famous tween actress-turned-singer (who, if the press was to be believed, hadn't ever drunk anything stronger than Gatorade; *yawn*). So far being a blogographer was like dating, but without any of the good parts—if Brooke had been a boy, Max would've broken up with her immediately.

But, *the salary.*

"I think…it will be okay?" Max attempted, easing herself down into the carpet. "I mean, you shared a room with her without killing her in her sleep. Surely I can hang out with her for a few hours."

"We survived being roommates, but that doesn't mean I'm not glad to be back in my own space," Molly said, relocating to the overstuffed red armchair in the corner of the room.

Max couldn't blame her. At her own house, noise reigned:

If it wasn't sirens roaring up Highland, it was her father's power tools or her mother's loud phone calls with pushy parents and harried teachers. By comparison, Molly's room—high atop Brick's giant brick and marble colonial mansion—felt like a spa. It was a third-story sanctuary painted a soothing dusty blue, much more relaxing than Max's frenetic paisley. The space looked straightforward but was somehow full of comfy nooks to sit and read, or do homework, and there was a towering antique book-shelf crammed with leather-bound tomes that Max could swear were first editions. Brick had obviously tried really hard to make it perfect. It also got fantastic light from sev-eral picture windows and a glass slider that led to a giant terrace that stretched the length of the house. Before becoming friends with Molly, Max had never ventured this far though the gates of Bel-Air—or indeed, through them at all—and she couldn't believe how lush and quiet it was, almost as if they were a hundred miles from a city instead of two minutes from UCLA.

Max kicked off Molly's insanely high shoes and lay back on the carpet, digging in with her fingers. "I might be a little nervous," she admitted. "I haven't written anything for publication before. And Brooke hasn't told me what she wants me to do yet. She just keeps yammering about *absorbing her essence.*"

Molly rubbed at the upholstery with her thumbnail. "I am concerned this is going to end with a straitjacket."

Max spread her hands helplessly. "I need the money,"

she said flatly. "I'm never going to make this much cash this fast unless I start working the pole or something. And I think we can all agree that would be *way* worse for my mental health."

"Well, it'll be nice to have you there tonight. I feel so weird at these parties," Molly said with a wince. "Remember the one Brick threw for me when I moved here?"

"Where you got totally wasted?"

"By accident!"

"And then passed out."

"A little."

"And then photos of Brooke beating your comatose body ran on every gossip blog in town."

"She was more pointing and laughing—"

"*Details*," Max said in her best Brooke impression.

Molly laughed. "I see your point. Compared to that, tonight should be a piece of cake."

"Yeah, just as long as you stay away from the bar," Max teased.

The intercom on Molly's landline buzzed angrily.

Molly grinned, punching the button to put the caller on speakerphone. "You rang, milady?"

"Is Max with you?" Brooke barked. "We only have two hours to get ready for this party, and I am very concerned that she's not treating this with the necessary gravitas."

Max made a gagging motion. *I'm not here*, she mouthed.

"She's sitting right next to me," Molly chirped. "Do you want to talk to her?"

59

Max bugged out her eyes and mimed choking herself.

"Or better, why don't I just send her across the hall," Molly said, stifling a laugh. "I know she's really eager to get going."

"Please do so," Brooke said superciliously. Then she paused. "Thanks, Mol," she sang before hanging up.

Max unsheathed an imaginary dagger, reached around herself, and pretended to plunge it into her back.

"And I thought Brooke was the drama queen," Molly said, kicking at Max's leg with her Converse. "Go get bloggy."

"You people and your made-up words," grumbled Max, reluctantly picking herself up off the carpet and stretching. "Fine, I'll go, but only because she's paying me to."

"You do realize you're quoting *Pretty Woman*, which makes you the prostitute."

Max stopped with her hand on the doorknob. "Unintentional. But appropriate," she said. Then she faltered. "I won't make an ass of myself, right?" she said, unconvincingly. "I mean, no one's going to read this thing."

"Damned if they do, damned if they don't, huh?" said Molly perceptively.

Max crossed the hall toward the imposing door with the pink velvet "B" charm hanging from the doorknob. She had never been in Brooke's room. Actually, she'd never been in most of the other rooms in Molly's house, because there were about fifty of them, and she was always afraid she'd accidentally walk in on Brick getting his back waxed or something.

She raised her hand to knock. The door burst open before her fist could even make contact.

"Let's get down to business," Brooke said.

Brooke's pink room was as vivid as Molly's was calming. There was a small sitting area near the TV, a workout station in the area Molly's stuff once occupied, a king-size bed dressed to coordinate with the walls, and a wing chair by the window. Framed memorabilia dotted the walls: pictures of Brooke as a kid with Brick, a magazine advertorial Molly had said featured Brooke's mother's once-famous hands, and a program commemorating Brooke's star turn in *My Fair Lady*. It appeared to be autographed by Brooke herself.

"Now," Brooke said, clapping. "Let's start with the obvious issue. What are you going to wear tonight?"

Max glanced down at her camouflage cargo pants and an old Cal Tech tee dating from when her father worked there. "This? Does it matter? Nobody will be looking at me."

Brooke burst into laughter that slowly died once she saw Max wasn't kidding. "This is exactly what I was afraid of. No one is going to believe you're just a friend of mine if you're dressed like a day laborer," she fretted. "Moxie Stilts might not even let you inside."

Max deployed her best "What have I done?" face, until

she remembered Molly wasn't there to appreciate it. Sarcasm could be so lonely.

"What does Moxie Stilts have to do with your dad, by the way?" Max asked, running a hand idly over a framed shot of seven-year-old Brooke at a movie premiere. Brick had barely aged. Brooke had no front teeth.

"Daddy wants her to be in the new ABC Family show he just sold," Brooke said, bodily relocating Max's hand to the wall and rubbing the glass frame with a baby wipe. "He's such a mogul."

"What's the show?"

"*Kamikaze Dad*," Brooke said. "He left the script in the printer last week. It's about a man named Stone Stuttgart"—here, Max swore she saw Brooke's eyes roll—"who inherits a daughter from the middle of nowhere, who constantly goads his other daughter by doing things like refusing to fix her bangs—"

"Some *slight* editorializing there, maybe..." Max murmured, flopping into Brooke's pink wing chair.

"—and then he saves the day through unconventional parenting," Brooke finished. "He said last fall he was going to do it, but I didn't think he was serious. He also once told me he was going to do a show about a hand model who abandons her family and then loses her arms in a bar fight, and that never happened."

"Too bad—I would've watched that," Max said. "But your mother probably would have sued. Which one of you does he want Moxie to play?"

"I'm not sure," Brooke said, scrunching up her face. "She's a big name, which is perfect for me, but Moxie's folksy accent thing might be better for someone from the sticks. No offense to Molly," she added, after a beat.

"She wouldn't care," Max said. "West Cairo *is* the sticks. She told me there is actually a bar there called The Sticks."

Brooke snickered, then tried to wave it off. "Don't try to distract me from the problem of . . . you," she said. "Can I offer you some shoes? A high heel can fix almost anything."

Max's toes obligingly went numb. There was a limit to how literally she was willing to be Brooke Berlin. "No," she said firmly. "No makeover."

"No makeover?" Brooke parroted, seeming galled. Then she tapped a finger against her well-glossed lip. "Interesting idea, actually. In those pants, you could very easily go unobserved if you need to crawl through the bushes to get a scoop."

Max again cursed that Molly hadn't come into the room, because all her psychic "girl, please" energies were being wasted.

"Maybe we should talk about what you actually expect me to do tonight," Max said. "I charge extra for shrubberies."

"Yes, let's talk plan of attack," Brooke said, beginning to pace across her room. "I've got the blog all ready to go, so all you have to do is e-mail me the first entry and I'll post it, after a thorough edit and study of your grammar, of course. You should follow me around tonight, but keep a safe distance so people don't suspect anything. Although if it's loud in there, it might be hard to hear, so maybe we need some kind of listening device...." She snapped her fingers. "Daddy has a working bug left over from *Amendment to Hell*. I could borrow it and—"

"Brooke," Max interrupted. "Are you off your meds? I'm not going to wear a wire to a party."

Brooke was silent for a second, picking at her bracelet. "Well, it's just that this is really important to me. It's..." She let out a long breath. "It has to work, is all."

"Okay, what's the deal with this?" Max asked, shifting so she could cross her legs in the chair. "Are you paying back a mafia debt or something?"

Brooke began to flap her hands a little. "I just...I thought being in *My Fair Lady* would somehow solve everything, but Daddy is still busy and my mother is still gone."

Oops. Max hadn't been prepared for an actual confidence. She'd assumed Brooke would confess that she'd never been the same, mentally, since she chipped her last pedicure. What did people say in these situations?

"Um," she said.

Way to go, wordsmith.

Brooke didn't seem to notice. "If I can do this, I'm not just some kid in a school play. I'm an Internet sensation. I'm in demand. And I think...I think Daddy would feel like he needed to be part of that."

Max was surprised to find herself without a glib comeback. She'd heard Molly talk about how hard it was on Brooke to have Brick fly off all the time without her,

64

ostensibly to protect her from the upheaval of his life, but in actuality ensuring he rarely saw her. Most kids probably dreamed of being left to their own devices in the plushest mansion money could build, but clearly it really bugged Brooke. Last fall, a cruel and unexpected public reading of Brooke's private e-mails had revealed what a crappy absentee mother she had, but obviously her absentee father stung the most. Max tried to imagine how that would feel, and couldn't: The farthest her father ever got was the garden shed, where he was usually taking apart various household objects and trying to merge them into a megainvention he could sell at Target. But that was just across the yard, and he still popped in to cook dinner (and steal the occasional toaster).

A strange calm settled over Max. "How about this," she began. "Instead of me transcribing everything you do and say, what about something more observational? About the scene, the people. But truthful, for a change."

"Like, ragging on them?" Brooke asked, worrying at her thumbnail before smacking it out of her mouth with her other hand.

"No, just…noticing," Max clarified. "And you wouldn't be lying, or talking about people who aren't in the public eye already. But everyone is sick of reading whitewashed BS about how all celebrities love each other. Like how everyone kisses Julia Roberts's ass anytime she even comes within sneezing distance of a movie set. I've eaten toffalo burgers that seem more authentic."

"So I'd be the honest insider," Brooke mused.

"Exactly."

Brooke looked up at Max and gave her a genuine smile, possibly the first real one of their entire shared history. "I like it. Bold and blunt."

"I'm on it," Max promised. "So please unclench. It's cracking your tan."

Brooke let slip a small snicker, then pushed out a crisp breath. "Great. You can go now. I have to cross-reference tonight's outfit with everything I've worn this past month just to make sure it's not repetitious." She shot Max an appraising look. "Your homework is to talk to Molly about the finer points of wearing shirts without writing on them. Rachel Zoe would die. And not in the good way."

Max watched Brooke disappear into her vast closet. "This ought to be interesting," she said aloud to no one.

✦ ✦ ✦

"Are you sure about this?"

Ari had asked Brooke that question earlier, and now—two hours after Max left her room—it rang in Brooke's head like a cowbell. *Of course* she wasn't sure. She'd been formulating this plan so fervently, and privately, for the past few months that it felt weird to be acting on it at long last. And with somebody with whom she'd historically exchanged more glares than words.

"She's just so *low-rent*," Jennifer Parker had said on the

phone earlier, when they'd three-way called with Arugula to discuss Brooke's outfit. "And she's always up in Jake's business. Why are you doing this to me?"

"She's not low-rent. She's...unvarnished," Brooke insisted. "I can handle that. And it's not about you, it's about my career, so I expect your full support. If you so much as breathe a word of this to anyone, even Jake—especially Jake—I swear to God I will find a way to lock you out of your IMDb page and put every infomercial you've ever done on there." Jen was silent. Brooke soldiered on. "Besides, it's too late now. I hired her. It's done."

"It's *not* too late," Arugula argued. "This is Hollywood, honey. People get terminated midsentence in this town. It's called a recast."

"Actually, I welcome the challenge," Brooke had said airily. "It would be boring if my blogographer were exactly like me."

She *almost* believed this. Although Max had been surprisingly comforting and in command earlier—never in a million years would Brooke have imagined she'd bare her soul to a person in cargo pants—now that it was zero hour and Brooke was applying the finishing touches to her makeup, she was still worried Max would turn out to be a surly loose cannon who only wanted to insult her trendy Louboutins, thus ruining Brooke's dream of having the designer name a pair after her.

On the other hand, hiring someone with a different worldview could be considered savvy, right? Brooke assured herself. *How else do you explain that Elisabeth Hasselbeck is still on* The View?

The bigger issue was that as much as Brooke felt her master plan was a theoretical stroke of genius, she also had no idea whether it would actually *work*. Phase One, at least, had gone well: Brick had been blown away by her performance as Eliza Doolittle. His unabashed paternal pride—attention she'd been craving her whole life while he was off shooting movies with other people's kids—was like a drug. Brooke wanted more. But scoring another hit was taking longer than she would've liked. *My Fair Lady* had been a wild success, but it was still just a school play. She needed a larger platform. A louder one.

And it was that epiphany, which came in part after Brooke realized that Kourtney Kardashian had two million Twitter followers just because she made bad relationship decisions in front of a camera crew, that led her to what she referred to in her head as the Big Idea: a blog. Something *good*, not just some random site where she uploaded pictures of herself in novelty sunglasses and then wrote about pants, or whatever. No, it had to get people talking. About *her*.

Brooke studied herself in the mirror. Her sleek navy backless Calvin Klein looked fantastic against her tan. Surely she already had enough going for her to stir up some buzz. Was she crazy to put her public image in the hands of a pale hobbit who probably hated her?

Stop it. This was ridiculous. They weren't covering the party for E! or *Hey!* or any of their exclamatory brethren. Max might not even write about any of tonight's events at all. It was just a test. Nobody at the party would know that her secret—and, she prayed, secretly brilliant—blog was even happening.

"You are going to be amazing," she told her reflection. "You need Max. And Max needs you. This is going to work."

It has to work.

SIX

AS THE CAR TURNED in through the front gate of an immense oceanside mansion, Max found herself wondering if Moxie Stilts had bought her house as a cutesy pun, as it was literally built on them. The Malibu manse was three stories of modern glass and steel, carved into a cliff and kept from tumbling into the waves below by a handful of what looked like Pixy Stix.

"I couldn't live here," Max said, peering out the window of Molly's SUV. "I would be down there all day staring at those things to see if they're still solid. What if there's a big storm?"

"Okay, for future reference, I do *not* want my blog to be full of boring commentary about architectural safety and, like, El Niño," Brooke said as Molly guided the car toward the party's valet-for-hire. She was clearly feeling like herself again. "Although, actually, maybe Daddy decided to come for research. They're already talking about an *Avalanche!* sequel called *Mudslide?!?*"

"That can't be. They only just finished shooting *Avalanche!* last week," Molly pointed out.

Brooke fiddled with the clasp of her silver evening clutch. "Well, I saw a script outline on Daddy's desk, and that's what it said. I don't make these things up. I just report them."

"You seem to do a lot of snooping around that office," Max noted.

Brooke turned around in her seat and glared at her. "I'm just observant," she said. "Like you're going to need to be if you're going to pull off being me."

"I think donating one percent of my working brain to the cause should cover it."

"*Zing,*" Brooke retorted sarcastically.

"Okay, everybody, retreat to your corners," Molly said, throwing the car into Park. "We're here."

The girls climbed out, gave their names to a ponytailed blonde wearing a black shift dress and holding a clipboard, and were waved up the gravel driveway toward a large amber-lit tent that had been erected on the house's massive side lawn. A convivial din emanated from behind the cloth as waiters bustled in and out, half of them ferrying snacks and full glasses of champagne, the others toting trays piled high with overturned plates and crumpled napkins.

Inside, chandeliers hung from the underside of the tent, throwing a dim, flattering light over the bar, a dance floor, and white-draped round tables topped with tight bunches of hyacinths. It echoed one of the receptions Max had read about in the copy of *InStyle Weddings* that had been in the Fu'd break room for the last six weeks. *Oh, please, can this be a surprise wedding?* That was almost as trendy as a secret baby. Writing about it would be a slam dunk.

"There he is," Brooke said, gesturing with her chin toward a tall, handsome fortysomething man in a tuxedo sitting at a corner table drinking a low-carb beer and staring suspiciously at a tiny hamburger from which he had taken one bite.

Brick Berlin visibly brightened and leaped to his feet. "Girls! Welcome! Group hug!"

He pulled Brooke and Molly into a tight embrace.

"Hi, Dad," Molly said, but it came out muffled because her mouth was covered by his giant biceps. "Burger no good?"

"Bad news, precious child—I tasted mayonnaise," he said. "Even though I specifically asked if they were condimented. People are so careless. My trainer says it takes a thousand crunches to offset a mayonnaise incident, and I already accidentally ate a tub of potato salad this week."

He peered over Brooke's blonde curls at Max.

"And who is this?" he asked. "Wait! Let me guess. You're the foreign exchange student Brooke sent away for!"

Brooke pulled away from her father. "Daddy, that was five years ago. This is Molly's friend. She comes over to the house, like, three times a week."

Recognition flooded Brick's face. "You mean the girl who's named after cheese?"

"I'm Max," said Max, wishing she had something more glamorous to offer.

Brick rubbed his hands together. "I'm not familiar with that one—sounds like one of the more exotic Bavarian cheeses, yes?"

In the face of his eager smile, Max felt flummoxed. Brick's freakishly charismatic enthusiasm had a way of sweeping people up, and the next thing you knew, you had agreed to something ridiculous. This explained why anyone was even considering a fifth Dirk Venom movie, and in that moment, his charm was hypnotizing Max into nodding dumbly. And then speaking dumbly.

"Yes," she heard herself say. "It's, um, Maxschtagen." *Huh?* "One of the rarer wax-coated cheeses." *What are you saying?* "It's very creamy, with a fruity bite." *Stop talking.* "It comes from the milk of mountain goats that are fed white chocolate and strawberries."

Brooke kicked the back of Max's foot. Max gratefully closed her mouth.

"That is fascinating, Max!" Brick boomed, clapping her on the back. "I feel enriched! Now, pardon me, but I have to go speak to someone about this condiment problem. You girls have fun. The rest of the kids are down in the guesthouse." He pressed his hands together. "But be on your guards. Trans fats lurk like a cat burglar."

"Goats fed white chocolate and strawberries?" Molly quoted as they exited the tent. "What was *that*?"

"I don't know," Max said defensively. "He thought I was Brie. I got all flustered."

"You are hideous under pressure," Brooke noted as they clambered down candlelit brick steps toward a giant guesthouse that was easily larger than Max's own home. "Although I appreciate the attempt to improv. Unfortunately, he's probably going to go home and try to order that cheese, and then I'll have to have a talk with him." She sighed. "Brick has loved exotic cheese ever since those three weeks he was on Atkins."

"Why is there a separate kids' party?" Max asked as they neared a set of French doors. "This feels like Thanksgiving at my grandmother's."

"That other one is for Moxie's parents, really," Brooke said. "An excuse to network and stuff, plus they can pretend to be chaperoning. *This* is the real thing." She stopped and grabbed Max's arm. "Are you ready? Maxine, this is important. I don't want you to be overwhelmed."

"Brooke, I've watched *Lust for Life* since the womb," Max said. "Nothing fazes me."

Brooke shrugged, then threw open the doors. A wall of sound hit them in the face—a mixture of aggressive hip-hop blaring from the deejay's deck and a thousand drunk, screaming conversations. If the event outside looked like a

74

wedding reception, then this was the bachelor party, complete with a stripper pole mounted in the corner of the dimly lit open-plan space. Max needed eight-inch leg extensions just to have a prayer of seeing through the crowd, but she could make out at least three teen stars in a twenty-foot radius alone, and—grossly—several actors well into their thirties. Nearby, a coffee table was chockablock with magazines Moxie had been in over the last two years, one of which bore a cover photo of her in a gingham blouse and the headline WHY I'M WAITING FOR MY WEDDING NIGHT.

"Whoa," Molly said. "This is . . . bold."

"This is *awesome*," Max corrected her. "I knew that whole 'Jesus is my talent manager' shtick was bogus. Seriously, I've never read an interview with her where she didn't use the word *amen*."

Brooke, totally unmoved, was idly filing a wayward nail.

"Where *is* Moxie, anyway?" Molly asked, craning her neck over the crowd. "I can't see her."

As if on cue, the place went dark. "Thanks for coming, everyone," Moxie Stilts's voice said from the vicinity of the sky. "I've got a treat for you."

As the moody piano strains from Moxie's hit song "Metaphor" played—it was a ballad about growing up that, ironically (and possibly unintentionally), was composed entirely of similes—a spotlight popped on and illuminated a swing hanging from the ceiling. Perched atop it was Moxie Stilts, wearing a bustier, fishnets, platform stilettos, and hair extensions so robust it looked like she'd scalped Ke$ha.

"Whoa. She's gone full *Burlesque*," Max breathed.

"I'm like a sapling busting open and trying to take rooooooot," Moxie crooned, wriggling coyly as the swing began to descend to the floor.

"Boring," Brooke said, yawning.

Molly and Max exchanged grins.

"What?" Brooke said. "If you've seen one repressed kiddie-TV starlet crack under pressure, you've seen them all."

"Well, *I* haven't seen it yet," Max said, as the backing track kicked into a club remix of "Metaphor." Moxie landed on the floor and slinked over to the stripper pole. "Not in person, anyway. What is she *thinking?*"

"Probably that she's not going to get a whole lot of work when she's twenty-five, if all she's ever known for is playing a teen clothing designer with a talking sewing machine," Brooke said, as Moxie bent over and swung her butt from side to side in time to the music. The crowd went nuts.

"Oh, my God, I can't look, but I can't *not* look." Molly grimaced.

"Fresh as a dewdrop, like a lie turning true, I am finding my meaning, baby, and the metaphor is you," Moxie panted. *She really should've lip-synched*, Max thought with uncharitable glee. As if in agreement, one of Moxie's stockings snapped in half across her thigh.

"Take it off!" shouted a guy Max was pretty sure had a daughter with one of the Pussycat Dolls.

Brooke looked pointedly at the part of her arm where a

watch would live, if she ever cared whether she was on time to anything. "How long is this going to go on?" she complained. "Downward spirals are so passé."

As if on cue, Moxie's music faded out and the latest hit from Justin Timberlake's new album came bursting over the speakers. Moxie took a distracted, sweaty bow.

"Finally!" Brooke said. "Okay, I see a guy from *The Wolf Pack* who almost certainly deserves to meet me. Don't forget to come find me, Max. Remember, this is work." And with that, she disappeared into the crowd.

"I don't know how she can see anything in here except a bunch of civil misdemeanors," Max said, gesturing at the writhing crowd. "I can't believe this is your life."

Molly pulled a face. "*This* isn't my life," she said. "I mean, I guess tangentially, because of Brooke and Brick, but not really. My actual life is, like, school and my family and you and Teddy and worrying about getting into college and stuff. Thank God you're here, or else Brooke would be forcing me to talk to that actor's grody wingman."

Max watched, a tad lost, as a clutch of revelers passed around a tray of brightly colored shots. Even at Colby-Randall, where Max belonged about as much as those thirtysomething pervs did at this party, she had never felt this out of her depth. High school was just something everyone did for a few years until their real lives started. But this madness *was* some people's real lives. How was she supposed to relate to this the way Brooke did? Brooke grew up with a pony, for Pete's sake. The only pony Max ever owned was Dallas, Barbie's Palomino, who eventually perished in a tragic weed-eater incident.

A good writer ought to be able to inhabit anyone else's brain, Teddy had told her earlier. The only problem was, Brooke's brain was across the room trying to get digits from a guy who'd just spent five episodes in a time-traveling coma that taught him life lessons, and Max didn't particularly want to go there.

"Don't freak out," Molly said, watching Max's face.

Max exhaled. "How could you tell?"

Molly smiled. "Your nostrils get all flare-y."

"I just want to do a good job." *For the money. And because if I can't manage to write a blog about someone whose only thoughts are about shoes, maybe I'm not cut out for NYU.*

"You'll be fine," Molly told her. "Don't think about what Brooke would want you to write. Think about what would make a fun read, and go from there."

"Well," Max said, "I guess the bathroom is as good a place to start as any. If people aren't debauching themselves in there, then this party is officially a failure."

Molly perched on the edge of a nearby leather sofa. She waved her phone. "I'll be right here, texting Teddy words that rhyme with *leggings.* I guess Bone wants to write a song about some girl he met at American Apparel."

Max tried to make herself as narrow as possible and plunged into the immense, noisy crowd, hoping it would carry her in a helpful direction. Instead the sea of bodies bounced her around as if she were caught in a riptide.

"—and then he said he couldn't date me because his boyfriend wouldn't like it. And I was, like, but it's the *Golden Globes*," Max overheard as she people-surfed past two tiny actresses she recognized from HBO. "It's not like I was going to have *sex* with him. Probably."

Next, she was whipsawed toward where Moxie had made her entrance, thus getting jostled by people scrambling to get a photo with the actress, and then past a woman in giant square glasses screaming into her phone about how childbirth was an unacceptable excuse for missing a script deadline. Max was dumbfounded at how many people were inside the guesthouse. It had to be violating the fire code ten times over, although maybe it just felt crowded because she kept somehow getting shoved back past the same crazy people.

"...But if I did sleep with him, do you think I could get him to change teams?"

"...Oh, please, you can still *type*, why do you think they invented C-sections?"

Max couldn't take it. Parties like this were why Valium was invented. She gave up on delicacy and barreled in a straight line until she couldn't feel flesh anymore. The mob spit her out near the kitchen, where an industrial-looking door was labeled MEN'S ROOM. Max cursed under her breath. But nobody was anywhere near it, so—after a look back at the suffocating crowd, and no sign of the ladies' room—Max decided this was the hand of fate at work again, this time giving her bladder a nudge. She yanked open the heavy metal door, found nobody in any of the three stalls (just how many guests did the Stilts family usually *have*, anyway?), and was in and out in a flash, drying her hands on her pants as she hurriedly threw her shoulder into the door. This time, instead of opening, it smacked into something squishy and soft. Surprised, she stopped dead halfway through the doorway, which promptly swung back at her and banged into her face.

"Ow!" Max said, stumbling backward, as a sharp pain shot through her sinuses, accompanied by fireworks behind her eyelids. She sank to her knees, holding her face.

"Holy crap," a male voice said from behind the door. Then he pulled it open and extracted Max while rubbing his own nose. "You okay?"

"Blurgh," was all Max could manage. Her vision was blurry. *Can you knock yourself blind?*

"Let me see your face," the man said, leading her into the kitchen. "Are you bleeding?"

Max leaned against something that she hoped was solid, since she still couldn't see very well. She gingerly touched her nose. "I don't think so."

The man hoisted himself up onto the kitchen counter and wiggled his own face. "Well, that cleared *my* sinuses."

Max blinked the last bit of water out of her eyes and looked up at him. To her surprise, he was actually not a man, but a boy about her own age—he had gray eyes and dark hair and was sort of on the short side, for a guy (although he still had several inches on Max).

"Can you breathe?" he asked.

Max took a deep breath.

"I meant through your nose," he clarified.

Duh. Maybe I have a concussion.

"Here, let me look," he said, pulling her toward him and prodding at her nose a little. He pressed on it carefully. "Does that hurt?"

"No, actually," Max said.

"Does it feel like your nose is stuffed up all of a sudden?"

"No."

The guy threw out his hands in a "ta-da" motion. "Excellent! I think you're still in one piece," he said.

"Are you some kind of boy-genius doctor?" Max asked. "How do you know so much about broken noses?"

He grinned. "This is Hollywood. I'm just *acting* like I know about broken noses. Also, I had mine broken at drama camp three years ago when part of the set for *Platoon: The Musical* fell on my face."

"Wow. War *is* dangerous."

"Apparently, so is going to the bathroom."

"I couldn't figure out where the ladies' room was," Max explained, nodding out the kitchen window toward the still stagnant queue. "And I couldn't handle the crowd anymore. I kept getting shoved up next to this pathetic actress who's trying to sleep with her gay friend."

The boy shook his head. "Actors are so irritating."

"Tell me about it," Max said. "I go to school with a girl

who actually entered our Speech Day contest with a monologue about flutes that her character delivered in *The Pied Viper.*"

His mouth fell open. "You go to school with Jennifer Parker?"

"You *know* her?"

"I've seen that movie like three times," the boy said. "It's what I watch if I'm depressed about my life. So that I know things could always be worse."

Holy crap, it's like I'm talking to myself. "I'll be sure to tell her you said that."

As they smiled at each other, Max became aware of the longish silence that had descended.

"I guess I should get back to my friend," she stammered. "I ditched her as soon as the pole-dancing wrapped up."

"At least you didn't abandon her in the middle of it," the boy said. "I'm only here because Moxie and my roommate share a manager. He ran up to her as soon as the spotlight came on. I spent the whole time wondering where I was supposed to look."

"What did you land on?"

He wiggled his iPhone. "Angry Birds," he said. "But I should probably go back to being a wingman. It was nice to meet you...um...?"

"Max," she said, sticking out her hand.

"Max," he repeated. "Explains why you were in the men's room." And with a wink, he hopped down and jogged outside, knocking into the door frame a bit on his way.

Max chuckled to herself and gave her nose one final, gentle squeeze. It seemed to be in working order, or at least it hadn't fallen off. Apparently this was a night of firsts for her: first insane Hollywood party, first time passing herself off as the namesake of a rare dairy product, first potential broken nose, first encounter with someone who similarly appreciated the awfulness of Jennifer's résumé. All that was left was her first Brooke Berlin blog entry. If only she could figure out how the hell to pull it off.

"I hope you had the tiiiime of your liiiiives," she could hear Moxie Stilts rapping from the guesthouse, in a mega-loud, mega-misguided cover of the Green Day high school graduation favorite.

With a bolstering nod, Max shoved her way back into the drunken abyss. Whatever she was going to write, it was probably going to start in there.

OPENBR👓KE.COM

MARCH 12

If you've found this blog, chances are—unless you were looking for information on German bodies of water and you're really terrible at Google—you already know a few things about me: I'm Brooke Berlin, I'm sixteen, my father is in at least one movie that's airing on TV right this second, and my mother is a hand model who ran off and left us without a word when I was a kid (no point in pretending you didn't see the *People* article). What you may not know: My mother is going to regret that; unlike half my peers in this town, I'm perfectly content to act sixteen and not twenty-six; I can pick exactly the right shoe to go with every outfit; I'm an actress; and even though I *am* naturally blonde, I also know how to use a semicolon.

I can also use hyphens—like, technically, I am a "student-actress"—but I chose not to mention that up top because the hyphen is the most overused punctuation mark in this entire town. I don't mean by the over-30 set; I am, after all, the offspring of a hyphenate. But my father worked as an actor for years before he added "director" and "producer" to it. In his case, I approve of the hyphen. He earned it. There is sweat on that hyphen, as opposed to the ones worn by most of Young Hollywood. They're all in a huge hurry to stuff their résumés and claim that they're model-actor-designers, or reality star-author-singers—or in the case of Moxie Stilts, an actress-singer-call girl, or at least I *assume* that's the message she was sending at her party this past weekend. Why else would she writhe around in lingerie, letting men twice

her age do shots of Cuervo out of her collar-
bone? (Memo to God: Despite what she tells
the magazines, Moxie is cheating on You with
half of Southern California. I assume You're
aware, but she sure had the rest of the world
fooled.)

So, my message to the junior hyphenates is:
Chill *out*. You're so busy cramming your résumés to the breaking point—paranoid everyone
will forget you exist unless you do everything,
everywhere, all the time—that you're losing
what there is about yourself that you actually
want us to remember. Like, does any little
kid wake up one morning and think, *When I
grow up, I want to have a really cheesy epony-
mous fashion line at Kmart?* No. They want
to be baseball players or rock stars or actors.
But my peers are all so obsessed with being
famous that they don't care anymore what
they're famous *for*; they just want attention.
Case in point: Name Moxie Stilts's last movie.
Now name her last TV commercial. I bet you
remembered her bacne-cream endorsement
first.

People like that are the reason you're probably reading this blog thinking, *Great, another idiot
wants her fifteen minutes.* But I don't want to be
tarred with that brush. I want to work. I am

capable of showing up on time, learning lines, arriving early and leaving late, and getting in and out of cars without flashing my underwear. (Somebody else at Moxie's party was not so lucky. I don't want to tell you who it was, but let's just say I saw more *pieces of her* than my retinas could handle.) And so I've started this blog to try to prove that we're not all alike. Let my fellow teen and twentysomething peers overextend themselves, act the fool, or peddle some false saintly image and then bust out of their petticoats as soon as they're legally able to seduce a backup dancer (*ahem*, Ms. Stilts). I just want to do *me*, and do it right. I'd rather have respect, self- and otherwise, than infamy. Why nobody else seems to feel that way is a mystery. But I'm coming. You're on notice.

And so are these people:

1) Confidential to HBO girl: HE'S GAY. ABAN-DON SHIP.

2) To the Cuervo lickers: Seriously? Half of you are married. I know this because a) you are recognizably famous, b) you left your rings on, and c) HELLO? WHAT PART ABOUT BEING RECOGNIZABLE DON'T YOU UNDERSTAND? Hope your prenups are airtight.

3) To Hollywood's divorce attorneys: Pursuant to the above, you might want to increase your hourly rate.

4) To Moxie: In addition to everything else, cool it with the eyeliner. You look like you face-planted into the La Brea Tar Pits.

Until next time,

B.

seven

MAX WOKE UP TO the sound of her cell phone buzzing somewhere near her left foot. She hadn't even realized she'd taken the phone to bed with her, the mystery of which was explained when Max figured out that she technically *hadn't*—she'd just left it in the pocket of the jeans that she never took off the night before. Blearily, she stared at the screen.

BROOKE BERLIN, it said, 6:24 AM.

"You've got to be kidding," Max muttered. *I am so not on the clock*, she thought, and hit Ignore.

She flopped onto her pillow. Despite Brooke's earlier assurance that Max could just e-mail her the entry, somehow they'd spent hours at the Berlin house the night before, poring over every last comma splice. But every time

Max felt herself getting irritated by Brooke's nitpickery—and occasional insistence on dangling participles—she reminded herself how much cash Brooke was forking over on a weekly basis. Max had always been disgusted by artists she thought were sellouts (people who agreed to have their music in a tampon ad, for example), but now that she herself had secretly sold out, she realized a fat paycheck really did make an irritating job much easier. Dennis might've had a happier workforce if he'd paid above minimum wage.

The phone buzzed again. BROOKE BERLIN, 6:26 AM.

I am not on call. I don't care how much you're paying me. I am keeping regular business hours.

She rolled over and tried to go back to sleep for the last sad thirty-four minutes before her alarm clock would sound. But behind her eyelids, Max was wide awake. And kind of nervous. She thought her blog entry was good. Molly had laughed out loud at it. But it was the first thing Max had ever written that might be seen by someone who wasn't biased in her favor, or contractually obligated to grade her. Strangers might read it. And hate it. And then leave rude comments telling her to shut her dumb face. Max groaned, remembering the many comments she herself had made on a variety of blogs in which she did things like correct the bloggers' grammar or wonder why anyone thought she might be interested in reading about, say, Jessica Alba's birthing plan. In retrospect, this all seemed karmically dangerous.

Her phone buzzed a third time. Max grabbed it angrily, but this time it was Molly.

"What the hell is going on over there?" Max answered. "It's practically still the middle of the night!"

"I knew you were awake!" Brooke said.

"I never would have fallen for that trick if I were really awake," Max groaned. "Does Molly even know you have her phone?"

"Of course not," Brooke said. "I snuck into her room and stole it. She sleeps *really* soundly. I'm worried she might have some kind of medical condition."

"I wish *I* had a medical condition. I would have loved to have slept through this."

"Whatever," Brooke said. "Anyway, do you think we should have given Moxie Stilts a fake name?"

Max flopped backward onto her bed. "We talked about this for *six hours* last night," she said. "To the point where I thought I was having a nightmare where all you did was stand in front of me and yap, and then I realized it was real."

"I had a dream that she sued me for calling her a fire-breathing ass-clown."

"We didn't call her a fire-breathing ass-clown," Max said, closing her eyes. Maybe she could snooze through this conversation.

"But—"

"Oh, my God, Brooke," Max groaned, almost involuntarily. "You have said more words to me in the last twenty-four hours than you have in five years."

"I don't know if you understand this, but my reputation is on the line here," Brooke said huffily.

"We didn't say anything that wasn't true," Max said, "*and* I doubt she's even going to read it."

"But—"

"Also, do you really think Moxie Stilts is going to sue Brick Berlin's daughter?" Max asked. This was her last-ditch argument. "She'd never work in this town again. I'd be more worried about having publicly insulted someone your dad wants to cast in a TV show."

She instantly regretted being so glib. There was a long moment of silence on the other end of the line. Max began to hope that Brooke had hung up on her.

"He won't care. Brick always says that the truth is the most powerful weapon we have, besides the P90X DVDs," Brooke said, although she sounded a bit wobbly. "Anyway. I'll see you at school. Go back to sleep, or you'll look like a puffer fish."

Max punched the End button and hurled her phone at the floor.

Beeeeeeeeeeeeeeeeep. Kevin and Bean, the morning guys on KROQ, came on her clock radio braying about something that had happened on *American Idol* the night before—apparently one of the contestants had sung an R. Kelly song while wearing a toga.

"Why, God?" Max wailed at her bedroom ceiling. About all of it.

God didn't respond, so Max rolled out of bed and went

to school. Unfortunately, Brooke was no easier to avoid there: She was waiting by Max's locker, impossible to miss in a brightly printed Peter Som minidress and clutching her iPad like a life preserver.

"We have three comments already," Brooke said softly by way of a greeting.

"How many of them are your aliases?" Max asked, twirling her padlock.

"None!" Brooke said, turning the tablet around so Max could see OpenBrooke.com's pink-themed home page. There were, as promised, three comments. The first one said, "Resplendent!"

"That's clearly Arugula," Max pointed out. "Doesn't count."

"But look at the other two! LOLWHATEVER98 wrote, '*You're* a tar pit.'"

"I don't think that's a compli—"

"And then right after that, Anonymous wrote, 'Nip-slip, please!'"

"Congratulations. You've really won over the heart of America." Max opened her locker and dumped her schoolbooks into a messy pile, on top of another messy pile.

Brooke hugged her iPad to her chest. "Everyone knows you're not really famous unless half the world wants to see you naked, and the other half hates your guts," she explained cheerfully. "So we're off to a good start. Don't forget, I'm expecting your pitches for my next three entries by noon today. You can e-mail me."

"'Don't forget'? You never told me that in the first place! We just finished *this* one," Max said, her voice rising a few notches.

"Shh, you're going to blow my cover," Brooke hissed. "And what did you think, we'd do one entry a month and be done with it? A successful blogographer's work is never done."

"Successful already, huh?" Molly asked, appearing at Max's side.

Brooke tapped her head. "Never doubt an evil genius," she said, setting off toward her class with a smug smile.

"Three comments and no lawsuits after being live for like twenty minutes," Max said, turning to Molly. "Does that sound successful?"

"Better than no comments and three lawsuits," Molly pointed out over the ringing of the first bell. "See you at lunch?"

"If I don't have to work," Max groused.

"Oh, you love it," Molly said, swinging past her toward homeroom.

Max looked down at her clean fingernails. *Three comments and counting.* Well, it was better than toham.

✦ ✦ ✦

Brooke refilled her glass of almond milk and slid back onto the brushed metal stool. The Berlin family kitchen was like a showpiece from a brochure, with Granny Smith apple–colored subway tile on the walls under the cabinets, white granite countertops, and modern metal furniture that complemented both the stainless-steel appliances and Brick's dizzying array of gadgets. They had an exotic coffeemaker whose nozzles and protuberances made it look like a Hindu deity; a machine that only existed to halve giant things, like butternut squashes or watermelons; a jar opener, a somewhat sarcastic gift from Brick's new trainer; and about ten things she knew Brick had bought from infomercials, including something called the Bacon Genie. The refrigerator was covered in calendars and diet plans, because Brick tried almost every fad diet known to man, including one that mandated eating nothing but homemade Fig Newtons. Brooke liked hanging out in the kitchen while the cook was on break before dinner, mostly because she enjoyed imagining herself as a young Gwyneth Paltrow, possessed of unforeseen culinary talents that would delight and amaze her soon-to-be-legions of fans, should she ever learn how to turn on the stove.

Today she didn't take any joy in imagining herself truffle-hunting with Mario Batali, though, because she was there waiting for Brick. He'd told her he wanted to talk, and it *had* to be about the blog, which she had *maybe* sort of forgotten to mention to him. Well, that wasn't strictly true. She had in passing expressed an interest in online self-publishing, and used the word *empire*, and Brick had made approving noises that she'd decided to consider a full endorsement. In truth, though, bringing it up while he was trying to grate a Pure Protein bar over his granola was a strategic move: It absolved her of any perceived lies of omission, but it also virtually guaranteed he hadn't heard or absorbed the words and therefore he wouldn't say anything to her that she didn't want to hear. Like her least favorite word, *No.*

Brooke nervously snuck a Soft Batch cookie out of the bag tucked away on the shelf by her knees and shoved it into her mouth. This conversation might not go as smoothly as that one had. It hadn't even occurred to Brooke until Max said something that maybe the blog's candor was a problem—that the observations about Moxie Stilts, however funny and accurate, would mess up Brick's project in development or make him an enemy he didn't want. Brooke hated it when her father was mad at her, not least because he had a bad habit of coming up with punishments that he considered creative and groundbreaking and Brooke considered social homicide.

Her phone buzzed. It was an alert letting her know she had five more comments on the blog. That made thirty today. On Day One. Surely Brick couldn't be upset if her blog turned into a raging success.

"Brookie," her father's voice boomed, on cue. "Are you in there? It's time for us to have that talk."

Brick bounded into the room (there was no door, but he had an energetic way of bursting through empty space, as if he were always two seconds away from yelling, "Ta-da!").

Opening the fridge, he grabbed a milk carton and a pre-portioned Ziploc bag that contained fresh berries, some powder, what looked like lawn clippings, and a melon baller–size scoop of peanut butter, all of which he scraped into the blender.

"How was school today?" he asked.

"Fumf," Brooke said, through a mouthful of cookie that stubbornly wasn't getting any smaller.

"Having a healthy snack, I hope," he said, pulsing the blender.

Brooke closed her eyes, chewed hard, and swallowed. "Took too big a bite of bran–acai berry muffin," she lied. "It was just so delicious."

Brick beamed and poured his smoothie into a glass. "Honey, I could talk about the mighty acai berry all day, but let's not beat around the bush," he said. "Caroline Goldberg showed me your blog."

Brooke took a deep breath and decided to meet his eyes. "I should have told you about it," she began.

"I also got a call from Travis Stilts telling me that Moxie is furious and doesn't feel she can work on *Kamikaze Dad* under the circumstances."

Brooke snorted before she could help herself. "Maybe she should've thought of that before she basically gave the entire room a lap dance."

"That is true," Brick said. "But it doesn't change the fact that what you do reflects on me."

Her phone buzzed. Brooke chanced a peek. Fifty comments. She swallowed her excitement and tried to focus on defusing the matter at hand.

"You're right, Daddy, and I didn't think about that," Brooke said, then took another deep breath and launched into her prepared speech. "But you have to understand, I can't sit idly by while my peers grapple with the trappings of fame. As a uniquely well-adjusted child of the industry, thanks to your sterling parental efforts, I think it's my duty to shine the light of truth on their struggles. It might heal them, and, more important, help others."

She finished this by leaning slightly forward, her hands spread on the countertop as if drawn there by the intensity of her do-gooder message. If there was one thing Brooke Berlin could do, it was monologue.

"This town only likes brutal honesty when it's behind people's backs," Brick said, sipping his smoothie. "You should have prepared me. I didn't like hearing about this from Caroline. And I didn't like even having to consider apologizing to Travis Stilts. That man was an athlete, and he accepted a canned-biscuit endorsement! Do you know how many calories are in those things?"

"I know, Daddy. I'm sorry."

"Luckily, Travis Stilts is a desperate washed-up baseball player who just let his daughter parade half-naked in front of most of Hollywood," Brick continued. "Who is he to question our integrity? I have three People's Choice awards. How's *that* for integrity?"

Brooke nodded vigorously, with a twinge of relief, as

Brick took another swig of his shake. If Brick was speechifying, it meant he wasn't brainstorming an elaborate punishment.

"So, instead of trying to make amends, I told him I had no interest in doing business with someone who is more interested in what *my* child is doing than his own," Brick said, after he swallowed.

"Also, I didn't lie," Brooke jumped in. "She *did* all that stuff. I was just telling the truth."

"Exactly," Brick said. "And it got me to thinking, there are worse things in the world than being known for someone who does not stand for baloney. Plus, you saved me a fortune in a contract buyout, since we don't want *Kamikaze Dad* associated with someone who doesn't wear pants."

"That's . . . great," Brooke offered.

"It can be a killer to get a reputation as someone who won't play the game of sweeping the ugly stuff under the rug," Brick said. He reached over and took her hand. "But I will not be killed. Instead we will battle for the truth. For justice. Sunshine, your writing is going to take the town by storm! No, the world! This could be huge!"

Brooke winced as a Brick gestured dramatically and took her arm with him. "Well, I'd rather simply be an example to others," she said, casting her eyes down modestly, "but of course if fame should come . . ."

"My daughter, an essayist!" Brick continued, as if he hadn't even heard her. "A freedom fighter!"

"That's true," Brooke said, feeling herself glow. "I don't like to use the word *heroic*, but..."

"Who's heroic?" Molly asked, bouncing into the kitchen and grabbing a Naked juice from the fridge.

"Your sister," Brick said. "She has an Internet blog!"

"It's just called a blog, Daddy," Brooke said.

"Ah, yes, the blog," Molly said. "It has like seventy comments now."

"It does?" Brooke squeaked. "I mean, it does. Of course it does."

"I sent it to all my buddies at the gym, and the guys who mix my bronzer," Brick said. "You would not *believe* their client list. You're going to be huge! A star who's a scholar!" He raised his smoothie glass. "To Brookie. Celebrity role model of our time."

Molly did a near-perfect spit-take of her juice. Brooke's phone buzzed. Seventy-five. She felt a frisson of excitement shoot through her veins.

"I'll drink to that," Brooke sang, with a confident, radiant smile.

eight

"SCOOT OVER. You are not going to believe this."

Max looked up from her lunch table at the lush Colby-Randall outdoor cafeteria and squinted into the glare. Either she was getting sunstroke, or Brooke Berlin was towering over her, waving that infernal iPad like she was signaling to a plane. *Has she had that thing surgically attached?*

When nobody moved, Brooke thwacked Teddy's shoulder with her hip and squeezed onto the small bench. "I'm serious, this is way more important than your taco salad," she said, shoving Teddy's lunch off to the left. "Also, I don't know how you can eat that."

"With a fork," Teddy responded mildly, taking a bite. Across from him, Molly reached over to scoop some for herself.

"Are you…*having lunch* with us?" Max asked, before she could help herself. Working for Brooke was about the limit of what she could handle in terms of changing the status quo.

Brooke furrowed her brow. "No," she said. "This is business. Max, your last couple entries got us into the big time. Look."

She shoved her iPad under Max's nose. Her browser was on something called Site Meter, and it showed that they'd already gotten more than fifty thousand visitors over the past week.

Holy shit.

"And there have only been ten comments calling me a she-male stank ho," Brooke said triumphantly. "The rest are all totally glowing. They want more insider dirt."

"How is this happening?" Max asked.

"People with desk jobs like to procrastinate," Brooke said gaily. "Plus, I posted several different links in the comments of one of Perez Hilton's entries. I am brilliant." She squinted at her tablet. "Also, according to this thing, Gawker and The Hollywood Reporter both linked to me."

"Damn. It's been, what, four days? You're going viral," Molly said.

Holy double-shit.

Max shoved her sandwich into her mouth to hide any of her potential facial expressions. Everything seemed to freeze. She was two parts terrified—what if Moxie Stilts *did* sue them?—and one part exhilarated. She'd *done* it.

She'd put words out there and people were reading them, and *liking* it, and she hadn't spontaneously combusted. Maybe all those authors who used pen names were on to something.

"This is even better than I'd expected," Brooke said. "Ari's mom has already gotten three calls from casting directors and producers wondering if I'd like to come in and read for things."

"Really?" Molly asked. "That fast?"

"Apparently, an attractive, articulate, well-groomed celebrity child with buzzworthy things to say is a desirable employee," Brooke said, glowing. "I hope you'll all acknowledge now that this idea was *genius*."

She stood up and brushed off the back of her short printed Alice + Olivia skirt. "And Max, tick tock, I need your ideas for my next entry ASAP. Seriously," she said in a low voice before scurrying off to her own, more centrally located lunch table. Jennifer Parker looked passionately annoyed. Arugula just looked right at Molly and scratched her nose with her middle finger. Apparently she was still bitter about losing out on Teddy.

Max's legs felt rubbery. "I will pay you both a dollar if we can get through the rest of this lunch break without mentioning blogs or Brooke Berlin."

"Sold," Teddy said.

"I'm fine with that," Molly agreed, taking a bite of her turkey sandwich. "Teddy has news, anyway."

Teddy cracked his knuckles. "It's seriously nothing," he

said. "Bone entered Mental Hygienist into some kind of Facebook contest that MTV is having, that's all. They're looking for a theme song for some new reality show."

"About teenage bullfighters," Molly interjected.

"They're saying it's like *Laguna Beach*, but with a slightly higher potential for someone to get gored," Teddy said. "Anyway, he entered us in the contest on the sly, but we made it into the semifinal round and now he thinks we're going to win."

"That rules!" Max crowed. "Maybe you *will*."

"We absolutely won't," Teddy said. "MTV will never use a song called 'Heat Me Up (Love Microwave).'"

"You don't know. These *are* the people making a show about teen bullfighters," Max pointed out.

Teddy snapped off a piece of his taco salad's shell. "There are a lot of great unsigned bands in Los Angeles, and I am okay with the fact that Mental Hygienist is not one of them," he said, scooping up some guacamole. "Bone has his hopes up, though. He told me yesterday that he really wants a Lamborghini."

He stuck out his hand. "Now, give me my dollar," he said. "That didn't have anything to do with You Know Who."

"Lord Voldemort?" Max asked, grinning.

"It wouldn't be the first time she's been called that," Molly noted. "Probably not even this week. But lunch isn't over yet."

It was the only time all day Max got a break from the words *Brooke Berlin*. People whispered incessantly, fervently, about Brooke's blog. It took all Max's inner fortitude to keep her poker face in place. She had just texted Molly that she was ditching the carnival meeting in favor of a nerve-soothing nap when—of course—her mother's head poked out the door of the main office.

"Maxine! You are headed in the wrong direction."

Max shuffled to a stop and reshouldered her backpack. "You mean, like, in a spiritual sense?"

"Cute. Mr. Kemp's room is that way."

"Mom, can't I skip this one?" she pleaded. "I was up so late working with Brooke on her bl—um, biology."

To keep her parents from asking questions, Max had told them she was tutoring Brooke in . . . well, everything. By the time her mother got wind that Brooke's grades were exactly the same—and, in fact, not sufficiently bad to require tutoring (the great surprise about Brooke was her solid GPA)—this whole blogographer thing probably would be over and Max would have enough cash to get out of Dodge for the summer.

"I am very proud of how industrious you are," Mrs. McCormack said. "And I am also totally unmoved. Go to the meeting. You will never get this wonderful high school time back."

Max just looked at her. Apparently, her mother's formative years were one big glossy picnic, where nobody threw elbows in the hallway, or thought "budget shopping" meant buying only *one* Issa dress, or got a huge zit on their noses that ended in half the grade calling them Mount

Kermitmonjaro (Chaz had been so pleased with that one). Max loved her mother, but she suspected that she would love her mother a thousand times more when the woman wasn't up in her grill every single day. *Like when I go to New York. If I go to New York.*

But all she said was, "Fine," then spun around on her boot and stomped toward Mr. Kemp's classroom.

"And so it is with deep regret that I must step down as the head of the Spring Carnival Planning Committee," she could hear Brooke saying. Max leaned against the doorjamb to watch. Anna Fury looked thrilled, and Jake was sitting with his back to Jennifer and texting someone, apparently not having heard a word of it.

"Oh, my God! That's just so sad for us!" Anna said, clicking into sycophant mode. "Are you okay?"

"I've never been better," Brooke said. "But, as I said in my statement, I simply have too many professional and creative obligations on my plate to give the Spring Carnival the attention it deserves. That being said, I am confident that I'm leaving you in good hands."

Anna's grin consumed her whole head. Brooke turned around and looked at the classroom's ticking clock.

"She ought to be here any minute," she said.

Anna's face fell. "Wait. Shouldn't we vote on—" she began.

"I'm here, Brooke," said a voice from behind Max. Brie squeezed past her with an apologetic smile.

"Excellent!" Brooke said, clapping her hands in a way

105

that reminded Max of Brick. She gave Brie her front-and-center spot. "You all know my assistant, Brie. As of today, she is the acting head of this planning committee. Brie will be reporting back to me, so it's not as if I'm completely abandoning you." She stood up. "Brie, is there anything you want to say before I go?"

Brie tapped Mr. Kemp's desk. "Um," she said, flushing and rubbing at the left lens of her bifocals.

"Well, that was compelling," Anna seethed.

"I've worked for Brooke for almost two years, so I know her vision," Brie began. "And I plan to execute the duties she set out for me to the best of my abilities. I'm sure we'll all work together to make this the best Spring Carnival yet."

"Obviously," Brooke said, pulling her glossy leather Louis Vuitton satchel out from under Mr. Kemp's desk. "My name *is* still on this thing." Suddenly she spotted Max still standing in the doorway. "Oh, Maxine," she said loudly. "A word, please, in the hallway."

Max backed out of the door frame. "What's wrong?" she whispered.

Brooke held up a finger. "Maxine, we need to talk about your raging attitude problems," she said loudly, aiming her mouth at the open door. To Max, she whispered, "Nothing. The audition requests are pouring in, so we need to get out of here. But we can't look too chummy."

"I—"

"Play along," Brooke urged her.

Max considered this. Maybe it would be therapeutic.

"I don't care what you say, Brooke. I am bored with your pointless carnival," she practically shouted. That *did* feel good. In a lower voice Max added, "My mother told me I had to come. She'll totally check in."

"That's why I have a plan," Brooke said, shaking her head. "You have *so much* to learn from me." Then Brooke raised her voice. "No wonder you never have a date," she all but yelled. "You're married to your own smug sense of superiority. I am taking you straight to your mother's office."

Max let out a melodramatically fatigued breath. "Fine," she boomed.

Brooke nodded briskly. "Your delivery needs work, but that should do it," she whispered, grabbing Max's arm and trotting off toward the main office. Max watched as Brooke stuck her head inside.

"Is she — Oh, hi, Headmistress McCormack," she heard Brooke say. "Groovy cardigan. I just wanted to let you know that Max and I are heading off campus to price some things for the carnival. Awesome! Thanks."

Brooke turned back to Max, looking self-satisfied. "See?" she whispered. "All taken care of. Now give me a ride home — we need to figure out how to run with my raging success."

Max felt a little buzzing in her head. It was either the fatigue or she was completely stoked. Possibly both. "Let's go kick some ass," she said.

nine

"JUST ONE MORE TIME."

"No, I haven't even had any caffeine yet," Max grunted, heaving her banged-up tan satchel onto the security table and walking through the metal detector.

"Pleeeeease?" Brooke wheedled from the other side of security.

A uniformed Warner Bros. guard rummaged through Max's bag, pulling out her Blistex, a torn spiral notebook, a half-eaten Luna Bar, a pair of sunglasses missing one lens, and three socks. He cocked an eyebrow.

Yeah, buddy? You should see my room.

"I promise this is the last time," Brooke said.

"That's because your audition is in, like, five minutes," Max pointed out, as the guard dumped everything back into her bag and handed it over with a curt nod. Max thanked him and shuffled onto the lot, rubbing her eyes. Apparently, in Brooke's dictionary of made-up words, *blogographer* also meant *lackey*. On this particular Saturday, she'd dragged Max out of bed at seven in the morning for a day of auditions—"I don't want you to miss any of the action!"—and in the last week alone Max had spent every waking hour forced to rehearse as a psychic, a detective, an evil twin (sort of fun), a good twin (completely *un*fun), and the main detective from *Bones*. At first Max amused herself by deploying a series of deliberately terrible accents. But then Brooke became compelled to try to coach memorable performances out of her, and Max didn't have the patience to morph herself into an actress on top of everything else.

At least the blog was going okay. Traffic was soaring. The other day Vixen.com had called Brooke the "celebutante Dorothy Parker of our time." The hyperbole had made Max want to barf a little—it was just a blog about random crap, half of which she made up—but then Brooke had given her a bonus. Maybe, Max thought as she trailed Brooke down a wide lane filled mostly with white vans, she should stop being such a crank. It wasn't *Brooke's* fault that Max's father had broken the coffeemaker when he'd tried to turn it into a cocktail shaker, and a sunny, crisp mid-March day rolling around the back lot of one of the biggest movie studios in Hollywood was bound to be more fun than her usual routine (sleeping until noon, picking a fight with her mother, staring at her still-blank NYU application, and then watching a crummy Drew Barrymore movie on HBO).

"Fine. One more time," Max said. "But just the part with your speech, okay? And you now owe me *two* coffees." She cleared her throat and read aloud, in the most deadpan voice she could muster, "Nancy, this is crazy."

"No, Ned. Crazy is me lying shivering and hungry on a bed made of the trash bags of *strangers*," Brooke replied, halting in front of a vending machine and reciting the line from memory. "Crazy is how all my bedtime stories came from the drug dealer selling crack outside my window. But finding the man who killed your father? Fighting for the truth? From where I'm sitting, Ned, that's the only thing that makes any sense at all."

A tear squeaked out of Brooke's left eye and rolled through her bronzer onto her chin.

"Not bad," Max offered, trying to take in the sights of the lot. She was pretty sure the parking spot they'd just passed said G. CLOONEY on it.

"Gee, thanks," Brooke snorted, turning away and breaking into a walk so speedy that Max could barely keep up. "Daddy always says, 'Nothing is *so* bad as something that is not-so-bad.'"

"I don't even know what that means."

"It means that if you can't be awesome, you're better off being awful, because at least awful is memorable," Brooke said from several feet down the road. "I mean, look at Keanu Reeves."

Max thought about the *Point Break* poster in her room. "Huh. I actually agree with you," Max said. "Okay, then, you were good. Very believable." And she meant it. "But the script is cracktacularly bad." She meant that, too.

Brooke sighed, and finally stopped to examine her lip gloss in the reflection of an office window. As Max caught up, a guy looked up from his computer and jumped in surprise when he saw them. *I feel you, dude,* she thought.

"No, Max. It's actually a really gritty look at the *Nancy Drew* mythos," Brooke explained, in words Max suspected she'd been fed by Caroline Goldberg. "Nancy is *the* hot role in town right now. They've been trying to cast her for months." She fluffed her hair. "It's a lot to expect my first time on the circuit, of course. Personally, I think I'd make a wonderful Bess. She *is* the pretty friend."

"I also seem to recall them calling her fat a lot of the time."

Brooke brightened. "Yes! A fat suit would be so humble. I mean, Nicole Kidman won an Oscar for going ugly, and that was just a fake nose and a bun."

A golf cart sped past them — was that Jeremy Renner? — as they trudged across the expansive studio lot. Max had only been there once before, when she was in sixth grade and her mother had insisted they go on the official tour. Like any kid that age being forced to sightsee, Max had spent the entire time staring at her sneakers and wishing she was somewhere else—specifically, a place where nobody used perky phrases like *movie magic* and meant them. So this was Max's first real look around the lot, which felt like it had been up and running for hours already, or maybe never shut down from the night before. Numbered soundstages loomed above them in endless, tidy rows, like gargantuan cream-colored versions of boxy Monopoly hotels. Their barnlike wooden doors hung open as men lugged ladders and lighting rigs through them; if she peeked inside at just the right angle, Max could see familiar living room sets and spy caves and schoolrooms, all of which looked impossibly small under the sound-stages' soaring ceilings, crisscrossed by complex wooden catwalks, tangled wires, and electronic equipment. Brooke swung left and detoured them through the lot's semireal-istic outdoor sets: fake brownstones, fake small-town America, fake big-city America. A parade of what *had* to be extras—on account of their animal costumes—marched toward Small Town U.S.A.'s gazebo, led by a harried girl holding a clipboard. The donkey nearest to Max carried a croissant in each hoof.

"The people-watching here is unbelievable," she said.

"Tell me about it," Brooke said. "A couple of years ago I came here for the Harry Potter costume exhibit, and I saw Shia LaBeouf sitting outside the commissary in his *Indiana Jones* costume, all fake-bloodied and dirty, as if that was totally normal." Brooke wrinkled her nose. "Except he was smoking, which is so *over*, like, hi, you're not Don Draper."

As Max took it all in—peeling shop windows dusted with fake frost and decorated for a Christmas movie, the diner on the corner that was Luke's when *Gilmore Girls* still existed and that now appeared to be (temporarily) a toy store, and crew members in headsets barking at one another—she felt goose bumps pop up on her arms. It seemed dorky to admit it, even to herself, but the air felt oddly electric—and it made her want to be part of it. To create. To write. For real.

"I bet it was fun growing up around all this," was all Max allowed herself to say.

"I didn't, really," Brooke said, sounding almost too casual. "Daddy didn't want me exposed to the industry until I was older, so I never came to set. He thought it would warp my brain or something. His assistant always showed me pictures, though, so...you know. It *seemed* super exciting."

There was a hint of loneliness in Brooke's voice.

"Here we are," Brooke said, effectively preventing Max from having to figure out how to react. She guided them toward a tall office building on the fringe of the lot. "Daddy rappelled down this building in the climactic scene of *Dirk Venom: Bite to Kill*," she said. "But it's actually just corporate offices."

They pushed through an incredibly heavy set of double doors and into a generic-looking lobby, albeit one with unusually flattering lighting and an expansive array of orchids on the reception desk. Brooke flashed an e-mail on her iPhone to the man behind the blooms, and he nodded toward the elevator. Max wondered if this was a private audition, a personal favor to Brick Berlin, because there was absolutely nobody else in sight. But as soon as the elevator doors slid open again, Max realized this wasn't just some random meeting: The fifth-floor lobby was crammed with easily two hundred girls, some naturally redheaded, some in wigs whose quality ranged from decent to Fell Off the Back of the *Annie* Tour Bus, all looking two seconds away from needing to breathe into a paper bag.

"Wow," Max said. "If this is how many they see in one day, how many did they see in months?"

"I told you, this is *the* part," Brooke said.

"Is that Emma Roberts?" Max asked, squinting down the hall.

"Probably," Brooke said. "Nobody saw her version of *Nancy Drew*. She might as well try again. Okay, stay put, I need to go let the coordinator know I'm here. It's supposed to be first come, first served, but...you know."

Max found a spot against the wall and slid down to the floor. Everyone in her vicinity was picking at scripts they'd nervously rolled into scrolls and then squeezed to death. Several were reciting lines under their breath, like a very superficial Gregorian chant. Suddenly, somebody burst out of a conference room door sobbing and ran to a hard-looking woman Max assumed was her mother.

"Let me guess—you blew it," the girl's mother scolded. "*Again*. You have no focus. Do you have any idea how much *money* we've spent on you? Acting lessons, and your chin job, and all that acne..."

The woman's nasty berating trailed off as they stepped into the elevator. There was something naggingly familiar about the pair. *Do I know them?*

A girl to her left nudged her. "Did you see? That was—"

"Carla Callahan," Max blurted. The last time Max had seen Carla in person, Carla was standing in front of their art class, announcing that she had landed a major TV role and telling everyone she hoped they, too, someday might beat the odds and amount to something. Max had gagged.

"This has happened with her every time since *iNeverland* got canceled," the girl said, picking at the ends of her long, sandy ponytail. "I've seen her on, like, ten auditions this year, and her mother always screams. Mrs. Callahan is the worst stage mom in town. Well. Actually, Jennifer Parker's is really mean, too."

"I go to school with Jennifer," Max said. "I didn't realize anyone knew who she was anymore."

"Oh, yeah," the girl said, warming up to her topic. "We all know each other. Half of us did guest spots when she was on *That's My Room!* It's so sad now, though. She auditions for *everything*. That's why you see her in so many late-night infomercials. Her mother is desperate to milk her for cash. Always tells her she should've gotten her teeth done. So mean."

But accurate.

"But accurate," the girl added suddenly. "So, what are you up for?"

"Oh, I'm not auditioning," Max said. "I'm just waiting for someone."

"Good." The girl exhaled. "In the script, Nancy lives in some kind of shanty in Baltimore, and with your hair and those boots you kind of *look* like a drug addict, so…"

"Thanks so much," Max said with a withering stare, her mind snapping shut again.

"God. Sorry. This whole competition thing messes with your head," the girl apologized. "I just meant…never mind. Who are you here with?"

"Brooke Berlin? She's—"

"Brick Berlin's daughter? *She's* up for this part?" the girl snapped. "The shallow blonde one, right? Not the boring new one with the terrible bangs?"

Max felt her hackles rise. "Have you even *met* either of them?" she asked.

"I don't need to," the girl said. "Those legacy kids are all alike. Dumb, strung out, and pretty sure they deserve to be famous just for being born."

"Brooke is a lot smarter than people give her credit for," Max said, suddenly feeling an urgent and inexplicable need to defend Brooke's honor. "I mean, her blog is a huge hit. That has to count for something."

"Please." The girl rolled her eyes. "I'm sorry, but it just sucks. Girls like her get everything handed to them, while talented people like me work really hard and get nowhere."

Max stood up hotly. "Brooke *does* work really hard. She can't help who her father is," she said. "And maybe if you spent less time being bitter about other people's successes, you'd find some of your own."

"What are you, like, on Brooke's payroll?" the girl snapped.

"She's my friend," said a voice, and both girls looked up to see Brooke standing above them looking very ticked off. "And my scene partner. And thanks to her, I just nailed it in there."

"You're done already?" Max asked.

"Yes. Obviously, they wanted to see me right away," Brooke said, then flashed a sweet smile at their cowed companion, who was suddenly extremely interested in examining her split ends. "And when I was done, they actually applauded. Good luck following that up. But don't worry. I'm sure you'll make a *great* extra."

Without looking back, they swept out of there. Well, Brooke swept. Max trotted behind her with as dignified a gait as she could manage.

"Did they really clap?" Max asked as soon as the elevator doors closed on them.

"No," Brooke said. "But it made a better story that way." She cast Max an odd look. "Thanks for sticking up for me."

"Don't worry about it," Max said.

In truth, she had surprised herself. But as they walked back out onto the lot toward the parking garage, Max realized what had rubbed her the wrong way: The girl was saying exactly the type of stuff Max usually said. And Max hadn't liked how it sounded.

✦ ✦ ✦

The rest of the day was as grim as Warner Bros. had been satisfying. From the vast, impressive studio, they'd driven across town to the *Rogue Justice* office, and found it in a windowless cube flanked by a pawn shop and a podiatrist's office on a pothole-marked stretch of Culver City. They visited two potential CW shows being developed in similarly depressing places, dropped by a well-known TV producer's offices that claimed to be "in the shadow of Paramount Pictures' iconic Melrose Avenue lot" but were in fact more of a neighbor to the Astro Burger's Dumpster, and were coming from a place in Beverly Hills that looked promising until they'd gone inside and seen that it contained no furniture. Brooke had read for the project— a *Saved by the Bell* reboot—sitting cross-legged on a scratchy brown Berber carpet while the producer, who Max could swear was one of the original cast members, flicked his cigarette into a bottle of Mountain Dew and asked her things like, "Yes, but dig deep—what is the bell saving your character *from?*"

They capped the day with a drive down Hollywood Boulevard, the eastern part of which was mostly latex-clothing stores and places that sold "hilarious" bongs. A sixtyish man in knee socks and sandals snapped a photo of his wife giving the thumbs-up sign to something on the sidewalk, while a nearby homeless man held up bunny ears.

"I can't imagine coming here as a tourist," Max said. "Hollywood is so *disappointing*. Do you think Audrey Hepburn would still want her star on the Walk of Fame if she knew it was in front of a place that hawks edible panties?"

"Oh, Max, don't be so literal," Brooke scoffed.

"What, they're not actually edible?"

"No, I mean, Hollywood isn't about the actual street, or geographical place. It's an idea. A concept."

"Well, *conceptually*, it needs to name itself after some-place more attractive," Max said. Then she paused. "I sound like you. We are spending too much time together already."

Brooke laughed, then grabbed the armrest as Max took a hard right down Gower Street. "Careful," Brooke scolded. "This isn't your old junkheap. This is a Lexus. It demands finesse. Wait, there it is. Pull over so we can switch."

"Fine, but don't go fifty miles an hour into the parking spot again," Max warned her. "If this thing has a scratch on it tomorrow, Molly is going to kill me."

Max parked by the sidewalk and hopped out of the car. After Max had driven Brooke home from school that one afternoon, Brooke announced she would never again grace Max's "unfumigated steel death trap" and brokered a deal with Molly wherein Max—as an actual licensed driver—chauffeured Brooke around town in the Lexus. But Brooke privately insisted that Max let her behind the wheel for all their arrivals and departures, claiming she needed to be seen as down-to-earth.

"Also, they need to know I can drive, for any potential chase scenes," she said brightly.

As if she were in one of them now, Brooke jammed the car into Drive and flew left through a broken guard gate, parking in front of an expanse of three-story buildings that had all the curb appeal of a prison.

"We're here!" Brooke said, brandishing the script sides for the reading.

"Thank God," Max said, wincing as she spied a gang tag. She'd had no idea that so many Hollywood producers worked out of such nickel-and-dime office spaces. At this rate their next stop would be a shed in the bowels of Sun Valley. "We should have called your blog 'Notes from the Underbelly.'"

"You can change it to that if I get *Saved by the Bell*," Brooke said.

Max laughed. "Funny and true," she said grudgingly.

"See? I'm actually a scintillating and witty person," Brooke said. "I just don't have time to type about it."

They entered a poorly lit office with dingy, off-white walls and dark blue industrial carpeting. Brooke exchanged a few words with the receptionist and immediately waved Max off, which Max knew meant she had finagled a meeting with the top honcho. Max retreated to the small waiting area, dotted with attractive people studying script sides in cheap-looking plastic chairs. Max slumped into a lime-colored one and closed her eyes. She never *had* gotten any coffee.

A voice said, "Long day?"

She opened an eye and saw a familiar-looking guy sitting to her right—cute, in a bookish way, and wearing faded cords and a vintage COKE IS IT T-shirt.

"The longest," she said. "I know you from somewhere, right?"

"Moxie Stilts's party," he said. "You're Max. We almost broke each other's noses."

"Oh, right, sorry—I didn't recognize you with the glasses," she said.

"I'm blind without them," he admitted. "The only reason I recognize you is that when that door hit my face, it gave me half an hour of twenty-twenty vision." He touched the thin black frames. "Do they make me look smarter?"

"Compared to who?" she teased.

"Don't you mean *whom*?" he retorted with twinkling eyes, tapping his glasses again.

"Yes, you're *such* a brainiac."

"I owed you one," he said, patting his nose exaggeratedly. "You almost destroyed the Sexy."

"Oh, you're fine. Cry me a river."

"I'm an *actor*," he said. "We're very sensitive. Especially about our faces."

Max sat up straight. "Wait, you told me at the party that you hate actors."

He scrunched up his face. "Welcome to my existential crisis," he said. "I really only got into acting by accident. I won a commercial-writing contest in Pittsburgh and then they made me star in it. One thing led to another and suddenly I'm doing incredibly prestigious roles like Third Altar Boy from the Left on a Very Special Episode of *Cougar Town*."

Max shook her head slowly. "I can't believe you let me sit there and say all actors are irritating. I feel so dumb now."

"But it's true!" he insisted. "My roommate is Method, so the time he got a part as a villain in *Spy Kidz 5: Look Who's Skulking*, he spent three weeks talking sports with me in a Russian accent. 'Steelers vill vin das Super Bowl, yes?'"

Max laughed. "You're making that up!"

"Scout's honor," he said, holding up the familiar two-fingered salute. "And I once had an audition for something set in Tennessee, so I ordered pizza from five different Domino's in a fake accent just to practice. Maybe *I'm* irritating. Who *does* that?"

"I used a British accent to call the library one time," Max admitted. "I owed late fees on a book and I was too embarrassed to talk to them about it as me."

"What book?"

"I'll never tell. You're too irritating," Max teased. "You won't even tell me your name."

He stuck out his hand. "Whoops. I'm Brady—Brady Swift."

Max took Brady's hand and shook it. He felt warm but a little rough, as if he wasn't the type of Hollywood pretty boy who got manicures or waxed his chest. Big points.

"*Of course* that's your name," she said. "That's the perfect actor name."

"Yes. That's another irritating thing about me," he said, fishing a Snickers bar out of his pants pocket and unwrapping it. "It's the perfect actor name because, like every third person in this business, it's not my real name. I had to change it."

Max raised a brow. "*Had* to?"

Brady took a bite of his candy bar. "Prepare yourself," he said, swallowing. "My real name is Taylor."

He looked at her expectantly.

"Taylor...?"

"...Swift?" he finished for her.

Max tried to make her mirth sound polite, but it was hard. "Wow, I'm really sorry it didn't work out with Jake Gyllenhaal. I was sure that was true love."

"That girl ruined my life," Brady said cheerfully. "So I used my mother's maiden name instead. I lobbied for Skippy, or Engelbert, but my mother said it would bring shame to my unborn children or something, as if that

Cougar Town episode isn't going to embarrass them enough."

Max's phone buzzed. She checked it; it was Jake. She felt rude reading a text, so she decided to deal with it later. (She hated people who were chained to their cells.)

"So, what are you auditioning for, Skippy?" she asked Brady, tossing the phone back into her bag.

He covered his face with his hands. *"Psychic Lifeguard,"* he said through his fingers. "Don't think less of me. I need to eat and pay for college."

"Shut up! I love that show," Max said. "How he runs up to people who are just sunbathing and tells them that in ten minutes he'll save their lives?"

"And they all go in the water anyway, because they are morons?" Brady chimed in, his gray eyes dancing. "It's the dumbest show on television. Totally brilliant."

He leaned forward for emphasis and accidentally bumped her shoe with one of his. Max felt a strange jolt and involuntarily tensed as her mouth went dry. She was almost relieved when her phone visibly buzzed again, so she could shift position under the guise of tucking it farther into her bag.

"So, what are you doing here?" Brady asked. "Are you an actress?"

"Oh, God, no. I'm clearly not irritating enough," Max said.

"Clearly," Brady echoed with a smirk.

"I'm just here with Brooke."

"Who's Brooke?"

"Didn't you see her come in?" Max asked. "Brooke Berlin. She's here reading for something."

Recognition flashed across Brady's face. "I knew she looked familiar," he said. "I just saw something she wrote online. It was really funny."

"Oh, thanks—I mean, on her behalf," Max said, feeling a warmth spread in her chest.

"She sounds cool. Takes guts to call out some of the lunatics in this town, especially when her dad is so famous."

A messy brunette in a belly shirt and a wrap skirt poked her head around the corner. "Brady Swift? They're ready for you."

He stood up and crumpled the Snickers wrapper in his hand. "Okay, wish me luck. I'm so sick of eating ramen noodles."

"Break a leg, Engelbert," Max said.

"Psychic Lifeguard would *never* allow that to happen," he deadpanned before disappearing around the corner.

Max leaned her head back against the wall and let her eyelids drift shut again. Her phone buzzed again but she was too tired to care. She made a mental note to check in with Jake later, just in case she'd missed something dramatic at all the Spring Carnival meetings she'd been blowing off to help Brooke rehearse.

"So, these guys totally dig the blog," Brooke announced as she reappeared. "People apparently think I'm 'bravely funny.'"

"I would agree with that," Max said, and smiled. "Are we done for the day, finally? Bravely funny blogs don't write themselves."

OPENBR👓KE.COM

MARCH 19

Lots of questions from readers after my last entry. Apparently none of you believe that I actually own shoes by Jessica Simpson, to which I say: Go try them on and then tell me who's crazy. And honestly, as much as I treasure my Jimmy Choos and my Blahniks, I have no patience for footwear elitism. A cute shoe is a cute shoe. Maybe that will be my new cause célèbre. It beats that made-up charity those boneheads from *Jugular* are pimping on the cover of *People* this week. Whoever heard of Juvenile Fang Syndrome? They're like the Hollywood version of that e-mail where a "prince" from Nigeria begs for financial help.

Let's take a look at the rest of the Open Brooke mailbag:

Q. Are you dating anyone?
A. I don't have time! My sister, Molly, is dating a guitar player (you might be familiar with

his band, Mental Hygienist, because they're in a Facebook contest right now that's looking for the theme song for MTV's new show *Bull-fight Club*), and so she's almost never around—having a boyfriend is like having a full-time job. So for me it, would be like a *third* career, behind school and acting. I'm not that industrious. Plus, half of young Hollywood has that Bieber hair that looks like someone dropped it on their heads from a high place. I can't date that. He would use all my product.

Q. Have you gotten any cool auditions lately?

A. Some cool, and some whose wretchedness defies description. I did a reading opposite the star of a popular teen soap who distracted me the entire time because she was wearing knit arm-warmers, a tank top, and shearling booty shorts. I'm not kidding—they were like Uggs for your butt. If Antarctica gets an NFL franchise, then I know what the cheerleaders will be wearing. She also kept spitting on every fourth word. Insider tip: If you're auditioning for her show, bring an umbrella. But I also read for what is going to be *the* teen girl part of the year, and just between us, I'm pretty sure I nailed it. (Of course, twenty thousand other aspiring actresses probably told their friends the same thing.) This movie is based on a popular book series, and so one of the stock "getting to know you" questions at the audition was about your favorite book with a teen-age protagonist. I wonder how many people answered *Twilight*, because when I told the casting people I loved *Catcher in the Rye*, one of them dropped her coffee. My pet theory is that the entire genesis of teen-centric entertainment— from, say, *Ferris Bueller* to the very existence of the CW—could be traced back to that book's success, and its welcome insistence on giving a teenage character the same intellectual and emotional heft as an adult one. And a snarky POV, of course. But they didn't get to hear my mad literary science, because they were too busy trying to mop up that woman's coffee mess. So you're getting it first.

Q. *Are you the answer to the blind item in last week's* Hey! *about the meth-head child of a major celebrity?*

A. It definitely sounded like it was supposed to be me. But as anyone who has ever seen me in person can attest, I've got the furthest thing from meth-face. Also: I've seen enough people in this town turn into drooling lunatics to know that I should avoid anything stronger than Advil.

However, I've got some juicy tidbits for you:

1) WHICH famous niece was sent packing after a *Nancy Drew* audition because "with her coloring she wouldn't work as a redhead"?

2) WHICH spunky starlet got a seriously lousy birthday present from one of her party guests? He took her to Crab Fest, and I'm not talking about Red Lobster.

3) WHICH former teen star's mom has turned into a mega-jackass? (No, it's not anybody in my social circle.) Listen: This city is all about rejection. So if you are a mom whose kid is putting him- or herself out there every day, trying to be the one in a million who hits it big, don't be a jerkwad. Imagine if you had the fate of your family's grocery budget on your shoulders at sixteen, when all you really wanted to be doing was day-dreaming about boys and maybe getting drunk on wine coolers at a college party. It would've sucked, right? So stop yelling. It's gross. Also, I hate your pants. I'm just saying.

Until next time,

B.

ten

"PICK UP YOUR FEET, McCormack!" the gym teacher, Coach Petit, yelled. "We're not paying you to chat!"

"You're not paying me to run, either," Max panted, infinitesimally increasing her pace around the Colby-Randall track. "I don't know how you deal with her every day in practice."

Molly, jogging alongside her for company, grimaced. "The beauty of cross-country is that it's based on running away from her for long periods of time."

"Where is Brooke, anyway?" Max crabbed. "I know Friday afternoon gym is totally lame, but she's already skipped it like ten times this year."

"She got a note from Brick's hypnotherapist. Something

about the prospect of group sports contributing to her claustrophobia."

"I have got to get in with her doctor," Max said. "I'm being crippled by how badly I need to take a nap."

Things had been crazy since OpenBrooke.com launched. And yet, weirdly fantastic—being so busy somehow made Max more productive. Her grades were up, because the little time she had to study, she had to maximize. She and Brooke had slipped into a pleasant social truce—they weren't sitting around braiding each other's hair and talking about their periods, but they weren't sniping at each other all the time, either. (Well, not in a mean way, anyhow. Max didn't think she could live in a world where she couldn't get in a couple of digs at Brooke Berlin every now and again—it was like getting a dog to unlearn how to bark—and she suspected Brooke felt the same about her.) And above all, the blog was exploding, thanks to a mention on *Conan*. Max loved hearing chatter about it everywhere she went, be it history class or Café Munch just off campus, or on her various errands with Brooke. It was addictive.

They rounded the top of the track, which was set into the base of one of the foothills Colby-Randall abutted. Cement benches had been erected at some point in the thirties, when the venue had been an outdoor amphitheater. While the junior class girls ran laps, the guys were running the stairs. Max and Molly reached them just as Jake Donovan finished.

"Max!" he yelled, trotting toward them. "Are you avoiding me?"

Max could feel Molly's eyes on her. And Jake's. And other people's. "No," she said, as Jake fell into stride with them.

"Hey, Dix," he said, leaning across her to greet Molly. "Do you think Max is avoiding me?"

"Why would you think that?" Molly asked him.

Jake made a "duh" face. "Well, because I've texted her about a hundred times and she never answers, and," he added, turning to Max, "you never go to the carnival planning meetings and it's *so boring,* especially now that Jennifer isn't speaking to me."

"Why isn't Jennifer talking to you this time?" Max asked.

"Dude, we *broke up.* For real. I even changed my Facebook status to single."

Max stopped, confused. How had she not noticed that? Come to think of it, when was the last time she'd checked Jake's Twitter? "I must have missed that," she said feebly.

"*Really?*" Molly said, then shot Max an apologetic look.

Jake beamed. "I took a stand," he said. "She was just always kinda mean to me. Coach told me I have to line up in the shotgun next season instead of under center, and she didn't even *care.*"

"I'm sorry," Max offered. It might have been the biggest lie she'd told all year, and based on the last two weeks alone, that was saying something.

Jake shook his head. "It's totally for the best. I have better people to hang out with. People who make me *happy*." He inched toward her. "But then I started worrying that you were mad at me or something."

"Me?" Max asked, confused. Suddenly she felt very conscious of smelling like... well, like gym class.

A wide, white-toothed grin spread across Jake's face. "Yeah, you, dummy," he said. "I really missed you."

"Missed *me*?" Max echoed again. Molly coughed lightly. "I mean, I'm sorry. I've just been really busy with an... outside project."

"McCormack, stop flirting and step it up!" Coach Petit screamed from across the track.

Jake jumped. "God, she's meaner than Coach," he said. "Anyway. I'm stoked we're cool." He did that boy thing where he turned his body so that he nudged her in the arm. "We should really hang out sometime."

"Yes, sometime," Max said, still discombobulated.

"Like, just the two of us."

Max begged her jaw to stay hinged. She could feel a flush climbing her cheeks. Molly stepped in and grabbed her. "Petit is going to kill you if you don't start running," she said, pushing Max forward.

Jake beamed and held out a hand, palm forward. "Don't leave me hanging, McCormack," he said, and Max gave him the world's most awkward high five before trotting away.

Molly turned to Max and raised her brows. "What just happened?"

Max shook her head. "I have no idea. Did he ... ?"

"I think he did," Molly said. "How did you not know they broke up? You usually monitor his social media like he's al-Qaeda and you're the CIA."

"I don't know," Max marveled. "I feel like I should get fired or something."

Molly grinned. "I guess you've been enjoying yourself too much with the blog to care."

"Yeah, right," Max scoffed, picking her pace up to a jog. "Like writing about Brooke's favorite toenail polish is so fun."

But, deep down, she knew Molly was right.

The last Friday of March was cloudy and gray, much like Brooke's mood. Two weeks had passed since her spate of auditions—not that much time in the Hollywood scheme of things, but an eternity in Brooke's universe, which mostly revolved around instant gratification (hence the size of her closet). She knew casting often took ages, but she also felt like Hollywood waited for no one, and her blog was hot *now*. Somebody needed to hurry up and snatch her out of the jaws of demi-obscurity before everyone lost interest in her natterings about Andrew Garfield's use of hair product.

Brooke distracted herself by blowing off school after lunch—running laps in gym class obviously would interfere with her digestion—and spending her afternoon on some hearty self-improvement. She'd begun with twenty minutes of yoga in her bedroom before she noticed a rogue cuticle that demanded immediate attention. That sucked her into the vortex of her bathroom, where she then accidentally spent twenty minutes hunting blackheads. Now, after doing some laps in a halfhearted attempt at cardio, she was standing in the middle of Brick's sauna in her sport bikini—she'd bought it when beach volleyball got popular for, like, half an hour during the Olympics; it made her feel like a serious athlete—trying to smoke out her pores while dry-brushing her thighs. *Cosmo* swore this would retard any lurking cellulite, but it felt weird and spartan, like some kind of Communist spa treatment. She had a moment of pause, wondering if this was too unglamorous an occupation for a budding star such as herself. However, she knew cellulite had no respect for a girl's fame level. Two seasons of the reality-hybrid *COPS: Jersey Shore* bore unfortunate witness to that.

At least she had the blog to cling to while she waited. Brooke loved how much people responded to it; there were three hundred comments alone on the entry in which Max confided "Brooke's" secret crush on Colin Firth no matter how jowly he was getting. Max had proved amazingly adept at assuming Brooke's basic tone and infusing it with a little of Arugula's braininess and Max's own sarcasm. Brooke might not be a household name yet, but she felt closer and closer every time someone quoted OpenBrooke.com on Twitter or UsMagazine.com linked to her in a roundup. It made her feel like a mogul—like a mini-Brick.

The door to the sauna burst open.

"You're late, Ari," Brooke said without looking. "Also, I think I might be giving myself a rash."

"Sunshine, drop whatever you are doing, unless it is biceps curls," her father boomed. "This is important."

Brooke whirled around and saw her father wiggling his iPhone at her. He pushed the FaceTime button, seeming a bit antsy. Caroline Goldberg's face appeared on the screen, looking—unusually for an agent—all business and no schmooze.

"Brooke," Caroline said crisply, "we need to discuss something."

Brooke looked from Caroline's slightly pixilated face to Brick's, which was drawn into an exaggerated stern expression. His lips were twitching like mad.

Oh, God. I didn't get any parts.

Caroline cleared her throat. "I hope you—"

"—feel comfortable answering to the name 'Nancy Drew'!" Brick finished in a volcanic torrent of speech, as if he could not possibly contain himself any longer. The phone clattered to the floor as he folded Brooke into his arms, squeezing so tightly that she sensed a decrease in her lung capacity.

"*Really?*" she squeaked.

"Really," Caroline's face said, staring straight up at them from the tile floor. "You're about to star in the biggest teen movie since *Twilight*. Can someone please pick up the phone? This is an unfortunate view."

Brick scooped it up. "Sorry, Caroline. We just needed to unleash our joy."

"That's touching," she said tersely. "Anyway, they think you're perfect for it. I believe their exact words were—"

"—that you had the ideal mix of brains and beauty to pull off the part!" Brick crowed, doing an endearing little hopping dance. All of a sudden, Brooke felt light-headed, as if someone had punched her in the stomach. *If I pass out and crack my head open and die in the sauna before I become a movie star, I am going to be so pissed.*

Brooke sank onto the cedar-plank bench and let out a breath. "Seriously?" she asked.

"Yes!" Brick said.

"Yes," Caroline reiterated. "Apparently, it came down to you and one other girl. They told me that what finally tilted them in your favor was—"

"—how savvy you seem on your blog!" Brick finished for her.

Caroline looked mildly annoyed. "Is there anything else you'd like to add, Brick?"

"Just that I always knew my Brookie was a wordsmith and a talent," he said fondly. "She's a chip off the old Brick."

"They want to get this signed quickly," Caroline said.

"I'll get going on the contract. Brick, you'll need to call your lawyers, and…"

Caroline kept talking—about on-set tutors and forms signed in triplicate and blah blah blah. But Brooke barely heard her. She felt like her blood had just started swirling twice as fast through her veins. Her thoughts were completely scrambled—if she were asked to transcribe them, they'd go something like, "*Ngvk4jn99434rnfnnfsgnanyohijhqwrk!!!!!1!!!*"

I got the part. I got the part. I got. The part.

"I got the paaaaaaaaart!" she screamed. Then she covered her mouth, embarrassed.

"Yes, I'm glad we're clear on that," Caroline said curtly.

"You knocked 'em dead, Sunshine!" Brick trilled, wrapping his arms around Brooke again, his phone still clutched in his hand.

"This is indeed a tender moment, but can we be done here?" Caroline said impatiently. "I have things to do that do not include a FaceTime chat with Brooke's rear end. Although I see you've been dry-brushing your thighs, Brooke. Don't. You'll get a rash."

Brick turned the phone upward. "Thanks for giving us the news, Caroline," he said, beaming. "And the grooming tips."

"No problem. Congratulations again, and be sure to keep that blog going, Brooke," she said.

Brick punched End and let out a whoop, then picked up Brooke and twirled her around the sauna, over and over, like she was seven again and he'd just returned home from shooting a movie on location. It was the best moment of Brooke's life. She closed her eyes and inhaled his familiar smell of chlorine, Brut, and a whiff of carrot juice, and wished this moment would never end.

eleven

MAX THREW HER SHOULDER into her mirrored closet door and pushed. It didn't budge. The damn thing never properly lived inside its plastic track, so it kept dragging against the carpet, making it almost impossible to get to the clothes on one side. She was due at a table read for *Nancy Drew* soon, her closet was a barely penetrable mess—not unlike her room—and she couldn't find anything to wear that wasn't dirty or suddenly totally horrible. She wished Molly would answer her phone. She needed advice. So far the only thing she'd unearthed was a relatively untarnished black denim skirt and a huge navy blue V-neck sweater that she was pretty sure she stole from Teddy.

Why do I even care? Maybe whatever makes Brooke so obsessed with her looks is contagious.

"What are you doing in there?" Teddy asked, nudging her in the butt with his toe.

Max jumped and glared at her brother. "Can you please announce yourself next time?" she said, annoyed. "What if I concussed myself on something?"

"I thought that *was* announcing myself," Teddy said. "But next time I'll have Jeeves make sure Milady is ready for visitors."

Max responded by flipping him the bird.

"Charming," Teddy said. "Don't strain the finger. It might inhibit your typing."

"You laugh," Max said, "but that's how I got out of picking up Brooke's dry cleaning the other day. Told her I couldn't risk my instrument."

"Trouble in bloggy paradise?" Teddy asked, watching Max paw through a pile of old shirts.

"She's not that bad," Max said, holding up a gray-and-black striped tee. It had a hole in the armpit. "She doesn't pull crap with me because I'm Molly's friend, and also because I hold the keys to her blog empire, so if I tell her to shove it she will be up a creek without a cell signal." She returned to digging through her clothes. "I can't believe this. I'm going to be late. I wish I had Brooke's closet. She's talking about getting this thing where all she has to do is push a button and everything starts rotating like at the dry cleaner's."

Teddy cocked his head. "I'm sorry, did I just hear you endorse a *motorized closet*? You, who once said that famous people are so dumb that you could shove a microchip in a Crisco jar and sell it to them for a grand?"

"Yeah, yeah," Max grumbled, backing out of her closet with two T-shirts. They turned out to be identical. She dove back into the abyss. Why were all her clothes dark? It was impossible to see what was what. "I'm just saying, maybe Dad could focus on inventing that, instead of whatever his gardening tool of the week is, so he could actually make some money."

She reemerged with a smirk. "But maybe with all your forthcoming band riches, all those problems will be solved."

Teddy groaned. "We're not in the finals yet," he said. "We have to send in another submission tape. Bone just wrote a song called 'Your Locker (Is Where Your Books and My Heart Are).' *Nobody* is going to want to listen to that."

"We'll just see," Max sang. "You got a ton of Facebook comments after I mentioned you on Open Brooke."

Teddy wrinkled his nose, then picked up an unfinished crossword from Max's bed and studied it absently. "Maybe I should go write some new songs just in case. Surely I can come up with something that outdoes the line, 'Six left, thirteen right, nine left; when you open your locker my heart leaves my chest.'"

"Good luck with that," Max said. She frowned. "What does a person wear to a table read, anyway?"

"Wow," Teddy said. "We are through the looking glass. Since when do you care what you wear to anything?"

"Since I started hanging out with a girl who's like six

feet tall and dresses like she owns stock in Prada," Max said. "And since I started having places to go that weren't, like, my bedroom. Since I got sucked into the vortex that is Brooke Berlin, basically. When we go anywhere together, I look like her Make-A-Wish kid. People seem disappointed when they find out I don't have cancer."

This was actually half-true. The other day Max and Brooke had been on Rodeo Drive—Brooke decreed Max needed to further her education in pointy-toed heels—and a salesman took one look at them, squeezed Brooke's shoulder, and said, "The needy are lucky to have you."

Teddy sat on the edge of Max's bed, shoving aside her quilt to expose her ratty old Garfield fitted sheet. "If you'd told me last year my band would blow up because of something you wrote on a blog where you're pretending to be Brooke Berlin, of all people, I would have told Mom to search your closet for drugs."

"Don't be silly. Mom would never look in here. It's a death trap," Max said, trying to disentangle a button-down shirt from her hair.

After a moment of silence, she looked up at Teddy, who seemed lost in thought.

"Teddy?" she prompted.

He shook his head. "Sorry," he said. "It's just so surreal—nobody had even heard of us until my sister, Fake Brooke Berlin, mentioned online that I'm dating the famously unfamous Berlin sibling. *Vortex* was the right word for what this is. It's an adjustment."

"This whole semester has been an adjustment," Max said. "I feel like I'm on some Oxygen show called *Touched by the Berlins*."

"No kidding," Teddy said. "Mostly, I can't believe Brooke's blog scheme actually *worked*. Next thing you know she'll sneeze and discover a cure for the common cold."

"Split ends are a cause dearer to her heart," Max snarked. "In all honesty, though, I don't think she can believe it, either. Not that she'd ever admit that."

Max had heard about Brooke's movie role after school the previous Friday, while she and Molly were browsing the stacks at Amoeba Music. Brooke's voice had caught a little when she recounted Brick's happy reaction to her big news, and it made Max think of Brooke's attempts not to sound lonely whenever she talked about never getting to see much of her father.

"So what now?" Teddy asked. "Are they going to let you hang around the set, or do you have to, like, skulk around the rafters?"

"She said something about getting me in the budget as her assistant," Max said with a grimace. "Honestly, I have no idea why I'm coming tonight—it's not like I can live-blog it while they sit there and read through the script. *Ugh*," she moaned, brandishing another shirt. This one was black-and-gray *plaid*. "I want to burn this entire closet and start over."

"It's just a reading. At a table. Don't go crazy," Teddy said, hopping up and heading for the door. "You're a good writer. I know it's not your ideal gig, but the blog is a fun read."

"I swear, you are so mushy now that you're all in love and stuff," Max scoffed, though she couldn't help feeling a little warm. "I liked you better when you were repressing your feelings. Now go away so I can get dressed."

"Okay." Teddy shrugged. "I guess I'll go make out with my girlfriend for a while."

Max balled up the offending plaid shirt and heaved it at him. "Ew, Teddy," she groaned. "Your tongue is not my business."

Teddy thudded down the hallway. Max resumed staring mournfully into her closet. Being the right hand of a self-proclaimed It Girl was a lot more stressful than she'd imagined. Nobody at school cared if she wore the same thing twice in a given week—half of them probably expected it. But now that she was spending so much more time outside her hovel, the usual rotation of jeans, black skirts, cargo pants, and T-shirts felt so stale and samey and depressing. She'd actually found herself idly browsing J.Crew's website the other day, as if she would ever wear an item of clothing called "café capris." Max decided to blame this on a fevered state brought on by writer's block, which itself was brought on by her evil NYU application essay that as of now contained only the words "Bob really *hated* peas."

Glancing at her watch, she realized that any other Tuesday, she'd be at Fu'd already for the dinner shift, getting a lecture from Dennis on how to clean the blender without using a lot of soap. And that she should've left two minutes ago if she wanted to get to Warner Bros. in time. Except she was still wearing sweatpants cut off at the knees and a tank top that read WANTED. Not good. Max sighed and grabbed her standby combat boots, some purple tights, a leather-looking skirt she'd found at Target for eleven dollars, and a striped tank top under a gray cardigan. It would rock nobody's world, but at least she wouldn't be naked.

Remember, nobody cares, Max told herself as she studied the outfit in the mirror. *This is what you wanted. An audience and anonymity all in one. Best of both worlds.*

✦ ✦ ✦

Max sprinted as fast as she could across the Warner Bros. lot. It wasn't really that far from her house, but she'd had to stop for gas, and in that time, apparently everyone in L.A. with a car hit the road. Max's fist had red marks on it from beating her horn so much, partly because a lot of people needed to be encouraged to use the accelerator, but mostly because her horn only worked about ten percent of the time.

She sped breathlessly around a corner onto the suburbia set—a curving road lined with a few all-American two-story clapboard houses. Max had seen at least ten episodes of television over the last month alone that used this outdoor location, but apparently one of the buildings was the *Nancy Drew* production office.

"*All* the houses are secretly offices," Brooke had told her. "They filmed bits of *Tequila Mockingbird* here, and Daddy said the staff of *Pals* ruined one of his takes because they were having a screaming fight over whether Rochelle and Ricky would ever get a parakeet."

"Well, they wouldn't, *obviously*," Max had said. "But it must be hard to get anything done with people shooting scenes in front of your window. I would totally be the writer who snapped and started dumping water balloons on the set."

"Somebody did throw a ham sandwich out the window," Brooke said. "One of the extras ate it."

Max hadn't known what to say—it rendered her mute that she and Brick shared a past of being molested by lunch meat. Now, she gazed up at the blue house Brooke's text message had directed her to and tried to catch her breath. She didn't want to go inside heaving like a low-rent phone-sex operator. Or even a high-rent one.

"Max?"

Shit. She'd been spotted. Max straightened up and came face-to-face with a grinning Brady Swift, a laptop bag slung across his body and a thick script in his hand.

"Fancy meeting you here," he said, giving Max a light hug. It was over almost before Max registered that it was happening, although she did catch a whiff of Right Guard deodorant and peppermint. "It's nice to see you again."

"Hi, Engelbert," Max said, suddenly feeling a bit clammy. *This* was why sweating was for suckers. She nodded at his script. "I'm guessing that's not for *Psychic Lifeguard*."

"You are wise," he said. "You're looking at Ned Nickerson, the earnest young student who discovers Nancy Drew huddled at a bus stop, falls in love with her, and then lets her help investigate his father's murder."

"No way! That's awesome!" Max said, spontaneously smacking him in the chest with the back of her hand. "I mean, not the plot. The plot is terrible. You would never let a homeless girl whose father makes meth poke around in your business."

"Idiocy," Brady agreed.

"And Ned was kind of a drag in the books," Max said. "I read them as a kid. He was like a tree with a mouth."

"The worst," he said amiably.

What are you doing? You need a rudeness alarm.

Max shook her head hard. "Sorry, I don't mean that *you* are a tree with a mouth. It's a great part," she amended. "This is a huge movie. You made it sound like you're just some schmo putting himself through school with glorified extra work."

"I am. Or, I was. I only got through one quarter of school before this happened," he said, sticking his hands deep into the pockets of his well-worn fleece pullover. "My agent called in a favor, so I read for this part about a month ago and never heard anything. Then they called last week and told me I was in." He lowered his voice. "I heard they had picked a big name but he wanted twenty million bucks, and they were like, 'Sorry, kid, but *Wall Street 2* should've gone straight to DVD.'"

"It'll be better with a cast of unknowns, anyway," Max said. She stopped and knocked on her forehead with her fist. "God, that sounded terrible."

"It's okay." Brady laughed. "I *am* a total unknown, except to psychotic fans of that episode of *Ghost Whisperer* where I got to yell at Jennifer Love Hewitt from the Other Side."

"Oi, mate, is this the *Nancy Drew* office?"

The accent was strange—faintly British, mostly weird—but the voice was unmistakable. As Carla Callahan drew closer to them, Max tried to picture the blonde beanpole she'd known in elementary school, but her memory wouldn't cooperate. It was like trying to draw somebody's portrait from a photocopy of a photocopy of a picture. Carla's chestnut pixie cut was an obvious attempt to copy Emma Watson's from the summer she wrapped Harry Potter, and she was clad in jeans tucked into shiny flat boots, a longish military-style blazer with giant brass buttons and epaulets, and a black fedora, like the Artful Dodger after raiding Neiman Marcus.

"Hi, Carla," Brady said pleasantly. "Brady Swift. We met a few years ago."

"Indeed! You read for a part on *iNeverland* and they decided you were too American-sounding," Carla Callahan beamed, rather too smugly for someone who Max knew had been born in the Valley. Apparently Carla was so Method she forgot she wasn't actually Wendy Darling, wasn't actually British, and wasn't actually still on that show, which itself wasn't actually even on TV anymore.

"Chuffed to see you again, love," Carla cooed, giving Brady two air kisses while putting a hand on his shoulder—no, almost putting it on his shoulder, but in fact leaving a sliver of air between it and her skin. "I never forget a face."

"So you're in this thing, too, huh?" Brady asked.

"Right-o, mate," Carla said. "I'm Nancy's best friend, George. Really knocked their blocks off at the audition."

Yeah, which must be why I saw you sobbing when you left the room, Max thought.

"George is ever so much more interesting than Nancy and Ned," Carla continued in her fake accent, which probably worked on people who didn't know she was born up the street. "She's just ripping, honestly. So nontraditional."

She's also the one the books say looks like a boy. Max was curious what would happen to Carla's voice when she started playing George, who was written as a hard-as-nails Bostonian running a girl gang.

"That's great, then," Brady said evenly. "Got what you wanted."

"Aces," Carla affirmed. Then she appeared to notice Max. "And you are?"

Max blinked. She wished she were better at this stuff—what exactly was she supposed to do when confronted with someone totally annoying from her youth who didn't even have the courtesy to recognize her? If this were *Lust for Life*, she would probably reach into her pocket and pull out a test tube of disfiguring acid. If it were *Dr. Phil*, she'd be expected to blather about her feelings and then give Carla a hug. Door No. 1 sounded more fun.

Luckily, Brady came to the rescue. "This is Max," he said. "She's, like, *the* top person in the Berlin empire. I heard from Brooke that she and her father wouldn't trust anyone else with, um, you know, all this...stuff."

Carla squinted at Max's face. "You look familiar." She snapped her fingers. "You were one of the autographs I signed at Comic-Con, right?"

"Close," Max said dryly. "We sat next to each other in art class a long time ago."

"Blimey, that's bonkers, Bob's your uncle," Carla said nonsensically, as if one could be British simply by blurting out random slang. "Max McCormack. You look...so..." Carla's voice faded.

Max caught her own eye in the window. Her green hair had gotten a bit matted from the sprinting, and her fair skin was flushed beet-red. She looked like Christmas in the rain. "I had to run here," she said lamely.

Carla cast her eyes over Max's outfit. "Actually, you look quite the same," she said, squeezing Max's arm like the two of them were sharing a little secret. "Can't think why I didn't spot you. Don't think you had green hair then. Go easy on the box dye, pet!"

Carla threw back her head and laughed. Max contemplated punching Carla in the neck.

"I think I hear someone calling for you," Brady said suddenly. "You'd better get upstairs. Oh, and don't listen to what anyone says—I think you *totally* have the right masculine essence to play George," he added in a tone of deepest support.

Carla turned as pale as she could underneath her suntan. "Lovely. Well, must dash..." she sputtered, gesturing vaguely toward the house before scurrying off.

"Wow," Max said under her breath. "So you're not just an actor; you also do pest control."

"And I might also be your stalker," Brady noted. "At this point, the only people I see more often than you are my three roommates and that homeless guy who lives in our Dumpster."

"Thanks for getting rid of her."

"No problem," he said. "I know her from the audition circuit, but I've never seen her be that...poncey." He shook his head. "I told you actors are lunatics. Run away while you still can."

Max grinned and caught sight of her reflection again. Her skin had finally returned to its normal color. "Too late, I've got a job to do," she said. "I'm supposed to meet Brooke."

"For the table read?" he asked, confused. "That's dedication. They don't usually let people in for that."

"Brooke must have pulled some strings. I'm her…moral support."

"Right. I mean, are you…You're not, like…are you two…" Brady seemed caught up in making a series of complicated, vaguely suggestive hand gestures.

It suddenly dawned on Max what he was trying to ask. "We are dating, yes," Max said. "We are so precious to each other."

Brady stopped at the house's front door and peered at Max's face. Then he broke into a grin. "Liar."

"I believe it's called *acting*," she said. "Really, I'm just her assistant. And her, um, friend. No benefits."

"Oh, good," Brady said, pulling open the door. "I mean…not that there's anything wrong with…if you were…never mind."

He looked slightly flustered. Max felt a weird ticklish sensation in her toes.

"I'm sort of curious to meet her, actually," Brady recovered, holding open the door so Max could go inside. "Her blog is something else. I love it when people surprise me."

"Thanks!" Max chirped. Then she caught herself. "For holding the door, I mean."

The blue house's ground floor was musty and barren, except for a back room that held office supplies, printers, and some computer equipment. But there was a din emanating from upstairs, and as Max and Brady trudged toward it, she saw that the top floor was all bustle: people passing out stapled papers, shaking hands, posing for pictures, and zooming in and out of rooms. There were a couple tiny white-walled offices, whose doors were ajar enough for Max to see messy couches, half-eaten bags of Cheetos, and wastebaskets overflowing with crumpled paper failures (Max knew the feeling), and a room with a large conference table and a wall of headshots—Brooke's and Brady's included—near several whiteboards covered in frantically scribbled phrases like "Act One: End at crack den?" and "Nancy = no dairy" and "Carson: Gay or just nice?"

Max felt a crackle in her veins. She envied these people. It made her want to go home and type something. Even if that something sucked. It couldn't be any worse than featuring a lactose-intolerant Nancy Drew—like, who wanted a subplot about a teen sleuth's intestinal drama? That would be like giving Dirk Venom a sinus infection in the long-rumored sequel *Dirk Venom: V Is for Five*.

"Wow," Brady breathed, backing out into the stairwell. "I'm...kind of nervous."

"Really? You?"

"Yeah, I mean, I always wanted to be a behind-the-scenes guy," he said, pointing to his laptop. "I snuck on the lot three hours early so I could work on my script at the commissary, because I always get good ideas from the extras milling around." He glanced queasily at the office door. "I've never done something like this. Usually I just show up in the middle of a shoot and say two lines and then go home to my Easy Mac."

"Well, the good news is you can probably afford spaghetti now," Max said. "Maybe even some sauce."

"Let's not get crazy," Brady said, taking off his glasses and nervously cleaning the lenses on his shirttails. "This is just big. And suddenly it feels big. Is it too late to blow this off and take up farming instead?"

"Relax. They hired you. They know what they were looking for," Max told him. "And when you become so famous that you can't leave the house without putting on dude-makeup, you can dry your tears with hundred-dollar bills. Now man up."

Brady blinked. "You're good," he said.

Max dragged him back into the production office and scanned the room for Brooke, who was in the middle of a circle of people, Carla Callahan among them. Brooke waved, then cocked an eyebrow at the sight of Brady and Max together and excused herself, making a beeline for them. Carla seemed surprised and slightly off-kilter, as if she'd been sure Brady was lying.

"I hope you brought a notebook," Brooke said cheerfully. "I need—" She caught herself, flicking her eyes over at Brady. "Um, I mean, Daddy needs you here as his proxy to take notes."

"Oh, yeah," Max said, opening her bag and digging through it, trying to hide the fact that she was carrying a copy of *The Awakening*, a giant biography of Truman Capote, and *In Touch* magazine's issue devoted to all the reasons Brad and Angelina were going to break up this week. Max felt like the contents of a girl's bag were as private as the contents of her bra. More so, maybe, because at least all boobs were variations on a theme.

Brady didn't miss a thing. "Just a little light reading?"

Max didn't like admitting to people what a bookworm she really was. It gave them ammo. "Um, you know, school stuff," she lied. "Brooke and I run...uh, a book club."

Brooke cleared her throat loudly, looking expectantly back and forth between Max and Brady.

"Oh, sorry, Brooke," Max said. "This is Brady. He's your boyfriend." *Wait, that didn't come out right.* "I mean, your fake boyfriend. He's Ned Nickerson."

Why are you so lame in public? Max scolded herself.

Brooke glanced down at Brady, bemused.

"Yeah, I'm short, but that's why God invented apple crates," he said.

"Either God or Ben Stiller," Max quipped. "Where are all the tall actors, anyway?"

"Tall guys have too much self-esteem to become actors," Brady said, with faux-seriousness. "You need self-loathing to vacate your own life so often. Look at Rob Pattinson. He seems miserable most of the time."

After a beat, Brooke gave him a warm smile. "Self-loathing. You're funny," she said, shaking his hand between both of hers.

"Thanks. Your blog cracks me up," Brady said. "It's much more satisfying than those celebrity Twitters that are all, like, barely concealed ads for weird weight-loss pills."

"Thank you, Brody," Brooke said.

Max bit back a correction.

"It makes sense that you're a big reader," Brady said to Brooke, nodding at the books Max was stuffing back into her purse. "That *Catcher in the Rye* comment was great. What other Salinger have you read?"

Brooke blinked. "Well, you know," she hedged, "*is* there any other Salinger, *really?*"

Max held her breath. But Brady just laughed. "True," he said. "It was never quite the same with his other stuff."

Phew. Maybe this would work yet.

"Well, I'd better go in and say hi before they start this thing," Brady said. "Awesome to meet you, Brooke, and awesome to see you, Max."

"Sure thing. And thanks for rescuing me back there," she said. "Enjoy your big-boy pasta."

Brady gave her a thumbs-up right before he got swarmed by people. They all took turns thumping him on the back and shaking his hand. Brady looked cutely bewildered by all the attention. Max guessed he was about eighteen, maybe nineteen, but he looked like a little kid on a playground for the first time. Complete with dimples. Deep ones.

"Well, well, well," Brooke said, a grin playing at her lips. "*Somebody* has a crush."

"What?" Max asked, snapping back to attention. "Who?"

"Oh, Maxine," Brooke said. "You are adorable."

"What?" Max protested.

"Big-boy pasta?"

"It was a joke from before, when—"

"'Thanks for rescuing me'?" Brooke quoted in an exaggerated femme fatale voice.

"I did not—"

"And he *loves* the blog."

"That's right. *Your* blog," Max said, feeling her neck get hot. "He thinks *you* are really smart and funny. Maybe *you* should have a crush on him."

"Please. He wears *glasses*, and he's, like, two feet shorter than me." Brooke shuddered. "Plus, I could never date another actor. They are way too self-involved. They always want the last word, and that totally flies in the face of all my best-planned exit lines." She smirked. "He's all yours."

For some reason Max felt itchy. "In case you haven't forgotten, I'm already married to my own sense of superiority."

Brooke snickered. Then she fell silent for a second. Max watched her as she gazed around the office, transfixed, as if she were already writing her memoir and didn't want to miss a single detail.

"I told you they hired me because they liked my point of view," she said softly. "And I know they think my blog is good PR for the movie. But just now, one of the writers told me that the fact that I'm smart gives my Nancy real credibility." Brooke cast a sidelong glance at Max. "They actually used the word *geek-chic* just now."

"I'm the geek and you're the chic," Max said. "That would be the tagline for our romantic comedy."

Brooke laughed again, and then let out a happy little sigh. "Daddy is making time to come to the set to watch some of the shooting," she said. "He told me last night that he wants to invest in my future." There was awe in her voice. Impulsively, she threw out an arm and squeezed Max around the shoulders. "Thank you," she said.

"Oh, uh...sure," Max said, taken aback. She could never read when someone was going to have a moment with her, and it made her feel like she wasn't holding up her end of the emotional bargain.

"Brooke!" said one of the executive producers, walking over and extending his hand. Despite the fact that he was easily in his midthirties, he was wearing a size-too-small T-shirt for Hall & Oates, accessorized with a wild thicket of dark hair and glasses with very chunky black frames, almost like Ray-Bans with the lenses popped out—a trend Max believed should have ended before it began.

"Zander Raymond. We met at the audition," said the hipster. "Let's get started. Here, I want you to take this CD. It's inspired by the script and it's a bunch of local Silver Lake bands and I really think it'll help you...."

As he led Brooke away, Brooke turned back and beckoned Max forward with a shining, joyful smile. Max couldn't help but return it. She might not be the one in the movie, but she couldn't help feeling like a piece of the success was hers.

twelve

"I SWEAR TO GOD, I will choke you to death with my bare hands," Max said.

"I'm not scared of you," Brooke responded.

"*Wrong*," Max said.

"What?" Brooke asked, sitting up on the green-and-white striped patio lounger and shooting Max an incredulous look, shading her eyes against the sun glinting off the Beverly Hills Hotel's swimming pool.

Max looked down at the chlorine-splattered script in her hands. "The line is, 'You don't scare me,' " she said. In front of them, two small children wearing floaties were beating each other with large, inflatable pigs.

Brooke groaned. "Close enough...?" she said, flopping back on the chair, her hands beating a nervous tattoo on her flat, tanned stomach. "What if it turns out that I have some kind of rare learning disability that prevents me from memorizing things?"

"You learned your lines for *My Fair Lady* without any problems."

Brooke jammed her sunglasses onto her face. "Maybe it's something that comes on suddenly," she mumbled. "Like appendicitis."

When Brooke had asked Max to run lines with her "by the pool," Max had assumed she meant the Berlins' own enormous one. But no, that would be too logical. Brooke had been waiting for her with a beach bag in one hand, the keys to the Lexus in the other, and the ready explanation that in order to *play* one of the people she needed to be *among* the people: "Daddy has a cabana permanently reserved for times like these." Apparently Brooke's version of "the people" was rich kids, models, and actors lounging poolside at the iconic, exclusive, and very pink hotel.

"Maybe you just need to go home and take a break. We've been at this since breakfast," Max said. Although, as it turned out, she didn't particularly want to go home. Being the plus-one of someone who had a permanent poolside hotel cabana wasn't exactly a hardship, even when that someone was Brooke, who Max suspected would faint in horror at her usual weekend view—namely, the McCormacks' weed-choked backyard. Every time Max stopped to take in these surroundings, she felt like she was living in a very elaborate chlorine-scented hallucination. If Max stopped moving long enough to take it all in, it felt a lot like she'd taken crazy pills.

Brooke stood. "What I need is another virgin daiquiri, but Sven is on break. I guess I'll just go to the pool bar." She slid on her espadrille wedges and pulled a robin's-egg blue cover-up over her tiny Missoni bikini. "Do you want another Arnold Palmer?"

Max eyed the tray table between them, which was littered with the detritus of the afternoon—the cap from a bottle of sunscreen, two lemon wedges, a chewed-on bendy straw, four empty glasses, the top page of Brooke's *Nancy Drew* script (which had gotten torn off in Max's backpack), and the most recent *Us Weekly*, which had a small piece about Brooke's casting coup.

"I think I'm good," she said.

"Are you sure? Dehydration is the number one cause of premature aging in women seventeen to twenty-four," Brooke said.

"I'll live on the edge."

"Suit yourself," Brooke said, and walked away toward the bar. Nearly everyone at the pool eyeballed her while pretending to be completely disinterested—exactly what Max and Molly used to do during their morning breakfast/ celeb-spotting sessions, except more openly—which was odd considering one of the gawkers looked eerily like Kate Bosworth.

Guess it's no surprise that everyone at the Beverly Hills Hotel has read Us Weekly.

Max was mentally writing her next blog post—something about how everyone in Hollywood spent most of their time pretending they weren't interested in the very thing they actually found *most* interesting—when someone sat down on the chaise next to her with a thump.

"Okay, this is just getting eerie," Brady Swift said.

Max jumped. "Whoa. What are you doing here? Um. I mean...hi, Skippy."

Brady laughed as he shrugged off a navy blue suit jacket. "Are you *sure* we're not secretly stalking each other? Or are you just a regular here? I guess you grew up around these parts, huh."

Max became acutely aware that she was wearing a four-year-old one-piece swimsuit and Umbros, as if this were summer camp and not the Beverly Freaking Hills Hotel.

"Only in a vague geographic sense," she said, self-consciously crossing her arms over her chest. "I've never been here before. Brooke brought me. She, um, likes the people-watching. Keen observer of humanity and all that."

"Nice work if you can get it," Brady said, loosening his necktie.

"I'm not complaining," Max admitted. "This is way nicer than being home working on my history paper. But seriously, what are you doing here?"

Brady raked a hand through his spiky black hair. "Valet-parking cars."

"Not in that suit."

"You're right. The valets here dress way nicer than I do."

Brady grinned, one half of his mouth twisting up sardoni-cally. "But I think I'd be more at home here if I were on staff. My agent wanted to buy me lunch to celebrate sign-ing my contract. I suggested Swingers diner. He laughed. So here I am. I saw your hair on my way out." He lowered his voice. "We were at the table next to Jack Nicholson."

"I would have spent the whole time trying to eavesdrop."

"I did," Brady said. "He was talking about the Lakers. *The entire lunch*." He fished around for some aviator sun-glasses in his jacket pocket. "How am I doing, trying to fit in?" he asked, putting them on and giving her some cheesy finger guns. "Do I look like an up-and-coming actor, or do I look like some dumbass whose hideous apartment in Marina del Rey doesn't have a coffee table or working air-conditioning?"

Max laughed and relaxed a little, scooting back on her chaise until they were sitting level with each other. "You're pulling it off," she said. "Just don't do an episode of *Cribs*."

One of Brady's brows cocked itself above the rims of his Ray-Bans. "Funny you should say that. My crazy manager wants Warner Brothers to rent a bungalow for me because the *L.A. Times* wants to write about actor bachelor pads." He took off his sunglasses and stared out at the pool. "I know Hollywood has a reputation for being appearance-obsessed, but I had hoped it was an exaggeration."

As if on cue, a fiftysomething blonde woman with huge fake breasts sauntered past them.

"Exhibit A," Max offered.

Brady shielded his eyes. "Horrifying," he said. "How'd you turn out so normal, growing up here?"

"It helps that my parents aren't in the business," she said. "But I still don't feel that normal."

He smiled. "I guess no one really feels normal. I never did, even back in Pittsburgh, where I was, like, *terminally* normal. Except for how I was That Freckled Eleven-Year-Old in the Life Cereal Ad." He sighed. "I was actually fourteen. Being short sucks."

"No kidding," Max deadpanned. "Just another apology my parents owe me." She curled up her legs and hugged them to her chest. "Living here, it sometimes feels like if you're not constantly trying to sell yourself, nobody thinks you're worth anything. I always feel like a sore thumb." She let out a harsh laugh. "A sore thumb on a fist that keeps punching people."

He looked sympathetic. "As someone who fell into this business ass-backward, I can say it doesn't feel much better from this side of things. I'd so much rather chuck it all and go write a book or something. But I kept telling myself I had to put myself through UCLA first, and now…" He gestured at the pool area, which was now pulsing with some trendy deejay's mash-up of Rihanna's latest with the German version of that old eighties song about red balloons.

"I'm doing the same thing," Max confessed before she even knew what she was doing. "I want to go to NYU this summer for a writing seminar, so I'm on Brooke's payroll."

She paused when he looked surprised. *Damn. I said too much.*

Brady looked at her for a long moment, his face inscrutable.

"That's fantastic," he finally said. "I think you'd be great at that, and Brooke's a good person to be hanging out with. She wrote something really funny the other day about how Elton John needs more friends his own age."

"Yes, right," Max said, hoping she successfully restrained herself from making a face.

"It's cool of her to do that for you," he said. "You guys *must* be really good friends."

"The best," Max said through clenched teeth.

"And it's great that you have each other," he said, fiddling with his cuffs. "I kind of miss that. My roommates are just random actors I got paired up with by my agency. We live together out of habit." He cocked his head as one of the guys in Kate Bosworth's posse stood up and rubbed Clarins tanner on his left pec. "It'd be nice to have a close friend out here to help keep me from freaking out."

"I don't mean to freak you out more, but that chick over there who looks like Jessica Biel is checking you out," Max noted, nodding to their left. "*Nancy Drew* is going to be big."

"Nobody cares that much about me, though. It's not *my* movie. I'm just...in it."

Max looked down at her unpedicured feet, resting on

top of a monogrammed Beverly Hills Hotel towel. "I think I know how you feel."

Brady tilted his head to the side, regarding her with... with what, exactly?

"Hey, do you like bad movies?" he asked suddenly.

"I almost exclusively like bad movies," Max said. "I watched *Wolf Trout* on Syfy last weekend twice in a row."

"Great, because I haven't been able to convince anyone to go see *The Room* with me, and I heard it's one of L.A.'s most iconic awful movies."

"It seriously is. I saw it over the summer," Max said. "You'll love it. If you need company, I don't think my brother's seen it yet. You'd like him—he's cool. But don't tell him I said that."

Brady half looked at her and then said, "Oh, great. Thanks."

The conversation seemed to hiccup. *Did I just do something wrong?* Max wondered.

"You don't scare me!"

Brooke's voice sliced between them, severing the moment like an ax murderer chopping a phone line at a remote forest cabin. She gracefully lowered herself onto her chaise without spilling a drop from the two giant fruit-festooned drinks in her hand, although her cover-up slid down her tanned shoulder a little.

"See? I remembered the line. And I got you a piña colada," she said, handing one to Max. "Coconut milk is full of electrolytes." She turned to Brady and hit him with a megawatt grin. "And you got *me* a costar. Want some? It's basically medicinal."

"I wish I could, but I have an acting class in"—he checked his watch—"damn, fifteen minutes." He winced. "My agent told me I have to hone my craft, or something. We're doing gender reversals. I have to read something from *The Vagina Monologues*." He looked vaguely queasy. "There is no way saying that sentence out loud is going to help my career. Maybe acting classes are just a big scam. Like valet parking, right, Brooke?"

"What? I valet all the time," Brooke said, blithely nibbling a strawberry.

Brady crinkled his brow. "Didn't you say on your blog the other day that you thought all the overpriced valets in Los Angeles were part of an elaborate scheme to lure the public into parking illegally so that the city could make big bucks off ticketing them?"

Brooke gave no sign that she was flustered by having forgotten this rant. "Just making sure you were paying attention," she said, removing her cover-up again and settling back into her chair with a grin.

She is a good actress.

"Always," Brady said, then donned his aviator shades and gave them both an ironic little salute.

"That's so *Top Gun*," Max said. "Be careful the paparazzi don't think you're Tom Cruise."

Brady straightened up. "Please," he said. "I'm at least two inches taller than that guy."

"I refuse to date an actor," Brooke said, lolling back on her chaise as he strolled out of earshot, "but Brady Swift cleans up nice."

"Aren't you betrothed to that octogenarian at the bar?" Max asked, maybe a bit quickly. "I saw you over there. He was really chatting you up."

Brooke rolled onto her stomach and laughed. "Ew, Max, he produced the Dirk Venom series. He's one of my god-fathers. Besides, if chatting someone up at the pool meant you were *involved*, I'd be asking when you and Brady were tying the knot."

Max felt heat climbing into her cheeks.

"Are you blushing?" Brooke asked.

"No! I think I'm sunburned," Max said, pretending to search for sunscreen.

"Uh-huh," Brooke said, mock-toasting Max with her daiquiri glass.

✦ ✦ ✦

It was almost dark when Max banged through her front door.

"Is that you, Maxine, or have we been invaded by elephants?"

Max rolled her eyes. "Sorry," she said, following the sound of her mother's voice into the kitchen. "I forgot your ears are so delicate."

Her mother was standing at the scratched porcelain

sink in their bright yellow kitchen, running some water over an extremely depressed cactus.

"I see you've met Irving," Max said.

Eileen McCormack glanced sideways at Max. "Who?" she asked, turning off the water.

"Irving," Max said, dumping her backpack on the linoleum. "My cactus."

"It's dead. It's an ex-cactus."

"I prefer to think of him as being chlorophyllically challenged."

Eileen smirked and put Irving back into the sink. "Sit down for a sec, honey."

Uh-oh. Does she know I ditched Spanish?

"Is everything okay?" Max asked, sliding into the country-style wooden chairs at their kitchen table, which her father had brought home from an estate sale and repainted a funky orange. It matched their KitchenAid mixer...and nothing else. Max loved that about her father. He didn't care about aesthetic rules.

"Everything is fine, except for the shocking state of your bedroom, as usual," Eileen said, pouring them each a mug of hot water and carrying them to the table along with two ginger tea bags. "As a matter of fact, your father and I are really proud of how hard you've been working."

"You are?" Max echoed.

"Absolutely. I always say that if you have a goal, you should stop at nothing until you achieve it, and I am very impressed with how completely you're pursuing this NYU program." Eileen's face took on a dreamy look. "You are displaying all the drive and determination of a true Colby-Randall achiever. Tutoring Brooke can't be easy, especially on top of carnival meetings and school and working at Fu'd."

Oops. Apparently, she'd forgotten to tell her mother that she'd quit.

"Although I should've known you had it in you," Mrs. McCormack continued, stirring her tea with a sly sidelong glance. "You were, ahem, *very* single-minded about getting the dissection portion of AP biology removed from the Colby-Randall curriculum."

"Well," Max said, taken aback by hearing compliments from her mother instead of promises of detentions or groundings. "It is barbaric. And gross."

Eileen chuckled. "And you won that round. But honey, we are *also* a bit concerned about you. We think you're working too hard."

"Since when is that phrase in your vocabulary?"

"You're rarely at home, Maxine. Trust me, one day you will wish you'd spent the springtime of your life enjoying having little or no real responsibilities instead of working yourself ragged."

"I can totally quit the carnival," Max offered. *Please, God, make her let me quit the stupid carnival.*

Eileen laughed. "Nice try," she said. "But we don't want you to spend all your teenage years slaving away."

"I don't—" Max began, but her mother held up a hand.

"I know it's been harder around here financially since your father got laid off. And despite his best efforts"— Eileen cast a despairing eye over to the white-tiled counter, on which sat the charred corpse of a hand mixer—"he hasn't sold an invention yet. But I want you to know we're still doing okay, moneywise. And your father has a lead on several part-time jobs to help supplement the fees for your NYU program, so you can quit working until next year."

Max sucked in a breath. This was as shocking to her as if Eileen had announced she was ditching academia to become a Lady Gaga impersonator. And two weeks earlier, Max would have been thrilled to hear it. Even today she was tempted. No more lying, no more tagging around after Brooke.

No more Brady, said a voice in her head.

Max shook it off. In two months he'd be too famous to talk to her, anyway, and this meant her free time and possibly NYU would be all hers. Finally.

"I really appreciate the gesture, Mom," Max began. "I don't know what to say. It's seriously amazing."

Eileen reached out and squeezed her hand. "Well, you are seriously amazing, and we are seriously serious about this."

Max took in her mother's earnest, warm eyes—identical to hers in shape and color—and saw the gray streaks shooting through her ash-blonde bun. Eileen looked tired. Max suspected she was sugarcoating how easy it would be to bring in extra cash and felt a wave of appreciation. The offer meant more to her than she could say. Which was precisely why she had to do the right thing and say no. Max knew she'd never be comfortable taking the help under false pretenses, not when it might make things harder for her family. Besides, for once, the right thing was also the easy thing. Posing as Brooke online had turned out to be not just profitable but...*fun*. She couldn't abandon OpenBrooke.com now.

"Thank you, but it's actually okay, Mom," Max said slowly. "I'm doing fine. I've almost got enough saved."

Eileen frowned. "Are you sure?"

Brady's face floated into Max's mind. She couldn't abandon him, either. He needed her. For eye-rolling purposes.

"I'm sure," Max said. "I promise. I've got this."

thirteen

"THIS IS NANCY'S BEDROOM," Brooke said, pulling her father by the hand toward a pile of garbage bags. "One of the first scenes we're doing tomorrow is the one where she's trying to read *Les Misérables* by candlelight but she keeps hearing gunshots."

"Powerful!" Brick intoned, squatting and running his hand over the bags, which were fluffed and rolled to look like a mattress with a pillow and a comforter. "In every slum, there is a hero."

He paused and fished around for one of his many phones, this time the BlackBerry. As he made a note of his brain wave, Brooke heard a snort from Max's direction — she was sitting in a chair in the corner of the soundstage *actually* reading *Les Misérables*, so that she could brief

Brooke on the specifics—but Brooke ignored it. The *Nancy Drew* script *was* a little bizarre in spots, but it had everything: tears, drugs, crime, love, dirt, and even a professionally choreographed nightclub scene. She would rock it. More important, Brick thought it would be a blockbuster, and he'd never been wrong (unless you counted that one astronaut film back in the early nineties, *Jupiter's Eye Needs Glasses*, although Brick always tersely insisted it was *supposed* to be funny). Brick had even cleared his schedule for a personal tour of the set. Brooke couldn't remember the last time he'd rearranged his agenda on the spot.

"And *this* is the Nickerson mansion set," she said, parading Brick toward a large makeshift living room, connected to a foyer and a double front door. "I'll be here for the scene where Nancy realizes there's cyanide in the carpet fibers because it triggers her rare skin allergy."

"Disease is an actor's greatest platform!" Brick boomed, following Brooke through the old soundstage. "Does it come with welts? Welts can be very evocative."

"I hope so!" Brooke said. "That reminds me, one of the producers has been dying to ask you something about prosthetic ears. Let me go find him."

Giddily, Brooke all but skipped away, leaving Brick to inspect the staircase in the Nickerson entryway that went only as high as the camera needed it to go. Today was the most fun she'd ever had, leading him around this fictional world that was all hers. He looked to *her* for information, he wanted to discuss *her* project, and he read and talked to her about *her* blog. When she'd told him that she got a hundred thousand hits the other day, he'd actually wiped a tear from his eye, handed her his last Clif Bar, and said she was turning into everything he'd hoped she'd be.

Except that Clif Bar should have gone to Max.

Brooke did not regret hiring Max. But every time her bosses praised Open Brooke or told her it was a key part of her getting hired, a super-annoying voice in her brain spoke up and reminded her that, technically, all of her happiness was based on a lie.

A very minor lie, though. Really quite small in the scheme of things. Max's writing was based on Brooke's experiences, after all. Lifetime movies were based on true stories, too, and nobody minded that the serial killers didn't write the scripts themselves. Brick himself had used a ghostwriter for his official autobiography, *Brick by Brick.* So Brooke decided OpenBrooke.com was simply ripped from the headlines of her own life the way *Law & Order* was ripped from the *New York Post.* Everything else was a tiny technicality. So her brain voice could shut its piehole.

Brooke couldn't find Zander or the other executive producer, Kyle, so she headed back toward the set. Brick's deep voice carried toward her, echoing against the backdrops.

"...the forgotten subtext of the movie," Brick was saying. "I'm impressed!"

As Brooke rounded the corner, she saw that he was

talking to Brady, who smiled at her shyly. Brooke allowed herself a moment to appreciate the effect she had on people. She *knew* this was a good hair day.

"Hi, Brady," she said. "What did I miss?"

"I was just telling your dad about a UCLA Extension course I'm taking on action films," Brady replied, his ears turning a tiny bit red. It was sort of sweet. "I'm doing a paper on themes of abandonment in the Dirk Venom movies, and I thought..."

Brick clapped a hand on Brady's back so hard that Brady coughed. "I was beginning to think nobody saw all the work I put into Dirk's backstory. I bet I have it all written down, still. Thirty pages of feelings. I actually called it *Thirty Pages of Feelings*. I should give it to you for your paper." He pulled out his phone. "I will e-mail myself a note."

"Thanks, sir. Um, so how are you doing, Brooke?" Brady asked, making brief eye contact and somewhat nervously picking at his pockets. "I saw Max had *The Hunger Games* in her bag the other day—are you guys reading that now?"

"Yes, of course," Brooke said, hooking her arm through Brick's. "Daddy and I make it a point to stay on top of the latest diet trends."

Brady seemed confused. Brooke wondered if she had made a mistake. Then he chuckled.

"Very funny," he said. "Can't wait to hear your take on the whole trilogy. I thought the ending was—well, I don't want to spoil it for you."

"A reader, eh?" Brick crowed. "Very impressive!" He thumped Brady on the back again. "Actors *should* be soldiers of academia. Our greatest tools are our brains."

Brooke could swear she heard another snort off in the distance.

Brady checked his watch. "Whoops, I'm due in wardrobe for a fitting," he said. "Always great to see you, Brooke. And it was nice to meet you, sir."

"Well, son, it was a pleasure to meet you," Brick said, thumping him again. "Call me Brick."

As Brady loped off toward the costumer's room, Brooke gazed curiously up at her father. He was beaming at Brady's back. "That is one impressive young man, Sunshine," he said. "It takes a very bright mind to pick up on my subtle subtext in Dirk Venom. Especially the second one." He winked at Brooke. "Nancy hooked a good one. Maybe life will imitate art, eh, Brookie? I've always wanted you to date someone as brilliant as you are."

"Daddy, you're so silly. I'm sure Brady doesn't think twice about me," Brooke twittered. She was mostly lying. She *was* Brooke Berlin, after all. Making guys think about her was in her DNA.

"Nonsense, Sunshine! He clearly appreciates your beautiful mind. A connection like that is too precious to waste," Brick said fondly. "Plus, get some lifts for his shoes and you'd look perfect together! A love story would be such great PR for the movie!"

Well, that much was true.

"And just think of the screenings we could have at our house!" Brick continued. "I could talk him through the scenes where Dirk Venom cleans his gun, and what it means about his relationship with his parents. And I could show him my custom Bowflex!"

"Then *you* date him, Daddy," Brooke said glibly.

"Don't be silly, Sunshine, he's not my type!" Brick chortled. "But just remember: An open mind leads to a full heart."

Brooke could tell what was coming next. "Wait, that would make a great slogan for the rom-com Heather Graham wants to do with me," Brick mused.

Brick's face glowed as he punched merrily at his Black-Berry. Brooke studied him for a few seconds and then smiled. It was obvious what she had to do.

✦ ✦ ✦

Max curled up and shifted in the armchair. The *Nancy Drew* soundstage also occasionally housed *Pretty Little Liars*, and she'd found a cozy chair from one of the girls' rooms that hadn't been put away yet. It made for a quiet place to read or do homework whenever she had nothing to do—which was frequently, since half the time Brooke dragged her out here for "research" and then just lay around on the meticulously made bed of trash bags, trying to absorb Nancy's aura.

In the weeks since Brooke got the part, Max was

increasingly glad she'd turned down her mother's offer of financial help. She'd started feeling less like an employee and more like a teammate. Brooke often pulled her aside for advice—granted, it was usually on something cosmetic and/or crazy, but she still *wanted* Max's opinion. Countless nights Molly had wandered into Brooke's room to find them with their heads together over the script or giggling over an idea for a blog entry.

"Max McCormack, are you actually starting to *like* my sister?" Molly had later wondered, amused. Max had just snorted and changed the subject, rather than admit that maybe this was a little bit true. She remembered Molly once noting that Brooke was entertaining when she wasn't being a total pain, and finally Max had begun to see it.

Max had also gotten to know the other key players pretty well, beyond just Brady. Zander, the hipster producer, was desperate for a vinyl copy of an old Rolling Stones album and nearly passed out with joy when Max found one at Amoeba. The other big boss, Kyle, wore a rubber band around his wrist and snapped it every time he cussed. He got around this by abbreviating everything—"g.d." this, "f'ing" that—but every so often he would let fly a four-letter pejorative and then thwack himself in the arm. He and Max had spent twenty minutes over sandwiches the other day, discussing whether *shiz* counted as a swear word (Max contended that no word with an artificially added *Z* counted as anything at all). Carla Callahan started sucking up incessantly once she saw how much time Max spent hanging out with Brooke, tagging after the two of them—"Oi, mates, fancy a brewsky?" she would bleat in faltering British tones that were blending with the Boston accent she was using for *Nancy Drew*. And Germain on Camera A had shown Max how to work the equipment and then secretly let her frame one of Brady's close-ups.

"Don't tell," he'd said, winking. "My union will kill me."

All told, between that and the never-ending process of script tweaks and rewrites, Max was absorbing a ton—*so* much more than just bits and bobs for blog ideas. The only frustration was that the more time she spent on set, the weirder it got when people quoted Max's own words at her, expecting her to agree that, yes, that paragraph she had slaved over *was* clever of Brooke. It was hard seeing Brooke praised for her blunt insights, while Max was being dispatched to get Brooke's coffee, or grab Brooke a banana, or make sure Brooke's trailer had toilet paper. When Max protested to Brooke that the movie had several PAs on staff whose sole job was to do these exact things, Brooke insisted that although she didn't feel good about it, either, Max had to keep up appearances—and if appearances were that she was a personal assistant, well, then it really didn't make sense for Max to refuse to make a Starbucks run for her.

"Channel your inner actress, Max," Brooke had urged her. "Channel your inner *me*."

"I thought I was already doing that," Max had replied with a sweet smile.

But the schlepping seemed like a decent trade for watching a movie get made (well, at least whatever parts were made between when school ended and Max's curfew). Despite her lifelong, self-proclaimed disdain for people who clamored to be in entertainment, Max had to admit it was fascinating. She could watch the director, Tad Cleary, all day. He was famous for directing *The Character Limit*, about the origins of Twitter, yet nobody knew much about Tad's personal life because he himself rarely made small talk, even when *not* making small talk was rude. When he did speak, it was at a pace three times faster than most people could even process, and he never sat still. Max had never seen Tad without three of those tiny 5-Hour Energy bottles in his hand. He was so wired one day that Max saw him walk smack into a set wall.

"What are you smiling about?" Brady asked, passing behind her and thwacking her gently on the back of her head with some script pages.

"Oh, I'm just reading this hilarious book," she said, waggling *Les Misérables* at him. "It's all about sick prostitutes and young guys getting themselves killed. It's a scream."

Brady peered into Max's bag. There were two other thick hardbacks in there. "Okay, I really think it's time you tell me why you carry fifty pounds of books everywhere. And don't say it's a book club. Nobody can read that much in one week."

Usually Max would've replied sarcastically, but after so many easy conversations, she had no trouble being herself with Brady. "This is grossly nerdy, but I'm kind of phobic about getting stuck somewhere without enough reading material," she said. "The last flight I took, I brought four books and seven magazines, and I still didn't let myself touch them until I'd read the Sky Mall catalog front to back."

"That's not nerdy, that's just common sense," Brady said. "Besides, the Sky Mall is full of useful things. Like that tiny-doughnut machine." He pursed his lips. "Actually, the first thing I buy with my *Nancy Drew* money might be the tiny-doughnut machine. Way better than a car."

"Oh, my God, speaking of, did you see somebody wants to remake *Back to the Future*, but with Zac Efron and a Mini Cooper?" Max said with a groan.

Brady winced. "Why do they ruin all the classics?" he asked. "Although it'd be nice if they shot it here, so we could have some kind of time travel–themed hot lunch at the commissary."

"I heard tomorrow's theme is *One Tree Hill*, and since a dog ate a guy's heart one time on that show, I am dying to find out what they're serving," Max said. "Are you going to be here? We have to go."

"I'll be here," he confirmed, brandishing a green-tinted call sheet. "Brooke and I are shooting Nancy's first visit to Ned's house." He fished around in his pocket. "According to the schedule, I have about two weeks to get comfortable standing next to her on an apple box before we have to make out."

Max's nostrils flared a little. "Congratulations," she said, her voice a bit testy.

Brady appeared not to notice. "It's weird," he said, rubbing his hair absently. "I feel like I know more about her from reading her website than from when we've talked in person." He shrugged. "Some people are just more comfortable in print than out loud. I was always that way."

"So of course you became an actor."

"By accident, remember?" he said. "And not a very successful one."

"Until now," Max pointed out.

"Jury's still out," Brady retorted. "My Razzie campaign for Worst Actor might still have some life."

"Max!" a voice called out. They looked up to see Brooke heading their way.

"Shoot, I told her I was due in wardrobe." Brady grinned sheepishly. "Brick is cool, but if he'd hit my back one more time, I think my spine would've come out my mouth. The guy is *strong*." He smacked her with the script again as he headed away. "We'll have to talk later about how I saw *Snakeacuda* on cable this weekend. You are going to love it."

As he walked away, Max tried to imagine him and Brooke making out for the cameras. It made her shudder. Brooke and Brady went together like peanut butter and herpes.

"Max!" Brooke hissed.

Max looked up to see Brooke standing right in front of her, hand on hip. "You really need to listen when I call you. What if it had been urgent?"

"There is no such thing as a blog emergency."

"You don't know that. And besides, it *is* vitally important." Brooke looked around the dusty area behind the set, seemingly trying not to breathe through her nose. "Stand up for a second," she said.

Max obliged, wondering if there was a bug on her chair or something. Brooke beamed. "Thank you," she said, sweeping into Max's seat.

"Hey!" Max protested.

"Max, I can't sit on the floor. This is a Phillip Lim," Brooke said, presumably as an apology. "Besides, with me sitting and you standing, we're more like eye-to-eye, right?" Brooke lowered her voice. "And I have a very, very big job for you."

"Please tell me it involves getting you another latte, so I can spit in it."

"Maxine, be serious. And hygienic." Brooke folded her hands in her lap and beckoned Max closer.

"I need you," Brooke began with a flourish, "to blog me a date."

Max blinked. "Those words don't make sense in that order."

"Look, Daddy just met Brady, and he, like, loved him. *Loved* him," Brooke said, a flush of excitement on her cheeks. "You should have seen it. You have to help me date him."

"Wait a minute," Max said, holding up her palms. "You said you wouldn't date short, bespectacled actors."

"Rules are made to be broken," Brooke said, waving her hands dismissively. "A precious connection is too smart to...wait, what was it he said? Anyway, whatever. The point is, Brady totally digs Internet Me, and he's all shy around Real Me, so I want you to use the blog to seal the deal."

"No way. No," Max said, feeling a creeping sensation in her limbs. "It doesn't seem fair to Brady. Do you even *like* him?"

Brooke looked thoughtful. "What's not to like? He's only short-*ish*, he's totally cute, he doesn't wear Drakkar Noir. And we'll totally be the new Kristen Stewart and Robert Pattinson. I definitely like him enough for that."

"So I should just sit by and let you trick him into thinking you're into him?"

"No, you should write an awesome blog entry that will totally help convince him to make a move, and then we'll just...play the roles."

"And you don't see anything morally wrong with this?" Max sputtered.

Brooke sniffled. "I just want Daddy...He was so thrilled at the idea, and...I just want him to..."

"No, you are not going to play the Poor Pitiful Princess Wants Daddy's Love card," Max groaned. "Not again."

"Okay, *fine*," Brooke pouted. "What if I promise not to date him for very long? Just enough so that Daddy can see me trying, and we maybe get a magazine cover?"

Max crossed her arms and frowned. Brooke narrowed her eyes.

"NYU will be awfully bummed if you get accepted and you can't afford tuition," she said softly.

Oh, God, so she played the trump card instead.

"Unless it's something else," Brooke mused, studying Max's face. "I asked you a few weeks ago if you were into Brady and you said no. Change of heart?"

"Don't be insane," Max huffed.

"Are you *jealous*?"

"I don't care who he hooks up with. He can do what he likes."

"Great, then it's a deal!" Brooke leaped up and hugged her. "Can't wait to read the entry!"

And she disappeared before Max could say another word.

✦ ✦ ✦

Max pulled into her gravel driveway—the best and loudest incentive against breaking curfew—and killed the car engine. The house was dark, except for two glowing porch lanterns, which illuminated her brother slumped in the swing and nursing a Dr Pepper.

"You look miserable," she said. "Did Molly finally notice

your freakishly long second toe and dump your mutant ass?"

"We made it." His voice was quiet.

"You...ew, Teddy, first of all, nobody says that outside a Judy Blume book, and second—"

"No, no, no, *the band*," Teddy said, exasperated. "We made the finals of the contest. We're playing the House of Blues."

"That's..." Max looked at her brother's long face. "Great?" she queried.

"It should be," he said. "But you know how I feel about Mental Hygienist. We're having fun, but I am not sure we should ever play those songs outside of Colby-Randall parties."

"Are you telling me you don't want to be the face of 'You (Rock)'?" Max quipped.

Teddy shook his head. "I tried to tell Bone that *righteous* doesn't rhyme with *ficus*, but he ignored me." He shifted in the swing so Max could sit down next to him. "Does this make me a dick?"

"Not when there are so many other things that make you a dick."

Teddy punched her shoulder. "Come on, I'm serious. The band was always just sort of a goof to me, like something to do before I went off to college. Now it's going to be on my permanent record."

"Is that such a bad thing?" Max asked. "I mean, Mark

Wahlberg rose above it. Bone isn't nearly as embarrassing as the Funky Bunch."

Teddy laughed grudgingly. "Point taken. It's not really my kind of music, though," he explained. "It's not *me*. I always figured I'd do something a little more unplugged. More Bon Iver than Bon Jovi."

"So what?" Max said. "Record execs know that people have more than one artist inside them. Remember when Molly showed us that Japanese *Vogue* where Lady Gaga pretended to be an Italian man named Jo? Just put on, like, a dirty tank top and grow a soul patch."

"You are *so* the wrong person to talk to about this."

"I'm sorry, I'm sorry. I can be serious," Max promised. "And I seriously believe you are overthinking this."

"Really?" Teddy stared out at the dark front lawn, on which a half-deconstructed wheelbarrow had been disintegrating for weeks. "I mean, did we even earn this? Our Facebook page got like twenty thousand more fans after you mentioned us on Brooke's blog. The Berlin stamp of approval might be swaying things a little."

"Probably," Max said, "but who cares? Take the opportunity while it's in front of you. Because who's to say you'll get another one? Maybe just do what it takes to get your foot in the door and *then* find a way to do your own thing. Maybe this is just the beginning."

Teddy pondered this for a moment. "My stomach hurts. Is this what riding on a Berlin girl's coattails feels like?"

"Hilarious," Max said. "And maybe that *is* what I'm doing, a little bit. But you aren't. You didn't ask me to mention you on the blog, and neither did Molly. I just did it. Think of me as, like, your in-house PR."

"Is it always going to be this weird?" Teddy mused. "You know, sitting around wondering if you're only getting your moment because of who you're dating, or who you know?"

"No idea—nobody sucks up to me," Max said, though she thought briefly of Carla. "Can you imagine how much it sucks to be an actual famous person? This is why half of them go to rehab."

"I know. I've been fame-adjacent for like five minutes, and it's already messing with my head," Teddy said. "Thank God Molly is so normal. I don't know how she does it. And you seem pretty much the same as you were before you became Brooke's new best friend."

"Yeah, I was a hot mess before, and I still am," Max joked. "And listen, for what it's worth, I really do think you're torturing yourself needlessly. You're not getting anything you don't deserve. It's not like you're the Kevin Federline in this situation."

Teddy drummed his thumbs against the wooden seat. "So I should just chill out, not care *why* we made the finals, and just support the band, and see where it takes me," he finally said.

"Yep. You have plenty of time to do *you* later. Do this first."

"That sounds sort of sensible, almost," Teddy said, feigning amazement. Or at least Max liked to think he was faking.

"Well, I am incredibly smart," she said. "Everyone who reads Brooke's blog says so. Indirectly."

Her brother ruffled her hair, probably because he knew she hated it. "Well, I will say it directly. You are smart," he said. "I think it's Brooke who's riding *your* coattails."

"I wear hoodies," Max demurred.

"Thank you, Maxine."

"You're welcome, Theodore. Now, if you'll excuse me, I'm very busy and important."

Max trudged up the stairs to her room and kicked shut the door, flinging her purse onto the bed. *You have plenty of time to do* you *later,* she repeated to herself. *Do what it takes to get your foot in the door.* All it would take was a blog entry or two, and the rest wasn't her responsibility. If Brady fell for it — for Brooke — then that wasn't her fault. And if Brooke fell for Brady, that wasn't her fault, either.

Take what's in front of you now.

Grabbing her phone, she checked the time: 10:05 PM. Jake would be up. She punched at his name on the screen.

"Hey, Jake, it's Max," she said, simultaneously waking up her computer and opening a blank blog window. "So, I've been thinking. Let's make plans to hang out." She paused. "Just the two of us, like you said."

APRIL 13

Greetings from the set of *Nancy Drew*, where we started shooting before dawn today. People who win movie awards never thank the real hero: caffeine. I have never been this productive before dawn in my entire life, unless you include a few all-nighters to finish my homework and that one time I got stuck in the Valley at a party for…well, I can't tell you, because her hit show won't want anyone to know that the *reason* we all got stuck was because her *secret life* involves getting hammered on wine coolers and then slashing everyone's tires. When are famous people going to realize that technology means there is a public record of just about everything? If you want to act like a college student, here's a thought: Go to college.

But it was a productive morning—we did a very intense scene that involved a lot of smeared mascara (I looked like Courtney Love, twenty years ago—and actually maybe also twenty hours ago). It's also Friday the 13th, so we spent all day walking around ladders and staying ten feet from any window and instituting a no-cat policy. Although when I went outside for a breather, I almost got run over by a golf cart driven by none other than Moxie Stilts. She was wearing a dress that I'm pretty sure was made of potholders (the skirt seriously had a thumb) and she looked *pissed*. Someone's either angling to get another shout-out here on Open Brooke (all press is good press?) or she's *really mad* that I told everyone about her drunky-funky birthday party. Listen, honey, if you don't want to get called out for taking off your pants in front of God and everyone, then *leave them on*. It's not hard.

But it's also not worth giving her that much attention, so let's talk about what I've learned my first day on the job:

1) Always make friends with the camera crew. The more they like you, the better you photograph. Funny how that works. Also: They have the good doughnuts.

2) I know my teen readers won't believe this, but on-set tutors might be worse than high school. Mine are nice, and there are some perks—no cafeteria food with suspicious hairs in it, no detention, no deputized but ultimately powerless student committees pretending they get to make decisions, when really the school board runs the show and the student "leaders" are stuck having to say things like "Please attend our

Dance-a-Thon benefiting Celebrities Climbing Mount Everest to Raise Awareness About Deadly Limb Sprains" with a straight face. But it turns out that being in class with other people is actually a plus: If you haven't read chapters seventeen and eighteen of *Chemistry: The Molecular Nature of Matter and Change*, there are other people to take the heat off you. As it stands here, I would have to fake a seizure.

3) According to the schedule, in a few days I shoot my first kissing scene. Again, being paid to make out with somebody probably sounds like bliss to you guys. And I'm sure it will be the best perk of the job. But I'm nervous about it (and no, not just because Brady Swift is kind of—okay, *really*—cute). Everyone keeps giving me tips about finding my light and not letting my nose get in the way and knowing which side I look better on when I'm kissing someone, and suddenly I have so much more to worry about than whether or not my breath is minty fresh.

4) My wig rules. I wasn't sure if I would work as a redhead. Would it be a gorgeous Amy Adams red, or more like the time Ashlee Simpson fried her hair crimson for *Melrose Place: Failed Reboot*? But I am loving it. When

I put it on, I can feel myself leaving behind Brooke Berlin and becoming somebody else. It's refreshing. Usually everyone expects me to be a certain sort of person, like a bimbo, or a snob (although I don't think I am either). This blog has been the best way to unleash the real parts of myself that people don't see—whether they're not looking or just don't want to—so thank you for reading, everyone; yes, even you, Commenter Who Keeps Asking if I Will Show You My Boobs. But I'll be honest, even with all this writing, it's still hard sometimes to share this side of myself out loud. Slipping into someone else's shoes and saying exactly the words everyone expects to hear can feel kind of like a vacation. I mean, it's not an over-water bungalow in Bora Bora—Nancy, after all, lives in a hovel in Baltimore—but it will do.

Now, if you'll excuse me, I might have to ask Brady if we can rehearse after work. That must be how rumors get started. I wonder how many of them eventually turn out to be true.

Hugs,

B.

fourteen

"ARE WE DISTURBING YOUR nap time, Maxine?"

Max jerked her head upward and tried to focus her eyes. What the hell? Why was Brooke suddenly back at school running meetings?

But it was Brie, standing at the front of the classroom with her hands on her hips, her hair teased into a curling ponytail, an alarmingly Brooke-ish glare on her face. Max felt picked on; Magnus Mitchell was clearly hypnotizing himself by staring at Mavis Moore's clicking knitting needles, and Brie didn't reprimand *him*.

"No, Brie, I'm captivated," Max sassed through a yawn. "Please continue. I'm dying to know if we're getting the twenty-foot or twenty-five-foot Ferris wheel."

Brie shot her one more imperious look, then continued on

her spiel, which appeared to involve a pie chart. She was running this Spring Carnival meeting with the kind of organized precision usually reserved for military invasions. But the kid deserved some credit: In the weeks since Max had been to one of these meetings, Brie had navigated the committee away from fantastical ideas, like *America's Next Top Model*–themed carnival rides or performances from a band consisting of rejected *Bachelor* contestants, and toward something that resembled a real, actual, old-fashioned carnival, apparently, by referring to it all as "retro-chic." Anna Fury was still trying to work in some kind of judicial theme—a carnival jail for miscreants, with a trial before their release—and Jennifer Parker kept furiously clicking her pen and sending Jake dirty looks. All in all, Max was not sorry she'd ditched. Only Colby-Randall would spend this much time discussing a theme, only to have the eventual outcome be "Hey, let's have a carnival-themed carnival."

Max tried to hold open her eyelids, but it was a losing effort. Brooke had made arrangements with Colby-Randall to complete her coursework without showing up on campus every day, but Max still had classes. Since she'd succumbed to financial pressure and written that Brady-baiting entry for Brooke, Max had figured she could just put down her head and push forward and not care, but instead it was getting *harder* to zip her lips about all of it: how she was working her ass off to give somebody else's reputation a boost and how every time Brady smiled at Brooke it was because of something *Max* had done.

Above all, Max resented these stupid committee meetings. But the welcoming look on Jake's face when she had walked in made it tolerable. Since their phone call the other week, in which both sides had agreed to Make Plans, they hadn't had time to follow through. Secretly, Max was relieved. Life was a lot easier when you could just shove your money under your mattress instead of putting it where your mouth was.

A note landed dead center on her desk with a gentle *thwack*. Jake's arm was perfect when it came to tossing notes in class—it was a shame that talent didn't extend to the football field (the Colby-Randall Megastars had finished the year 2–8).

WHATCHA DOIN TONIGHT.

Max sucked in her breath. Was this it? Was he making plans...in a *note*? Using the word *whatcha*? Or was that all super casual because he didn't want her to think it was a date, because even though he said he missed her, he then also high-fived her, and therefore maybe he just thought of her as a very brightly colored little brother?

Either way, she couldn't very well be honest and reply, *Getting paid to pretend to be Brooke.* Max uncapped her pen with her teeth and wrote:

Can't. Plans with Molly.

"Furthermore," Brie was saying, whacking the chart with a pointer she picked up off the desk, "I'm concerned that we've all forgotten that this carnival raises money for charity. Last night, I did some research on local causes, and I think—"

Thwack.

DITCH HER. GOING TO THE MOVIES. COME WITH.

Max glanced around, wishing Molly were there to help her parse this. But the closest possible substitute was Mavis, and she was elbow-deep in the large intestine, which Magnus Mitchell kept nudging with his toe. This note *sounded* datey, but it also sounded like maybe Jake already had plans to go independently of her. What should she do? She had never more heartily wished she had ESP. There was nothing worse than not knowing where you stood with someone, and flat-out asking him was not an option. Because if Jake didn't like her, she would look ridiculous for thinking he did, and then Chaz Kelly would be all, *Kermit, dude, are you high? He's the quarterback and you're a potted plant.* And then all the effort she'd put into removing herself from Colby-Randall society to avoid such hideous embarrassments would have been wasted, and she'd have to run off and raise goats in darkest Manitoba.

"At the next meeting, we'll be voting for which charity to support, so please give this some serious thought in the interim," Brie said, flipping her hair over her unusually tan shoulder in a very familiar way. "No time for questions— I'm running late for my facial."

Brie started packing up her bag—Max noticed that her

Target tote had been replaced with a Kate Spade—and the room erupted into chitchat. Jennifer leaped up from her seat and ran out of the room like her feet were on fire.

"Dude, what's up with Molly that's so important?" Jake asked, handing Max her backpack.

Max silently apologized to the universe for her umpteenth lie. "Girl stuff."

"Well, whatever, it's okay," Jake said. "I didn't really want to see that Matthew McConaughey romantic thingy anyway. Bro might have great abs, but he seems stoned all the time. It makes me tired."

It was a date. It totally was a date. "I wouldn't have made you see that," Max ventured. "I like explosions and gore, myself. I think Michael Bay movies are the greatest thing ever."

"And that is why you're the bomb, Max," Jake said, hugging her to him. Max was so surprised by this display of affection that all she could do was stand there.

Jake crinkled up his face. "What about this weekend? Can we go out then? Will your girl stuff be over?" He frowned. "Molly's not having trouble with your brother, is she? Do I need to crack some skulls?"

"Oh, no, it's fine," Max said quickly, mentally kicking herself. "He's just stressed about this band thing this weekend."

"Dude, we should go watch him play!" Jake beamed. "That's Saturday, right? It's a date." Max felt a hot flush crawl up her face. His smile was as swoon-worthy as ever.

"Okay! I gotta go talk to Coach about how much he's making me lift."

And off he went, and that was that. But it was okay. Max wasn't a sweet-nothings kind of girl. Or at least she didn't think she was. *Guess I'll find out. Finally.*

Max's phone buzzed in the pocket of her cardigan. It was Brooke.

WHERE ARE YOU? BOY PROBLEMS.

Having a double life was stressful. How did spies do it?

✦ ✦ ✦

By the time Max finally trotted into Stage 32, any good mood that had been created by Jake's attention had been replaced by the kind of bone-deep crabbiness only L.A. traffic could create. Other people appeared to be having similar issues.

"Why don't people just use their g.d. accelerators?" Kyle was booming at Germain, who gave Max a little wave and a covert eye-roll. "And why don't we ever have any f'ing bagels left? These people are actors—they don't eat carbs!"

Brooke, however, seemed to be in a great mood. Judging from the fact that she was perched beside Brady on a black leather sofa next to some wardrobe racks, her mythical boy problems had clearly solved themselves. The two of them had their heads bowed over a folded magazine. Watching them, Max felt uncomfortable and short of breath, like she'd accidentally put on a too-small pair of Spanx.

Brooke threw back her head and laughed. Max saw she was wearing a trendy pair of black-framed reading glasses. *Since when?*

"Max!" Brooke chirped, catching sight of her. "There you are! Where have you been?"

Max rearranged her face into what she hoped was a neutral expression. "Sorry. Traffic was crazy."

"When I think about how those emissions are poisoning our lungs..." Brooke said with a tsking noise, cocking her head toward Brady in such a way that a curly lock dropped gracefully onto his shoulder.

"Hey, Max," he said, unfazed. "Did you know that Brooke was so into French history as a child that she named her pony after Joan of Arc?"

"That is news to me," Max said, carefully. This was technically true: Brooke's pony had actually been named Mr. Pickles.

Brooke pushed up her glasses and rubbed her nose. Max was unreasonably pleased to see they had left a mark. "We're trying to get in some quality bonding time," Brooke said, giving Brady a flirtatious elbow and Max a pointed look. "Tad has us doing our first kissing scene next week, and it's just been so nice to try to get to know Brady a little bit before we get so *intimate*."

"Yeah, my personal rule is never to kiss a girl before you know her middle name," Brady said. "Apparently Brooke has two, which would make her porn-star name, what? Ophelia Mayflower of Arc? That's fantastic."

Brooke giggled and leaned over Brady's lap toward where Max was standing. "Did you know Brady once almost choked to death on a sandwich?"

"It's true," he affirmed. "Ruined my appetite for pastrami. I can only eat it once a week now."

Brooke slung her arm casually around Brady's neck. "See? It's so valuable to get close like this," she said. "If we don't get comfortable giving up our personal space for each other, then scene fifty-two will be a bit of a shock."

They grinned at each other. *Kill me now*, Max thought. Apparently her powers of persuasion matched well with Brooke's... well, *powers*.

A harried production assistant stormed over to them. "We need Brady," she told them, without looking up from her clipboard.

Brady stood and pushed his (hideous) argyle sweater sleeves up over his elbows. "Ned Nickerson is about to find out that his father was in league with the crack dealers in Nancy's hood," he said. "I get to punch someone from my apple crate." He cracked his knuckles. "That thing is in so many scenes with me, I feel like I should name it. Any suggestions?"

"Mr. Pickles?" Max muttered before she could stop herself.

"Brady, I'll come watch in a minute," Brooke interjected, leaping to her feet and nudging herself between them. "First, Max and I have to talk about what we're going to read next for our book group. I really want to do *The Rise and Fall of the Roman Empire*, but she keeps agitating for *Sweet Valley Confidential*."

Max opened her mouth and then shut it.

"I used to sneak Sweet Valley High books out of my sister's room when I was a kid," Brady said. "That's how I learned that if you wake up from a coma with someone else's personality, the easiest cure is to hit your head on the coffee table."

"Brady," the PA repeated flatly. "They're waiting."

He grimaced. "Look at what a diva I'm turning into already. Nice to see you, Max."

"So what do you think?" Brooke whispered as soon as Brady was out of earshot. "Is this working? He always just wants to talk. It's been four days and he's had tons of opportunities to accidentally put a hand on my knee, or something, but he's not making a move. Is it me? Is my breath secretly bad?"

She exhaled lightly in Max's face, a warm vanilla-spearmint breeze.

"Can I get my paycheck?" Max asked. "I have a ton of homework tonight."

"He's just so gentlemanly. You don't think he's *gay*, do you?" Brooke suddenly gaped. "I mean, not that I mind being someone's beard, but I'd just like to know. It totally affects what eyelashes I wear."

"Paycheck," Max repeated flatly.

"Oh, *fine*," Brooke said. "I just thought you'd want to hear about how your plan is going. The check is in my trailer."

"It's your plan, not mine," Max said, following her through the cold and slightly dank soundstage and then outside to where the Airstreams were parked.

"Same difference," Brooke said, opening the door and ushering her inside.

Brooke's trailer was as cozy as Stage 32 was cavernous. Persian rugs hid the linoleum, and a queen-size daybed in the back room was decked out with a royal blue velvet duvet and multiple bright silk throw pillows. The perfunctory but functional kitchen in the middle faced a small table with bench seats in deep chocolate leather, and whatever wall space was available had been covered with framed vintage movie posters. Turned out living in a trailer wasn't so bad when you were doing it on a billionaire's dime.

"I've got your money in here somewhere," Brooke said, rooting through some books on a long counter under the window. They included *The Corrections*, *Literature of the Western World*, Volume II, and *Ulysses*, all stacked in a failed attempt to hide *The Secret*.

"A little light reading?" Max asked, thinking of when Brady had used those exact words with her.

"I have to keep up appearances!" Brooke beamed. "Mostly I just use them as free weights." She put her hands on her hips and frowned. "*Where* did I put that check? Can you check the bedroom, under my vanity? Daddy said I shouldn't be careless with my knees."

Max swallowed a groan and pushed through the curtain, squeezing between the bed and the table and searching for anything resembling an envelope. All she found were some Kleenex that had been used to blot lipstick and a loose subscriber card from an issue of *Self*.

As she twisted herself back upright, Max heard low voices coming from the main room. She cracked open the curtain and saw Brady leaning against the trailer door, speaking earnestly as Brooke beamed. Max shrank back just enough that she could watch undetected. *It's for research*, she told herself.

"...supposed to be one of the worst movies you can see in L.A.," Brady was saying. "I'm dying to go."

Apparently he still hadn't gone to see *The Room*. Brooke looked at him a bit blankly even though it was one of the most infamous activities in town.

"You should be seeing *good* movies, to figure out which screenwriters you want to work with next," she instructed him. "I've also been wanting to see that one where Cameron Diaz gives a kidney to Zach Galifianakis and then they take over each other's personalities. It's supposed to be hilarious."

"Oh, well, sure," Brady said, flustered. "I guess I just thought it might be fun to go see something hilariously *bad*. You know, escape from the business for a while."

Brooke grabbed Brady's arm and smiled up at him.

"You're right, of course," she said. "Does this mean you're asking me out on a date, Brady Swift?"

The imaginary Spanx roared back, strangling Max's gut more ruthlessly than before.

Brady flushed. "Well, I just think you were right before," he said. "It's hard to get to know somebody with all this going on, and if we're going to work together—"

"*Intimately*," Brooke interrupted him, pointedly.

"—well, yeah, so I think we should probably hang out on our own, you know, where no one is screaming at us to go to set, and I'm not wearing eyeliner."

Brooke batted her lashes. "I would *love* to go out with you. Our conversations have become so *important* to me, even if they're short."

Brady flashed Brooke a self-conscious grin. His dimples were so deep, you could ask him to stash your car keys in them. "Well, okay then," he said.

Max pinched shut the curtain. She didn't want to see any more.

fifteen

Heath wasn't like any pirate Francesca had ever seen. Lean and pale, with a shock of brown hair and milky brown eyes, he was intense and hungry and oh my god he was Edward Cullen flarrrrgh.

Max punched the delete key with abandon. She didn't care if it broke off and smashed into a million pieces. Half the point of taking on Brooke's blog had been to unlock Max's own creative process. Instead, her NYU writing sample got worse every time she restarted it. And it didn't help that Teddy was upstairs playing the same riff on his guitar over and over and over again.

"A little variety, please, maestro?" she bellowed in the

general direction of Teddy's upstairs turret room. He thumped the floor and kept playing.

Max looked out her bedroom window and saw her dad puttering around with something that looked like an old-fashioned hand-push lawn mower with an oscillating fan attached, presumably to keep the person mowing the lawn from getting overheated. They were in the middle of a heat wave — the WeatherBug on Max's computer claimed Los Angeles had hit a hundred degrees that day — and with the air still unpleasantly oppressive, Max was beginning to regret not taking Molly up on her offer of a post-school swim at her place. But Max felt too antsy to relax on an inflatable raft.

"I have to work on my application," was her excuse. Which of course meant rewriting the opening sentences about seventy-five times, reading all the comments on Open Brooke.com (the last entry, about how "if it zips, it fits" is not a proper style mantra, had gotten more than four hundred), and flipping between the Lifetime Movie Network and info-mercials. She'd stopped even pretending to work when she discovered a Colon Zap ad starring Jennifer Parker.

Brooke called. Max sent her to voice mail.

Vampires didn't scare Francesca. Neither did werewolves. No, what she really feared were robot zombie werevamps. And dying alone in her garret never having left Los Angeles and doing nothing but writing a dumb blog. THE END.

209

A box popped up on her computer screen. It was a video-chat request from Molly. Max clicked Accept, and Brooke, wearing an orange bathing suit with a cardigan pulled over it, appeared on-screen.

"Gotcha," Brooke said, grinning.

Dammit. Will I ever learn?

"Oh, my God. Your room is a *mess*," Brooke added, trying to peer around Max's body as if video chat allowed for a fully three-dimensional perspective. Without makeup and with her hair pulled back into a ponytail, she actually looked like a regular, wholesome sixteen-year-old who could as easily have come from basketball practice as from a movie set.

"Hello to you, too, Brooke," Max said, reaching up to adjust her webcam so that Brooke couldn't see the pile of dirty laundry on top of Max's bed. "What do you want? And why are we video-chatting now?"

"Does Brady like red? Or is that too obvious?"

"How should I know?" Max felt prickly.

"Well, you two are all chatty all the time," Brooke said. "I just assumed you'd found out the basics—favorite color, favorite sushi roll, favorite cut of jeans. Brick is *really* excited that Brady and I are going out, and I think he might be tipping off a reporter from *In Touch*. So this has to look good."

"Lucky Brady," Max said before she could stop herself.

Brooke rolled her eyes. "Maybe you should switch to herbal teas to cure your mood problems," she said. "Is Molly there?"

"No, I thought she was at your place."

"She was, but she said she was heading over to your house for moral support," Brooke said. "I assumed she meant for you, like maybe you were going to color your hair or something..." Her voice took on a hopeful note.

"No such luck, Brooke," Max said. "Try her cell?"

"That's so 2009." Brooke peered through the screen at something on Max's desk. "Please at least throw out that apple. It's practically a fossil." She punched her mouse pertly and Skype made its signature sign-off blurping noise.

"Yes, *boss*," Max sang to the blank screen. Glaring at the shriveled, slightly imploded apple, she contemplated hurling it at the ceiling to make Teddy stop his infernal twanging, but the backsplash would make her the actual victim. So she carefully carried it to her wastebasket and shoved it inside an empty Kleenex box for protection, then grabbed a shoe and threw it at the spot on the ceiling where Teddy's music seemed the loudest.

"Some of us are trying to use our delete key down here," she shouted.

A knock came at the door. Max jumped. That was fast. "Go away," she yelled.

The door opened and Molly stuck in her head. "Really?"

"Oh, it's you. No, you can stay," Max said, flopping down on the bed and staring at the ceiling again. There was now a dirty spot on it in the shape of her sneaker. "But I'm warning you, Teddy has been playing the same half of a song for two hours and it might make you stabby."

"I was just up there," Molly said. "I guess he's getting press attention because of what you wrote about him in Brooke's blog, so now the band has decided to play one of his songs and one of Bone's. He's stressing. I decided to leave him alone."

"Great. So we both have writer's block." Max rubbed her temple. "Sorry," she yelled up at the ceiling. There was a pause, and then they heard a short acoustic version of the chorus to Cee Lo Green's "Forget You."

Max laughed. "Well played," she shouted.

Molly curled up in Max's desk chair and peered at the screen. "Why is Francesca writing Brooke's blog now?" she asked.

"Crap, I thought I deleted that," Max said. "I keep getting halfway through the opening of a story and then I get so mad at how bad it is that I start typing nonsense. It's seriously bumming me out."

"Well, at least you have one thing to look forward to," Molly said.

Max snorted. "I've seen Mental Hygienist play before."

"No, not the contest. Your date. With Jake. Saturday."

Max sat up abruptly. "Oh, right."

Molly looked shocked. "You *forgot*? You were so in love with him six months ago that you let him call you Mary, and you *forgot that he asked you out?*"

"No, it's just... well, okay, maybe a bit," Max said sheepishly. "I just lost track of what day it is."

"Are you not into him anymore?" Molly asked, furrowing her brow.

"I'm just...I don't know." Max rolled onto her side and picked at a stray thread on her quilt. "My foot won't stay still. It keeps twitching. I can't concentrate. I feel really weird."

"That happened to me once when I drank an entire two-liter of Diet Coke in one sitting," Molly said. "Except I know that's not what you did, so what's the deal?"

"I don't know," Max moaned melodramatically.

"Okay, *Brooke*."

Max shot Molly a halfhearted dirty look. "Fine. Let's take stock," she said, holding up her fingers to tick off the points on the list. "I write a popular blog. I'm paid pretty well to do it, and so if I get into the NYU thing I can actually *go*, and still pay for food. And the quarterback I've been in love with for years finally broke up with his girlfriend and asked me out because he 'misses me.'" When she finished the air quotes, she spread her hands wide. "That's everything I've always wanted, right? So what's my deal? Shouldn't I be totally stoked?" She swallowed hard. "Do you think I'm cold and dead inside?"

"Isn't that pretty much the first line on your résumé?"

Max frowned. "I prefer sarcasm when it's not directed at me," she said. Then she sighed. "All the false pretenses are just kind of starting to bug me. And I feel so *lame* that it bugs me. I knew what I was signing up for, and now I feel like a whiny little kid asking to be noticed, which is so dumb because I *never* care if anyone notices me."

"Uh-huh," Molly said, a note of skepticism in her voice. Max chose to ignore it.

"The thing is, I don't usually let people get to know me," she barreled on. "And you know that. But now I'm meeting all these people, but of course they think all these little parts of me that I'm putting out there for the world to read on the blog are really *Brooke*, so they still don't really see *me*. And maybe it offends me a little that they believe it all so easily." She shook her head. "Has *nobody* noticed that those glasses came out of nowhere?"

"Wow," Molly said, uncurling her legs and propping them up on the bed. "That was a lot to keep bottled up. But I get it." She tucked her bangs behind her ear. "You know, when I first moved here, the hardest thing was feeling like I had to become someone else, either to survive Hurricane Brooke or to get Brick to like me, or both."

"But you were always normal around me and Teddy."

"Yeah, and I *still* almost got swallowed up by all the me-versus-Brooke stuff," Molly said. "I'm doing so much better now, and it's because I'm just being *me*, and not whatever version of me was trying to please Brick or beat Brooke at her own game. That got so exhausting."

"I don't even know what version of me to be anymore," Max moped. "And now I've let her drag Brady into this mess. He doesn't deserve that. He's so into her writing and—"

"*Your* writing."

"My writing, and her *everything else*," Max said. "And she wants him, so she'll get him. But that's not the point."

"Are you sure about that?" Molly asked.

The way Molly was looking at her, Max knew she couldn't get away with a half-truth. She took a deep breath.

"Even if I did think he was kind of cool, he's obviously crazy about Brooke," she said. "She's Barbie and I'm a troll."

"Don't be ridiculous. You are not."

"You know what I mean," Max insisted. "I can't compete with that. Besides, I've been obsessed with Jake since junior high, and he's here *now*. So maybe he doesn't read much. And his grammar is awful. And he dated that crazy bitch for the last few years. But he's nice, and he's *really* hot, and I make him laugh. *I* do that. Me."

"As opposed to Brady, who thinks it's Brooke making him laugh."

"If you bring up Brady again I am going to throw my other shoe at you," Max warned. Molly grabbed a Kleenex off Max's desk and waved it in faux-surrender as Max added, "Jake was always what I wanted, and now he wants to go out, and that's great. I'm just a little wonky right now, is all."

Molly nodded sympathetically. "It must be hard living a lie."

"*Lust for Life* makes it look easy."

"Yes, and *Lust for Life* is noted for its documentary approach to social situations."

The girls swapped smiles, but Max couldn't contain a deep groan. "I miss old Max. I miss not caring."

"Oh, come on, you cared," Molly said. "Nobody who genuinely doesn't care fights that hard to *look* like they don't care. And now you just happen to care about something that's all jacked up with little white lies, so you don't know how to feel."

"Thanks, doc," Max said. "Do you charge by the hour?"

"I wish I knew what else to tell you," Molly said. "Psychic identity theft is complicated."

Abruptly Max sat up. "I *am* doing the right thing, though," she insisted. "Right? Not quitting the blog? I mean, I am getting published. If NYU isn't meant to be, then at least I have that."

"I trust your judgment," Molly said sincerely.

"So I will just chill out and keep rolling with it. Whatever it is," Max stated, almost like a resolution.

Her phone rang. JAKE DONOVAN, it read. Max picked it up and waved it at Molly. "See? The universe agrees with me."

Max accepted the call. "Hey, Jake!" she said. "Awesome to hear from you!" Then she recoiled a little inside—it sounded too hearty, too false.

"Hey! So we're still on for Saturday, right?" he asked.

"Yep," she said, trying to sound supremely relaxed and confident.

sixteen

"...AND SO THEN ANNA FURY was, like, 'I hold you in *contempt*,' and I had to be, like, 'Honey, you are not your mother, and these people are not here because one of them is suing a roommate for puking in the dishwasher,' and Justine was all, 'Oh, snap,' and then I adjourned the meeting and came here. And that's all you missed."

"Interesting," Brooke said, eyeing her apprentice. "Did you change your hair, Brie?"

Brie touched her head gingerly. Her light brown locks, once straight, had been jazzed up with golden highlights, curls, and what looked like extensions. "Do you like it?" she asked. "I just felt like I needed something more... authoritative."

"Everyone listens more to blondes," Brooke averred.

Brie crossed her arms proudly. "I even got a near-unanimous majority when we voted on the theme."

Brooke covered her eyes. "Please tell me they didn't pick the one where Mavis Moore wanted every ride to be named after an internal organ. That girl is so weird."

"As if," Brie said. "We actually went with my idea for a regular carnival. I won everyone over by saying we could have a Hollywood bit at the entrance—like, a patch of red carpet so people can get fake-papped on their way in, and then a booth where you can put on loaner gowns and get your picture taken to see if they're see-through. That sort of stuff."

"We should invite some *real* celebrities to that," Brooke said. "Did you see what that chick who used to be on *Greek* wore to The Ivy last weekend?"

"Right? I saw more nipple than her gynecologist does," Brie said, sitting down on Brooke's chaise longue and crossing her legs.

Brooke snorted. "You sound like me."

Brie gave her a hopeful smile. "That's the idea!"

Brooke stood up and stretched. "Well, that should do it," she said. "Thanks for the update. Now I need complete solitude to prepare for my date tonight. It's very important."

Brie stood back up, gathered her stuff, and headed for Brooke's door. "It'll be great, no matter what you wear," she said loyally. "That boy doesn't stand a chance."

"*Obviously*," Brooke said, with a tinkling laugh.

But as soon as the bedroom door closed, Brooke headed

straight to her picture window for some therapeutic pacing (well, as therapeutic as it could be in four-inch Brian Atwoods; Brooke never went long without wearing stilettos, in case her arches got complacent). She was nervous. And tired. It was her first day off after a triumphant week of shooting, and instead of going with Arugula to Burke Williams for a massage and a mud bath, she was gearing up for more acting—this time, on her big date with Brady.

She had total confidence that she'd nail the visuals. Wearing a wig every day, rather than styling her own hair, left her blonde tresses less overworked and a bit shinier than usual. She'd double-dipped on the Crest Whitestrips that morning and had one more set ready to go, to negate any negative effects from her 4 PM Diet Coke. She'd squeezed in a quick leg wax on the way home from the studio yesterday, and she'd picked out the perfect dress: a gray ombre Elizabeth and James silk-satin shift that made her blue eyes pop, and which looked relaxed but chic when she added a wide belt and booties. Those Olsen twins might look like pint-sized Wiccan hobos in person, but they definitely knew how to design a dress.

The other part of the date, the actual *out loud* part, was causing Brooke more stress. All week she'd seen Brady having animated chats with Brick—who had brought Brady a custom Green Tea Power Bar to try, which was basically the equivalent of adopting him—and laughing in corners with Max about whatever Syfy movie about mutant eels had just aired. But she herself had only grabbed Brady for very brief exchanges so far. In part, that was because every day had been just busy enough that they kept getting interrupted—either she was on set, or he was, or both of them were—but mostly, to be honest, Brooke deliberately kept things light and short. She secretly liked how it felt when Brady asked her intelligent questions and expected her to know the answers. Unfortunately, she sometimes didn't. He hadn't tripped her up yet, but what if she burned through all her good luck? She wanted to save up all her universe-allotted high-IQ moments for when they were out alone, so that she didn't find herself sitting at Craft staring stupidly at one of Tom Colicchio's steaks. Because she *wasn't* stupid. She just wasn't Max.

Brooke rested her head on the sliding door out to the balcony and heard a stream of chatter through the glass.

Max.

Brooke pasted on her most accessible, innocent smile and flounced onto the patio. Max and Molly were sitting on Molly's end, sorting through an enormous pile of clothes.

"Making a Goodwill run?" Brooke asked sunnily. "I'm pretty sure I have some Marc Jacobs stuff that needs to be evicted."

Max glowered at her. "These are my actual clothes. We're...going through them." She shivered. "I had to get out of my house. Teddy is driving me insane. He's so nervous about the band competition tonight that he drank four Red Bulls in a row."

"Shouldn't you be over there with him, soothing his troubled brow or whatever it is that devoted girlfriends are supposed to do?" Brooke asked Molly.

Molly shook her head. "He said he wants to focus. So I'm meeting up with Max and Jake at the House of Blues for the show, and I'll see him then."

Max looked horrified. "I told you not to say anything about Jake in front of her."

"Relax," Brooke said. "You're forgetting that I'm friends with Jake's ex-girlfriend. Jennifer screamed at me about your date for an hour last night. Something about him not valuing her enough to wait a month before his rebound girl."

"Brooke," Molly warned, as Max's expression turned slightly queasy.

"Not that I think you are a rebound," Brooke amended sweetly, sitting down on one of the patio chairs. "*She* said that. She's a little insane right now. I wouldn't be surprised if she stalks you around town the whole night."

Max looked stricken. "Maybe this is a bad idea."

"Oh, *please*," Brooke said. "Twitter was invented to find out what celebrities eat for lunch, not for yelling at your boyfriend. I love Jennifer, but she deserved to get dumped. Now, what do we have here?"

She reached into the pile, then thought better of it and grabbed a pair of tweezers she'd left sitting on the table. "What *is* this?" she asked, using them to lift up something stripey.

"Tights," Max said.

"No," Brooke said, throwing them off to the side. "You are not in a Tim Burton movie. Next?"

Max dug around and pulled out a T-shirt whose sleeves were covered in grommets, as Brooke's tweezers hooked one that said GOOD GRAMMAR COSTS NOTHING.

"No, and no," Brooke said again. "You are not a walking PSA, and you are also not looking for a curtain rod to hang from." She sighed. "This is a mess. You need help. You need..." Her face darkened, then lit up so brightly the sun would've felt irrelevant. She had her plan. "You need *me*."

"Oh, God, here we go," Molly muttered.

"No way," Max said. "No makeovers, remember?"

"Come on, just this one time?" Brooke wheedled. "You want to knock Jake off his feet, right? You want this to be memorable, right?" Max appeared to be listening. "And you want to know he's not going to look at you all night and think, *Man, Jennifer's hair was such a nice, normal color*, right?" she pressed.

"Seriously, Brooke, lay off," Molly said.

"I'm just saying, this is big. And so I think she should bring in the big guns." Brooke looked triumphant. "And I am heavy artillery. I am, like, the bazooka of makeovers."

"She kind of has a point," Max said, turning to Molly. "I mean, I brought half my closet over here in a duffel bag because I couldn't deal with this on my own."

"Then you definitely need my help," Brooke said. "And you'd only need to do, like, one *tiny* thing for me in return."

"I knew it," Molly said.

Brooke made them wait another second for dramatic effect—she considered it good practice for her day job—and then announced, "You have to make it a double date with me and Brady."

Max stood up and went a little white. Well, *whiter*. "What? No."

"It'll be fun!" Brooke said, even starting to believe it. Now that she'd thought of this, it seemed like she couldn't *not* take Max, in case she got into some kind of intellectual muddle.

"What, the four of us sitting at a table pretending it isn't totally *awkward* that we're on a group first date? Yeah, that sounds super fun," Max said sarcastically. "My presence will really add to the ambience when you're sitting in Brady's lap feeding him fries or whatever."

"It's just that you're so *smart*," Brooke began in earnest.

"So is Arugula. Take her."

Brooke rolled her eyes. "She doesn't even know Brady. And she'd probably bring some boring science major from UCLA and then talk to us for three hours about how her dad invented a new kind of lettuce."

"Not my problem. I'm not going with you."

"Pleeeeeease?"

"I don't need to watch you lead him on."

"Don't be so dramatic," Brooke said crossly. "This is just a casual getting-to-know-you. I'm sure nothing's actually going to happen."

"Does *he* know that?"

Brooke waved her hand. "Details," she said. "It's more convincing this way, which is good for publicity." *And for Brick. And for me.* She raised her right hand. "I swear on some invisible religious text that I won't lead him on in any way. Does that help?"

"I'm still not coming."

Brooke sprang off the edge of her patio lounger and walked to the railing, where she stared down at the pool. She knew Max being less than pliable was a good thing for their joint project, but she found that trait frustrating when it meant that she couldn't BS her way through moments like this. To Brooke, honesty was rarely the best policy; it usually was more like ammunition for the enemy. She would know. She'd been on the firing squad before. Still, with no other options...

"I can't believe you're going to make me say this," she said, pouting. "But... fine. I feel like I might screw this up if you're not there to bail me out. Like, what if he asks me about *Hunger Games* again? I only read the first and last chapters."

"You're an actress," Max said. "Fake it."

"I don't think you realize how much acting I'm already *doing*," Brooke whined.

"That's not my problem! I'm not going to be some kind of intellectual translator service," Max said. "Anyway, I'm sure the first time you bat your eyelashes he'll get so distracted that you could answer him in Farsi and be fine."

Brooke considered this. It was possible. But while she firmly believed that her eyelashes had powers, she didn't fancy her chances of rendering him mute for *that* many hours.

"No. I need the help," she said plainly. "Daddy gave him a limited-edition Power Bar, Max. I can't blow this."

Silence. Max wasn't budging. Brooke simply stared at her, trying to read her face (or intimidate her into saying yes). Why was Max being so stubborn? She was acting like a jealous... *Oh, God. Of course.*

"I asked if you liked him and you said no," Brooke said. "Was that a lie? Are you the one leading somebody on here? Do I need to call Jennifer?"

"Give her a break, Brooke," Molly intervened. "She doesn't want to do it."

"But what is her hang-up? She was on board enough to help arrange this thing in the first place." Brooke turned to Max, exasperated. She wasn't used to not getting her way, and it was making her bratty. "Listen, Brady will thank us when the *Us Weekly* coverage lands him on the B-plus-list," she insisted. "It's what every actor wants. And don't you think it'd hurt him more if this evening goes badly and then he's stuck working with me every day? It might tank his performance, Max. So do this for *him*."

Max tensed her jaw, and then finally she looked up at Brooke with a resigned expression on her face. "Maybe I *can* make you a cheat sheet or something," she said. "But that's as far as I go."

Brooke clasped her hands together, thrilled. "Really? Max, you are the best," she crowed. "But let's not call it a cheat sheet, okay? It sounds so lowbrow."

Max rolled her eyes. "Fine. Flash cards," she said. "I'll write down a couple things you might want to know, or something you can talk about, and whenever you get stuck, just pretend you're looking for your lip gloss in your purse and then read one. Is that enough? Can we please stop all this blah-blah about a double date?"

Brooke beamed. "Whatever you say," she said. "And in return, you get the full Brooke Berlin glamour treatment." Max started to back away but Brooke grabbed her by the sleeve. "I insist," she said. "It's the least I can do. Come with me."

"Am I going to regret this?" Max asked.

Brooke placed her hands on Max's shoulders. "Beautification is my specialty, Max. Let me use *my* talent for *you*," she said, feeling a burst of altruism. Brooke Berlin, social philanthropist. "Just leave it to me. Jake won't know what hit him."

And neither will Brady.

In a totally platonic, publicity-friendly way, of course.

seventeen

"YEEEEEEE-HAAAAAAAW!" SCREECHED THE GIRL on the mechanical bull, just before it bucked her off and she tumbled onto the padded floor in a flurry of limbs and toned belly flesh. There was a moment of silence as she rubbed her head before she threw up her arms and screamed, "Go Lakers! Touchdooooown!" The spectators ringing the bull pen toasted her and whooped.

And I didn't think my life could get weirder, Max thought.

When planning their date, Jake had suggested grabbing dinner at one of his favorite spots before they headed to the House of Blues for the band contest. This was how Max had ended up at the dreaded Saddle Ranch, a cheesy faux-Western tourist trap on Sunset, which Max knew of chiefly from its appearance in about eighty percent of all reality shows—including, inevitably, its own. In fact, *something* was filming that night. Max knew she'd visibly balked when she saw the wide-area release—noting that simply walking inside was tantamount to consenting to appear on camera—because Jake had stopped to sling a supportive arm around her shoulder and say, "Now *everyone* will get to see how great you are." Little did he know this was precisely Max's fear. The idea of his friends, her friends, Molly's friend Charmaine in Indiana—hell, even some random Jane in Topeka—watching her pretend to belong on the arm of the quarterback was vomit-inducing.

Everyone inside seemed a lot more enthused than she was. Mostly, they were already cast on the show, hoped to be on the show, or had already been on a different show. (Max recognized their waitress, Brandelle—a very skinny, very tan, very fake redhead in a pair of painted-on jeans— from *Real World: Daytona Beach*, on which she had filled up a hot tub with tequila, climbed inside with a straw and four people, and then drank it.) Everyone else was a mixture of sunburned tourists and Ed Hardy enthusiasts.

"This is…really interesting," Max managed to say to Jake, slumping down in her seat reflexively as two cameramen followed a tattooed bartender and a screaming customer out onto the patio.

"I should've called to see if they were filming," Jake said apologetically. "I just got excited. This is my favorite restaurant in Los Angeles, and Jen would never come with me. She said she was worried that she was going to catch a fungus from the napkin dispenser." He leaned across the table. "Are you okay with staying here? We can go somewhere else."

Looking around the restaurant, with its sawdust-covered concrete floor and vaguely grimy walls, Max reflected that this might have been the only time ever that she and Jennifer Parker agreed on anything. But Jake's face was so earnest; he was really trying to make her happy.

"No, it's cool. The people-watching is great," she offered gamely, watching as another drunk girl climbed on the bull, her lacy pink thong peeking out the back of her jeans.

"It really is," Jake said, looking intently at Max. "And I am watching you look seriously awesome."

Max felt herself blushing.

"Um, can you excuse me for a second? I'll be right back," she said.

"Sure!" Jake chirped. "I'll order appetizers!"

"Great." Max forced a smile and grabbed her caramel suede clutch (picked out by Brooke) before tottering down the hallway on her new knee-high boots (ditto) and banging through the ladies' room door. She headed straight to the sink and leaned both hands on the cool porcelain, hoping that maybe it would unfluster her.

But the face that looked back at her from the mirror over the sink belonged to a stranger. Brooke had talked her into dying her hair a glossy, warm chestnut and then shaping it into a tidy banged bob that evoked an old silent-movie star from the 1920s; then she'd squeezed her into a halter top and a pair of dark-wash skinny jeans that may have cost more than Max's car. She looked sleek and polished, every inch a Maxine instead of a Max, which she imagined was exactly what Brooke had yearned for ever since they'd started this blog project together. Max felt sort of dorky for allowing this—she hadn't had a hair color other than green in years—but Brooke had cut to her core when she talked about impressing Jake. In all her years of crushing on Jake Donovan, Max had assumed he was unattainable, and so never imagined what they'd do on an actual date. She cursed her lack of psychic powers.

I wonder what Brooke and Brady are doing.

Max rolled her eyes the instant she thought it. Who cared what they were doing? Jake was *amazing*. He'd been entranced by her makeover. Before they'd even sat down, he'd gravely asked Brandelle the Waitress to make double sure Max's food wasn't cooked within a foot of any meat. He'd held doors, pulled out her chair, and, best of all, chosen a polo shirt that was satisfyingly snug around his biceps. So the fact that Max had spent the last forty-five minutes feeling more awkward than pants on a cat was entirely her own fault. She silently cursed Molly for making her admit she'd had a curiosity about Brady.

Pull it together. This is what you've wanted since you were thirteen years old. In fact, technically, this was Max's first real, official, Drive Together in a Car Alone and Eat Dinner Together date. *So stop acting like you've been lobotomized and enjoy it.*

She returned to the booth to find Jake sitting in front of two massive baskets of fried food. "I ordered curly fries and onion rings," he announced with a mixture of glee and hesitation.

"Awesome," Max said.

"Are you sure?"

"Well, yeah," Max said. "I love onion rings." She tried to grin. "No meat, right?"

Jake looked thrilled. "Jen always used to get upset if I ordered fried things for her. She said it made her wonder if I was trying to sabotage her diet, and if so, *why*."

"I'm not on a diet," Max said, picking up a ring and shoving it in her mouth.

"Good. You shouldn't be," Jake declared. His fingers inched toward hers, which had a vise grip on her water glass. "There is nothing hotter than a girl who will eat an onion ring in front of you."

Jake's eyes were glowing at her in a way that, even a month ago, would've melted off her matte black toenail polish, but tonight Max was grateful for the mouthful of food that kept her from having to respond to his flirting. She scanned the room for good conversation pieces, and settled on a girl wearing a terrycloth tube top who was drinking a Flaming Dr Pepper shot while six guys banged on the bar in unison. "I guess she wore the towel to catch the drips," Max said. "By the end of the night you could probably wring that thing out into a glass and get drunk just off that."

"I think I saw Chaz do that at a party one time," Jake said. "But it was with the towels we kept around the keg."

"Ew, really?" Max gaped.

"Really," Jake said. "I think maybe the padding in his helmet needs to be thicker."

"True." Max felt that one word kill the momentum. "Um, so speaking of football, how's that going? Spring scrimmages are soon, huh?" she asked, hoping that this sounded like a smooth segue.

"Yeah, but it's hard to get motivated before, like, August," Jake said. "I was supposed to go to the gym with Magnus today, but instead I stayed home and watched TV."

"That sounds fun," Max said. "What did you watch?"

He looked pleased. "You're not mad?"

"Why would I be mad? TV is pretty much my number one hobby. Other than writing," she added impulsively, as a test balloon.

Jake blew out a breath. "Jen always got on my case about not working out all the time!" he crowed, in his relief totally missing her revelation. "She said it was ruining my shot at getting recruited to a top-tier football school."

No, being on a terrible football team is ruining your shot at getting recruited to a top-tier football school, Max thought. Her inner monologue was crabby tonight.

"You have to take a day off now and again," she said instead, trying to sound reassuring (rather than relieved he hadn't picked up on her possibly premature comment about her writing aspirations).

"You are so supportive and nice."

"Thank you," Max said, feeling bad about her Mind Bitch. Her guilty silence ground things to a halt again. *How do people ever get married, if this is what dating is like? Is it too soon to decide to be a nun?*

The girl on the bull was laughing uncontrollably, her giggles getting higher and higher in pitch until she was mercifully bucked to the ground and into silence. "She signed a release, right?" the bull operator called out, sounding kind of worried.

"I really like your hair," Jake said. "It brings out your eyes."

Max smoothed it down self-consciously. She kept forgetting it had changed, until she caught a glimpse of herself in random reflective surfaces. "Thank you," she repeated.

Jake dug his cell phone out of his pocket. "Dude! I totally forgot to check in on foursquare," he said. "What if some of my bros are in the area?"

Dear Jesus, please don't let any of his bros be in the area.

"Check it, I'm the mayor of the Saddle Ranch!" Jake crowed, holding out his phone so she could see. "And my Facebook says, 'Jake is having a great time with beautiful Max at Saddle Ranch!'"

Max took his phone from him and looked down at it. "And just now Jennifer commented that she hopes you get trampled by the fake bull."

"Typical," Jake said, taking the phone back and beginning

to tap at it furiously. "Oh, and Magnus wrote that he's going to meet us at the concert!"

"Great," Max said. She shoved an entire onion ring into her mouth.

"Yeah, he and Chaz went to elementary school with some dudes whose band made it, too. Unsinkable Panty Line. *Super* intense, although the name kind of sounds like something in the Victoria's Secret catalog."

"Wow." Max let out a genuine giggle that, in her heightened nervous state, quickly turned bubblier than she'd intended. *Great, now I sound vacuous. And could I possibly manage to say more than one word at once?* "I'm not sure that Chaz and Magnus are going to be that into hanging out with me," she ventured.

Jake set the phone down. "I know they're jerk-offs a lot of the time," he said. "But they're not that bad once you get to know them, and they will like you because I like you."

He flashed his heart-stopping grin. Max felt her Mind Bitch recede a bit. Okay, a lot.

"It's so great going out with someone I can really *talk* to," Jake said, his giant right hand finally making it all the way to her tiny left one, which he covered warmly. "I like that. Change is good."

As she looked into his eager eyes, which pulled her in like a tractor beam, Max felt a tiny flare of optimism. Maybe he was right. Maybe Jake Donovan was the change she'd needed.

"And so then I was like, 'Bro, he's never going to learn the pistol offense *that way*!' " Jake burst into a truly delighted guffaw.

Max joined in, weakly, and then resumed playing with the straw in her lemonade while Jake launched into Chapter Two of this story, which had begun over s'mores at the Saddle Ranch and then continued as they trotted the half block west down Sunset and across to the House of Blues and found a table near the stage. It had something to do with his football squad, their coach, and the pistol versus the shotgun versus something else that wasn't named after a weapon. And apparently it was very, very funny. Max couldn't follow it at all, so she just laughed whenever Jake did. This must've been what it was like for Brooke whenever Brady tried to talk to her about, like, the tonal difference between Joss Whedon's graphic novels and his movie scripts. Brooke hadn't been kidding: It was *exhausting* pretending to know what someone else was talking about when in fact you were totally lost and thinking about shoes (although in Max's case, these footwear thoughts were about why she'd let Brooke talk her into heeled boots, because her toes had already developed screaming blisters). Her earlier optimism had dampened somewhat now that she wasn't under the thrall of his blue eyes. Had he *always* talked about football so much?

"I'm sorry, I must be boring you," Jake said, as if he'd read her mind. "Blah blah blah about football."

"Not at all," Max lied politely, swinging her legs on the tall stool. She was too short to plant her feet against the footrest.

"I'd rather focus on you for a bit," Jake said, his eyes twinkling. "You said something about writing at dinner, right? What sort of stuff do you write? Screenplays?"

"Oh, you know, just…" she began.

"*Jake!* Fancy meeting you here!"

Max looked up just in time to see a nearly six-foot blonde creature swoop over and plant her red patent clutch dead center on the tall, tiny cocktail table she and Jake had snagged near stage left.

Brooke.

And standing slightly behind her, looking slightly befuddled in cords and a close-cut navy sweater, was Brady.

eighteen

AT THE SIGHT OF BROOKE clutching Brady Swift's arm
to her chest like a child cradling a beloved stuffed animal,
Max was torn: Part of her wanted to thank Brooke for
sparing her any further uncomfortable one-on-one conversation with Jake, and the rest of her wanted to pull out
Brooke's hair for dragging Max into their evening and thus
into something that would hurt a very nice guy's feelings.

You mean, more into it than you already were, her subconscious needled her.

Shut up, Max scolded it.

"Bro!" Jake said, filling the silence by leaping out of his
seat and raising a fist for Brooke to bump. "Ha! Get it? You're
Brooke? And you're my bro? What are you doing here?"

Brooke burst into a gale of innocent laughter that Max

had heard often enough to know it was forced. Apparently she was leaving all her actual acting energy on the Warner Bros. lot.

"Brady and I were going to go to the movies, but I realized I just couldn't possibly *not* come out and support my beloved sister's boyfriend," Brooke gushed. "How amazing to randomly bump into you two!"

You lying liar who lies, Max thought. *You have been planning this since you woke up this morning.*

Brooke pulled Brady toward the table. Designed for two, it was extremely tight quarters for twice that, and Max found herself squashed between the boys. Brady smelled faintly, warmly, like soap. "Brady, this is my dear friend from school, Jake Donovan," Brooke said. "Brady is my love interest in *Nancy Drew*."

Max shrank back as the boys reached across her to shake hands.

"Nice to meet you," Brady said, then turned his outstretched hand to Max as if to shake hers.

"Oh, my God, Brady, that's *Max*," Brooke said, chortling.

Max smiled weakly and watched as recognition and then, briefly, shock washed over his face. "Whoa," he blurted. "What did you do to your hair?"

"A return to the natural look for Maxine," Brooke narrated. "Doesn't she look great?"

"Of course," he said, a little wistfully. There was something in his eyes, deep down, that seemed a little confused. "Sorry, that was unsmooth. I just...liked the green."

"Me, too," Max admitted before she could help herself.

"Well, it's good to see you anyway," he added, with another glance at her head. "But I should have known you'd be here. You two are attached at the hip."

Jake burst into laughter. "You," he said to Brady with a jaunty finger gun, "are one funny dude."

"I...don't get it," Brady said, looking from Max to Brooke, whose nostrils were flaring—a sign Max had learned meant trouble. In this case, they were like a tiny SOS, asking Max how to get them out of this one. "I see them together, like, every day."

Jake kept on laughing and shaking his head. "Man, you should do stand-up."

"Jake, you are as unobservant as ever," Brooke said lightly—and very quickly. "Apparently, the increase in head injuries at the high school football level really *is* causing serious problems."

"You play?" Jake asked Brady.

"I tried, but I could never throw a spiral. My dad said I looked like I was trying to throw an egg."

"Bro, it's easy, you just put your pointer finger on the—"

"You two stay here and chat. We'll go get drinks," Brooke said, grabbing Max's arm. Max opened her eyes really wide at Brooke, hoping this would convey the message *Do you really think we should leave them alone?* But all Brooke did was open her eyes wide in return.

"Fine. We'll be right back," Max said. "Jake, why don't

you tell Brady that story you were telling me about the...
handgun thing?"

"Oh, right! The pistol offense! Okay, so..." Jake turned
to Brady, a look of adorable enthusiasm on his face, as
Brooke dragged Max across the darkened club's uneven
wooden floorboards. Max hated siccing Jake and his football obsession on Brady, but it was the only way she could
think of to distract Jake from asking Brady why he thought
she and Brooke were so buddy-buddy, when in fact everyone at Colby-Randall knew they couldn't stand each other.

"What are you *really* doing here?" Max snapped at
Brooke, as soon as they reached the long wooden bar.

Brooke waved at the bartender. "What do you mean?"
she said blithely. "I really did think Molly could use my
sisterly support. Where is she, anyway?"

"Backstage with Teddy," Max said. "And you are a terrible liar. I *told you* not to make this a double date."

"Two couples happening to find themselves at the same
concert is *not* a double date. It is a coincidence," Brooke
insisted. "Besides, I *really* need your help."

"I knew it," Max said, resisting the urge to throttle
Brooke with one of her long blonde curls as the bartender
looked expectantly at them.

"Two Cokes, a Diet Coke, and..." Brooke looked at Max
questioningly.

"A lemonade, and you're paying," Max said. "What happened? This had better be good."

"Well," Brooke began, fanning both her hands out—a

gesture that Max knew meant she was about to launch into one of her more complicated tales.

"The short version," she interrupted. "We can't leave them alone for long."

"Okay, you're right," Brooke said. "Everything was going fine. We went to this amazing little Indian place Brady picked out where you actually get to sit on these fabulous throw pillows and there's a fire pit, and I wasn't sure what to get that wouldn't stain my teeth, so—"

"Seriously, *this* is the short version? Is the long version a three-day television event?"

"I had to set the scene!" Brooke protested. "Anyway. The flash cards were working great, right? That whole bit about not being able to take that guy from the *Hunger Games* seriously because his name is terrible—what was it? Something with bread."

"Peeta," Max supplied. "It sounds so dumb out loud."

"Exactly! He ate that up. I even used your line about it making you want to dip things in hummus."

"Okay..." Max said, sensing things were about to turn left.

"And *then* we were talking about places we'd traveled, and he was going on about Mount Rushmore, and he asked me which one of the presidents on there was my favorite, and that's not on the flash cards, Max," Brooke said, the words tumbling out of her mouth. "So I made up some answer about Justin Bieber and he sort of laughed, and then he asked if I'd ever been to Paris, and I accidentally

241

said yes, since, you know, I've seen it in tons of movies, so I figured I could wing it, and then he asked me this question about the Paris catacombs, and I had no idea what he was talking about...." She heaved a sigh. "I just panicked, and then I felt really stupid. I *whiffed it.*"

"Calm down," Max said. "It's going to be okay. You don't need to know everything, Brooke. No one knows *everything.*"

"You do," Brooke pouted, handing the bartender a credit card.

Max laughed. "Brooke! I've never been to Paris. I couldn't have had that conversation, either. You just need to chill. Make up a story about a crepe stand or something."

Brooke bit her lip. "I just don't want to look like an idiot," she admitted. "I freaked out, and I figured you could fix it."

"Well," Max finally said, feeling satisfyingly magnanimous, "first dates are hard."

I should know.

"But you and Jake seem to be having fun," Brooke said, handing Max two drinks.

"Oh, sure," Max said vaguely, not wanting to get into gory detail with someone whose loyalties were not guaranteed. She was saving that conversation for Molly.

Brooke took a long look at Max. "You look great," she said. "I can tell Jake is really digging you. I hope it works out."

Max felt the frost layer she'd put up start to melt. Brooke wasn't all bad—a little schemey, maybe, but it seemed to come from a place of insecurity. Maybe she really just needed the help. Besides, she'd sworn this was just for show with Brady, and she'd made good on her other promises, *and* she was being nice....It would only be a few hours. Max gulped and resolved to make it through without exploding.

When they got back to the table, the boys were laughing so hard that Jake actually smacked the table with the palm of his hand.

"Did you understand that story?" Max hissed as she slid in between the boys, under Brooke's chattering.

"I'm an *actor*," Brady replied under his breath. "Okay, so I've been needing to talk to you about the script my agent got the other day. Two words: *possum farmer*."

"Are you up for the possum or the farmer?"

"Even better. The possum farmer's blind son. Who is... wait for it...a possum *whisperer*."

"Have them throw in a prosthetic limb and your Oscar is in the bag," Max cracked.

As they smiled at each other, Brooke hooked an arm possessively though Brady's. "You should show the script to me," she said. "I have a lot of experience. I read all Daddy's scripts."

"Okay, sure," Brady said. To Max, he added, "You are going to love how awful it is. There's this particular kind of soil, right, and—"

Jake made a loud *pshaw* noise. "Nah, man, nobody wants to watch a movie about dirt," he said. He nudged Max flirtatiously. "Maybe you should write him something." Then he turned to Brooke and Brady and said proudly, "Max was just telling me how she wants to be a writer."

"She mentioned that. I think it's great," Brady said. "We need another Great American Novel."

"Yeah, but nobody reads books anymore," Jake said, curling his hand around Max's and squeezing. "Not when there's Twitter."

"I don't know; I feel like I need something more pretentious," Max jumped in before Jake could expound on that. "Like an obnoxiously navel-gazing indie flick starring, like, Zach Braff and Maggie Gyllenhaal and that random third Olsen sister."

"No, no, go the other way—sell out and do a Michael Bay movie, those are the best," Brady said. *"Transformers 5: More."*

Max pretended to think about it. "I *would* be really good at coming up with multiple scenarios in which people get crushed by robots."

"And then the hero launches the Eiffel Tower into space to plug a hole in the moon."

"And the president is played by Julianne Hough."

"And then the moon explodes over the Super Bowl!"

That last one was Jake. He threw up his fist for a celebratory bump. Max blinked. Out of the corner of her eye, she noticed that Brooke seemed bored and had crumpled her drink straw so much that it looked more like a question mark. Max had forgotten the two of them were even there.

"Right!" she said, covering by making a fist and thumping Jake's. He grabbed it and unfolded it, twining their fingers.

"That's my girl," he said fondly. "Max is super hilarious."

"She is," Brady agreed.

Jake pulled Max to his chest for a snuggle. Flustered, she stared straight ahead, trying to look pleasant. She couldn't help chancing a peek at Brady. He was smiling as amiably as ever, although she did detect a bit of bemusement in his eyes. What was he thinking?

"So, when are the bands going on?" Brooke chirped, springing to life and nuzzling Brady's shoulder with her cheek.

"Soon, I think," Max said, trying not to look at them so she could concentrate on stringing words together. "Teddy told me the first band is supposed to play at nine, and then Mental Hygienist goes on...third? Or fourth?"

"I haven't seen a show here in ages," Brady said, looking around the dark, cramped club with fondness. "Brooke, you saw Super Diamond here last year, right?"

Brooke looked blank.

No, that was me, Max thought. *And that was also not on a flash card.*

"I think I read that on your blog," Jake said. "In that post about jumpsuits."

"I *hate* jumpsuits," Brooke said, clearly relieved to be back on safer ground.

"Unless they're being worn by the world's greatest Neil

Diamond cover band, obviously," Max said, nudging Brooke's shin.

"Oh, yes! Of course!" Brooke said. "Super Diamond. He is...so *super.*"

"They," Max coughed.

"*They* are so super," Brooke corrected herself. Brady shot Max a perplexed look out of the corner of his eye, but Jake seemed distracted by his cell phone. "Gosh, I'm so spacey tonight," Brooke continued. "I must be dehydrated."

She took a huge sip of her Diet Coke.

"So Brooke was just telling me that you've been to Paris," Max said to Brady, as Jake unexpectedly slung his arm around Max's shoulders.

"Yeah, my parents took me a couple years ago, after I booked my first national ad. It was kind of an 'I hope you've enjoyed living rent-free because now it's time to get your own place' present," he said dryly. "It's an amazing city."

"I've never been," Max continued. She felt the weight and warmth of Jake's arm pressing down on her. "I've heard the Louvre is really worth the trip," she added, looking pointedly at Brooke.

"Oh, it is," Brooke said, flashing Max a grateful smile. "But the better thing is this, um, crepe stand across the way..."

Brady shot Brooke an eager smile. "Banana and Nutella!" he said. "I wonder if we went to the same cart."

As the two of them chattered about crepe fillings, Jake let out a happy murmur.

"Brooke's boyfriend seems nice. You should see if he wants to come to the spring football scrimmage. He really wanted to see the pistol offense in action, and playing against ourselves is my best shot at winning," Jake said with a self-deprecating wince. "And he can keep you company in the stands. I always reserve the best seats for my girlfriend and my parents. They're..."

As he talked, Max felt a pang. They'd been dating—if that's what this was—for about three hours, and already she was on his personal pep squad in the bleachers, when deep down she knew she'd rather be in her room writing, or talking about Paris with Brady. But Jake was so sweet, so attentive.... Max resolved to get through the rest of the night as convivially as she could, for both their sakes. Give it one more chance. Besides, how much weirder could it get?

"And then there's Homecoming," Jake was saying, still stroking her arm. "We should rent a limo. Magnus's dad got us a stretch Hummer for the winter formal, and it had a hot tub in the back. We all took it up to Mulholland and parked it for a while. Way romantic."

Max felt his eyes burning into the side of her face. It was alarmingly similar to the sensation she got when she knew guys in the car next to her at a stoplight were checking her out.

"I'm having such a good time," he husked, leaning toward her. "I'm so glad we did this."

Oh, my God, is he going to kiss me?

Oh, my God.

Oh, my God, Jake Donovan is kissing me.

✦ ✦ ✦

Max was so stunned by the feeling of Jake's lips on her own that she had already pulled away from him and leaped off her bar stool in a panic before she even processed that she'd moved at all.

"I just remembered, I have to go backstage and wish my brother good luck before he goes on," she stammered.

"Good idea," Jake said, beaming. "Let's go say hi. See you on the flip side," he said to Brady and Brooke, who were still discussing crepes, acting like they hadn't noticed a thing.

Max could barely manage not to make a horrified expression. She needed distance from Jake so she could piece together what her head and her heart and her mouth were all screaming at her. But he was so damn agreeable there was no way around taking him with her, so she grabbed Jake's arm and turned to look for the entrance to the backstage area—she had no idea where it was, and she probably wasn't on the list to get back there, anyway. All she knew was that kissing Jake made her feel off-kilter and uneasy, and she didn't think she wanted to do it again tonight, at least not in public. In front of Brooke. And Brady. Who now thought she was *dating* this beautiful dunderhead instead of *on* a date with him. The distinction was suddenly important to Max.

Instead of finding the backstage door, Max saw Molly heading in their direction, but with an expression on her face that Max knew meant she a) had seen the kiss and b) was unsure if Max felt she needed to be rescued or not.

"Molly!" Max yelled, waving. "Over here!"

"They're about to start," Molly said, joining them. "I felt like too much of a groupie hanging out backstage all by myself."

"We were just about to go back there," Max sputtered. "I didn't even get to tell Teddy to break a leg."

Molly shook her head. "Don't worry about it. He's really nervous. He wouldn't have even heard you. I could have told him I was having Jay Leno's love child and he would have been totally fine with it."

Max looked around the club, which was by that point crammed with teenagers, adults who looked like they might be in the record industry, and, in the far corner of the room, Magnus Mitchell and Chaz Kelly. She prayed they wouldn't come over to fist-bump Jake or anything. Especially if they'd seen him kiss her.

God, what if they saw him kiss me?

"Where's Brooke?" Molly asked. "She just texted me that she was here."

"She and that dude were sitting over there," Jake said, pointing. "But I don't see them. Maybe they went to buy a T-shirt."

"Um, right, yeah," Molly said. "Brooke loves T-shirts. Listen, is it okay if I hang out with you guys? I don't want to be the fifth wheel or anything, but I feel like if I'm standing alone at the front of the stage people will think I'm pathetic."

"*Please* hang out with us," Max said.

"We're only two wheels, anyway," Jake pointed out. "Like a bike. You will make us a trike."

Molly shot Max a wry look as the curtain opened and the host of the event—an MTV regular Max recognized from the time she fell asleep watching a *Jersey Shore* marathon and woke up to see him leading a roundtable discussion about Sammi and Ron—welcomed them all to the contest.

"Are you guys *ready to par-taaaay?*" he asked, and the crowd cheered.

But Max barely heard him, nor the ensuing musical stylings of Unsinkable Panty Line. Her mind was racing: *I can't believe Jake kissed me. I can't believe I didn't enjoy it when Jake kissed me. I can't believe I was thinking about what Brady might be thinking when Jake kissed me. If thirteen-year-old me found out about this, she'd want to punch me in the face.*

After what seemed like half a lifetime of "intense" "singing," Unsinkable Panty Line ran offstage. They were followed by a jug band called Uncle Grandma, and then a fivesome by the name of Plush that included a woman in a rabbit suit hopping around the stage and beating her chest between handstands.

"Well, they're not much competition," Molly noted.

"Are you kidding? I wish we were the Colby-Randall Rabbits," Jake said. "That thing would make a rad mascot."

Mental Hygienist was next. Molly and Max cheered as Teddy ran onstage, holding his guitar, wearing a fedora, and looking pale.

"What's with the hat?" Max whispered.

Molly rolled her eyes. "Bone decided they needed to be more visually arresting, or something," she said as the band launched into its first song, "Knead Your Love (I Need It [Love Bread])."

Whether it was the hats or just the fact that anyone would have been better than Plush, the crowd immediately took to Mental Hygienist. Max never would have admitted it to anyone, especially to Teddy, but the first song was kind of good. The lyrics were incredibly stupid, obviously, but the chorus was buoyant and the tune was catchy. Even the adults in the audience were bobbing their heads to the beat.

"Thank you, Hollywoooooood!" Bone yelled over the applause as the last notes died out. "We are Mental Hygienist, and we are so excited to be here! I'm your lead singer, Bone Johnson!"

He took a bow as the crowd applauded, flipping his long bangs out of his eyes when he righted himself—an affectation Max knew from Teddy that he'd been practicing for months. Max and Molly clapped wildly as he introduced the rest of the band, especially for Teddy, who lifted his hat in a halfhearted salute. Out of the corner of her eye, Max thought she saw some people taking camera-phone pictures of Molly cheering. It was always weird to remember that, depending on who else was in the room, Brick Berlin's surprise daughter Molly Dix was considered a semi–celebrity sighting.

"Thanks, everyone," Teddy said, stepping up to his micro-phone. "We're gonna try something a little different now."

With that, he launched into the song Max had heard him practicing endlessly in his room. It was slow, roman-tic, acoustic—and totally wrong for the audience, which had been pumped up by Mental Hygienist's perky first number.

Molly shot Max a concerned look. Teddy was already losing the crowd; people had started to chat among them-selves, and several spectators around them had abandoned ship to refill their drinks. Even Jake was suddenly nowhere to be seen. Max peered through the half light at the peo-ple around them, but she couldn't find him.

"Where did Jake go?" she asked Molly.

Molly looked around. "He was here like two seconds ago. Did he leave?"

"I have no idea," Max said.

"I saw you guys—"

"*Yeah*," Max said.

"Oh, wait," Molly said. "Isn't that him?"

Max followed Molly's outstretched finger all the way across the club to a darkened corner, where Jake was in a heated discussion with a very angry-looking Jennifer Parker.

"What is she doing here?" Molly asked, but the bulk of her attention was clearly drifting back to Teddy, who was valiantly pressing forward with his ballad.

"She's probably here to choke me out," Max muttered. She knew she should be annoyed at the prospect of being on a collision course with Jake's ex, especially since the two of them were such enthusiastic public arguers, but she was more curious as to when exactly Jennifer had arrived on the scene. Because as much as she was terrible at reading people's signals, she was pretty sure Jake had chosen a really random moment to go in for their first kiss. *Maybe he was making a point,* she thought. Rather than get caught staring at Jake and Jennifer, who were getting right up in each other's faces and making violent gestures, Max turned back to Teddy. As she did so, a flash of blonde hair caught her eye. *There* was Brooke, leaning up against a wall at the back of the club. At least, it sure looked like Brooke. It was hard to tell—some of her was blocked from view because she was...

Because she's making out.

It was like a giant stone dropping into her solar plexus, a sudden jealousy that was an actual physical presence in Max's body. Brooke Berlin was kissing Brady Swift. And it ejected all thoughts of Jake Donovan kissing Max McCormack from Max's mind.

I am so stupid. So, so stupid.

Up until now, Max had wanted to believe that she was only mildly intrigued by Brady—and that it didn't matter that he was probably into Brooke, because Brooke was, well, *Brooke*, and people like Max didn't stand a chance in the face of all that hair and height and skin and batted eyelashes. But as she watched Brooke touch Brady's neck, the full force of every conversation, every joke, even their excitement at making fun of the possum farmer thing, hit Max at once. It was a massive wallop of adoration, exhilaration, envy, agony, and regret.

It's so obvious. I don't just want to be with some guy like Brady. I want to be with actual *Brady. And now he's kissing Brooke, because of me. I made this happen. I am the stupidest girl in the world.*

"Sorry about that," Jake said, popping back up at her side. "I had to deal with an unwelcome guest."

Max barely registered him, or that Teddy's song was over, or the audience's halfhearted applause. She needed to go somewhere to breathe. She spun around, almost in a panic, trying to scope out the exit.

"Max, it's okay, I got rid of Jennifer," Jake called out to her. "Told her this was none of her business. Wait, where are you going?"

Max wasn't sure. All she knew was that she had to get out of the club, away from everyone, immediately. She mumbled something to Jake that she hoped sounded like "Be right back" and pushed away through the crowd, not stopping until she'd burst out of the heavy double doors leading to the parking lot and collapsed against the wall.

All her other emotions were quickly being supplanted by resentment. Brooke had asked her several times if she was into Brady. Clearly, she had seen something Max herself hadn't.

And yet she did this anyway, Max raged to herself. *She told me it was for publicity. She told me she didn't like him. She told me she wasn't going to lead him on. And now she's making out with him in public. She lied. Brooke Berlin is not my friend. Brooke Berlin has never been my friend.*

"Max," Brooke's voice said.

Max looked up and her eyes slowly focused on Brooke's perfectly painted, very satisfied face. She had her arm wrapped around the waist of a flushed, slightly embarrassed-looking Brady.

"What a night, right?" Brooke chirped.

"You could say that," Max said, staring at her shoes. She didn't want either of them to see her face. Because then surely they would know. For all her crowing about her poker face, Max had no idea how to hide what she was feeling right now.

Why didn't I quit this stupid job when my mother gave me the chance?

"We're off—early call times tomorrow," Brooke said. "See you on set!"

As they walked away, Brooke suddenly stopped and said something Max couldn't hear, then ran back to Max.

"Did you see?" Brooke whispered excitedly. "Mission

accomplished! The tabloids are going to go nuts." She squeezed Max's hand. "Just remember, you made it happen!"

And with that, she scurried back to Brady and dragged him to the valet stand. Max just watched them go.

I made this happen.

In the distance, Brooke rummaged through her purse and briefly unearthed the edge of what looked like one of Max's flash cards before hastily stuffing it back inside. A slow smile spread across Max's face.

Yeah, I made this happen, she thought spitefully. *And I can make it un-happen.*

nineteen

"THE NERVE OF THAT GIRL," seethed Jennifer Parker.

"Mmm," Brooke said. *Damn, he's cute. And those dimples.*

"I ran into her at Barneys, talking to *your* regular shoe salesman and trying on those YSL boots that *you* saw in *Vogue* and said you liked," Jennifer nattered. "And when I went up to confront her she blew me off! Can you believe it? Doesn't she know who I am?"

"Mmm." *He's like Ryan Gosling combined with that hottie from* White Collar. *How did I not notice this before?*

"And then she cut off Rene's head with a sales receipt and made it into a purse."

"Great." *I wonder what our Hollywood couple nickname will be. Brooky? Bralin? Brake? Broke? Ew, no.*

"Brooke!" Jennifer shouted peevishly, snapping her fingers in front of Brooke's face.

"What? Sorry, Jen. What were you saying about Brady?"

"I wasn't saying anything about him," Jen huffed. "I was talking about your disrespectful little assistant."

"What did Max do now?"

"Not her," Jen spat. "Brie. As if they'd even *let* Max into Barneys."

Brooke resettled herself against the huge old maple tree on Colby-Randall's main lawn and tried to focus on what Jennifer was saying, but her mind was elsewhere. Specifically, in Brady Swift's mouth. "So what's the problem? Brie didn't want to talk?"

"She should treat me with respect," Jennifer said, tugging some grass out of the ground in irritation. "She is your employee, and I am one of your oldest and dearest and most loyal friends. She doesn't get to say, 'Jennifer, I don't have time for this, I have a manicure.'"

Brooke shrugged. "Maybe she really had a manicure." At Jen's furious expression, she quickly added, "But I will make sure she knows that if she runs into you again at Barneys, she should cancel it."

"That's the least she should do," Jennifer said airily. Then she added, "But since you brought up Max..."

Brooke stretched lazily. "I can't control who she goes out with, Jen."

"It's so *rude*." Grass was being uprooted by the violent

fistful now. "She's dating my ex! Of, like, a week! That violates the Girl Code, doesn't it?"

"It would, *if* you had ever been friends," pointed out Arugula, who had been absorbed in her iPhone on Jen's other side. "But you loathe each other. Ergo, I'm confident the only code you have in common is the penal code preventing you from running each other over with your respective cars."

"She was so *in my face* about it, too! Kissing him in the bar…" Jen's tone went from aggressive to wounded. "It really sucked, seeing that. I didn't think…" Her face crumbled as she trailed off into silence.

Brooke sat up. "I'm sorry, Jen," she said sincerely, feeling slightly guilty for her small (*very* small, though, really) part in encouraging Max and Jake. She rubbed Jen's arm sympathetically. "I've been kind of caught up in my own stuff."

"It's okay," Jen said quietly. "I understand. You have a big movie taking up all your time." Her voice took on a wistful tone. "Jake was kind of all I had to focus on."

Brooke didn't know what to say. Now she felt massively guilty for her somewhat larger than "very small" part in encouraging Max and Jake.

"First of all, every woman should have something to sustain her emotionally other than just some man," Arugula said. "Second, at least you got to yell at him about it."

"That's true," Jen allowed, twisting a strand of brown

hair around her finger. "It was kind of like old times." She brightened. "Maybe it'll make him nostalgic! He always liked it when we fought."

At that moment, two of the school's basketball players crossed the quad. "Hey, Maneater," one yelled, and wolf-whistled. Brooke blushed prettily and waved.

"Oh, right, how many hits has the YouTube video gotten?" Jen asked, a bit peppier now.

Ari pecked at her phone. "Fifty thousand so far," she said. "How many of them were you, Brooke?"

"Only about twelve," she lied. It was more like fifty. But she couldn't help it—whoever had gotten the cell-phone video of her and Brady making out had been at a really advantageous angle. She looked great—her nose wasn't in the way at *all*, although she had mild concerns about her chin—and it perfectly captured the heat of the moment. Brooke could still feel his kiss all the way to her toes.

"Way to go, Berlin!" Chaz Kelly shouted, giving her a chunky thumbs-up from the parking lot. "You're an animal!"

"The commenters aren't so charitably disposed," Ari said, skimming the page.

Brooke blanched. "What are they saying?" she squeaked, snatching the phone from Ari. "Is it my chin? I knew it was my chin."

"Oh, they aren't talking about you," Ari said. "They're *murdering* the song that's playing. The one Teddy McCor-mack wrote."

Brooke scrolled down and read a few of them. "Artless whining from a nasal loser," she read aloud. "Oh, God, this one called it 'eunuch rock.'" She frowned. "Poor Teddy. Molly said he worked really hard on that."

"Well, that doesn't change the fact that he's an 'emo angst bag,'" Arugula quoted. Brooke glared at her. "I didn't write it," Ari protested. Then she paused. "But I may have written the eunuch one."

"That's my sister's boyfriend you're talking about," Brooke huffed. "Kindly leave out the snide comments."

Brooke stood up and brushed off her pleated DKNY mini. "Okay, I'm off—I have to turn in this week's homework to Headmistress McCormack and then I'm due on set." She smiled. "Nancy solves the mystery today, in an actual dress. Such a nice break from my homeless rags."

"I know what you mean," Jen said, scooping up her books. "On Thursday I did an infomercial for a company that makes neti pots and they put me in a shirt from Wet Seal. I mean, can you imagine?"

The three of them headed into the main building. Brooke hadn't been on campus much in the past month, and it was satisfying to find her old stomping grounds totally unchanged: The student din nearly overshadowed the light classical music piped in on the PA system, the air still smelled like Lysol and chalk, and people continued to gawk and whisper whenever she passed. Maybe even more than usual, now that she was Hollywood's most promising up-and-comer.

In fact, something was definitely different about their attention today. Instead of seeing the standard cocktail of admiration and mild fear in her fellow classmates' eyes, Brooke saw confusion, with traces of...*amusement?*

"Excuse me, Brooke?" said a smooth, cold voice from over her shoulder. Brooke whirled around to face the most wretched human being on the planet: her longtime archnemesis Shelby Kendall, the anchor of the school's TV station and heiress to the tabloid *Hey!*, a blisteringly (and inconveniently) beautiful Angelina Jolie in a world of Paris Hiltons, and a daily thorn in Brooke's side. Shelby's red Serious News blazer matched her lipstick to a T; she wore it over white skinny jeans with leopard pumps.

"Shelby," Brooke said pleasantly. "Trying to make the eighties happen *again*, I see."

"We're on live for CR-One, covering Colby-Randall's most cherished blogger and member of the literati," Shelby sneered coolly, jamming a microphone into Brooke's face. "We're just all so inspired today by your brave antitechnology stance—what prompted it?"

Brooke looked blankly at Shelby. "Have you hit your head recently?" she asked.

"I might ask you the same," Shelby said, tilting her head in faux-concern. "For someone who has *cleaved* to the Internet so intimately this past month, I thought calling it a 'succubus' was a surprising choice." Shelby shot her a smug smile. "Would you care to elaborate?"

Brooke's mind spun wildly. She hadn't taken a single sip of alcohol on her date with Brady. She hadn't gone anywhere the following day except to get her brows waxed. As far as she knew, nothing Shelby was yammering about had anything to do with her.

Ari finagled a spot in her peripheral vision. *The blog*, Ari mouthed, waving her phone in the air. Brooke realized she hadn't checked it yet that day. She'd been letting Max go on autopilot after the success of their first several entries. Suddenly, it seemed urgent that she escape and see what "Brooke" was talking about today.

"Shelby, if you need help with your reading comprehension, I'd be happy to lend you one of my on-set tutors," Brooke said, turning to leave. "Ian once taught a chimp to read, so hopefully he won't have too much trouble with you."

"Such *warm beauty* in your words," Shelby said, catching Brooke with her hand and squeezing her arm. The assembled crowd tittered. Brooke felt herself go pale. For the first time possibly in her entire life, she was the only person not in on the joke.

"I don't have time for an interview, actually," she fumbled, shaking off Shelby and scurrying away.

"Of course," Shelby called after her. "So much *typing* to do. Ta-ta!"

Brooke didn't give Shelby a backward glance; instead, she stormed into the principal's office and dumped her file folder of homework papers on the receptionist's vacant desk. Ari followed and silently handed Brooke her phone, cued up to OpenBrooke.com's latest:

OPENBRᴏᴏKE.COM

Precious Open Brookers, I've got an English assignment you might feel compelled to embrace to your collective bosoms: I'm to take a novel and imagine how it would be changed if social media existed in its universe. At first, of course, I aimed to cleave to my old favorite, my comrade-in-snark, my friend-against-phonies, the dearly departed but ne'er forgotten J. D. Salinger, but it's simply too easy to envision the indolent existentialist funk into which Holden Caulfield would descend upon being forced to parse his worldview into 140 characters or less.

Heathcliff and Cathy could have sated their guttural yen to sup on each other's spirits by DMing their love letters on Twitter—private passion naught but an Internet outage could intercept, thus irretrievably and detrimentally changing the course of *Wuthering Heights* from a searing lovelorn drama to a lukewarm revision of *You've Got Mail*. How about Jane Austen? Wayward Lydia in *Pride and Prejudice*, who disappeared with the sly knave Wickham, would be unable to resist making herself the mayor of Gretna Green on foursquare, and would have been dragged back to Longbourn well before dawn. And imagine the Facebook stalking between Jane and the Bingleys, or how Darcy might've vanished for good after Lizzie excoriated him on her Wall for his aloof prejudice and impenetrable pride. It would rend their romantic journeys into shattered oddments of a story arc. Or, take *To Kill a Mockingbird*: Scout would've had an online journal recounting her travails (much like this one, but spiced with her unique flavor of innocence), but the inevitable parody Boo Radley Twitter feeds would demystify the man and his magnetic myth! Each of these tomes would have been the poorer—a shadow, a joke—for the inclusion of these modern miracles of connectivity.

Indeed, it causes one pause: If social media would have laid waste to the purity of our classic love stories, mutilated our morality plays, and turned starkly simple coming-of-age moments into chilly digital snapshots that couldn't equal the warm beauty of the thousand words, then what is it doing to us—ourselves—in this very moment? In yearning to know more, are we condemning ourselves to settle for less?

With our hands overflowing with technology, yoking us to the superhighway succubus, are our hearts and minds the emptier for it? Or is being able to intertwine fingers with one another from thousands of miles apart worth pouring out our souls through our laptops and not our eyes?

Pensively,

B.

After a long moment, Brooke realized that her mouth was hanging open. Nobody—except maybe Arugula—used so many SAT words, sentence after sentence. In fact, that entry read like a cracked-out, pretentious parody of Arugula. Had Max totally lost her mind? What was going on with her?

Brooke forced herself to relax her face (nothing was serious enough to court wrinkles). She and Max had been getting along fine; Brooke had even started to enjoy the friendly bantering that had grown from their bickering. The makeover she'd given her had been fantastic. And Max herself had been very helpful in keeping Brooke's conversations with Brady on track once they'd met up the night of the concert. In fact, Max's smoothness had probably paved the way for Brooke and Brady's lip-lock, and that wasn't the sort of favor you did for someone you hated. But as Brooke reread and reread this pompous entry, she couldn't help thinking that it had been written to make her look like an idiot. To wound her.

And it had worked. Brooke had never anticipated that Max McCormack, of all people, would turn into someone who had the capacity to hurt her. It was a very unwelcome surprise.

"Brooke!" a voice said warmly.

Brooke snapped her head up and saw Headmistress McCormack walking out of her office, followed by Max, who was cradling her own cell phone as if it had just been returned to her after a long confiscation (which, given what Brooke knew of Max's disciplinary history, it probably had been). The light in Max's eyes seemed to dim a bit when she saw Brooke's face.

Guilty, Brooke thought. *Guilty, guilty, guilty.*

"So nice to see you being so conscientious about turning in your assignments," Mrs. McCormack said, blithely picking up Brooke's folder, unaware of the simmering tension between the girls. "I hope Maxine's tutelage has been helpful."

"Oh, yes," Brooke said, never taking her eyes off Max. "Max has been *unbelievable.*"

Max's eyes flickered with what Brooke would swear was defiance. "Anytime," she said, with exaggerated sweetness. "I just hate to see a fellow student suffer from her own academic inertia."

So it was *deliberate,* Brooke realized. *She knew people would think the entry was absurd.*

The two stared at each other for several awkward seconds. Brooke tried to pour a gallon of betrayal into her face, punctuated with some hurt and a little rage. Max simply wore an innocent expression that seemed to become more angelic the more Brooke allowed herself to seethe.

I am going to kill her.

"Well, this has been great, but I have to go," Max said. "I'll be late for gym. See you later, Brooke!"

"Drop by the set later, sweetie," Brooke replied, her eyes flashing with subtle menace. "We have *so much* to discuss!"

If she wasn't mistaken, Max looked a little scared.

Good.

twenty

MAX PULLED INTO THE parking lot of the Miauhaus photo studio just off La Brea and gazed up at the ivy-covered building, fronted by a huge sign with a rotating black-and-white cat logo, so familiar to her after seeing it approximately a hundred and thirty-seven times on *America's Next Top Model*.

Remind me again what you're doing here?!? her brain screamed.

This was a good question. Max hated confrontation—well, okay, that wasn't totally true. She loved confrontation when it happened in front of her, and it involved other people. But it was harder to hide behind flip remarks when the drama was her own. And as soon as Max had hit Publish on that entry in the wee hours of Monday morning, she'd known there would be consequences. The comments on it were hilarious: Some people were hailing Brooke as a florid genius, a true new-age wordsmith, but most of them were wondering if she'd fallen and cracked her head on a thesaurus. One had posted simply, "HEROIN," in all caps, forty-three times (Max had counted twice).

Max didn't regret posting it one bit. After using Brady like that, Brooke deserved to take a little heat. But Max's allergy to melodrama meant that after Monday's accidental run-in with Brooke in her mother's office, Max spent the subsequent two days studiously dodging her; however, today Brooke had texted Max to reiterate that she needed her at Miauhaus because *Vanity Fair* was doing a photo shoot for a big, splashy article about the *Nancy Drew* cast, and Brooke wanted her official blogographer to chronicle that milestone. It may have been a ploy to draw Max out of hiding, but Max's lingering financial issues meant that she had to suck it up and report for duty, and stop pretending nothing had happened. And, accordingly, face whatever came at her.

She won't fire me. She needs me too much.

Max pushed open the glass doors and sidled inside the cavernous white-walled building. A security guard pointed her toward a door labeled PLAYHAUS. Inside, a small snack table was set up in front of a brightly colored wall, starkly contrasting the sterile contours of the photo-shoot set—a white floor and backdrop were joined with a gentle curve instead of a right-angle corner, which Max assumed was to avoid casting strange shadows but which also made it look like a piece of paper caught in a gust of wind. Kyle and Zander were chortling and patting each other's backs while Tad Cleary talked to a woman wearing a pencil skirt and a smart white blouse—evidently, this was the reporter, armed with a tape recorder, which would be handy later because Tad was talking so fast his face had turned purple. Several of the younger cast members, perched in tall folding director's chairs over by a faux-brick corner that was doubling as a makeup area, were garbed in 1930s-era fashions as a nod to when the *Nancy Drew* book series first debuted. Brooke was nowhere to be seen, but Brick was standing just off set in track pants and a white Hanes tee, munching on trail mix and then punching the caloric information into an app on his phone. His face fell.

"Raisins," he said sadly to the table, throwing a handful of trail mix in the trash. "The silent killer."

Max decided not to go hunting for Brooke. Instead, she checked around for a low-key place to sit. The reporter was conducting interviews before the shoot, and Max wanted to see Brooke dance around questions about her blog, satisfying that dark part of her soul that thought Brooke deserved a little trial-by-fire after coasting so far on all the credit for OpenBrooke.com. A sofa near a kelly-green wall seemed like a promising place to go unnoticed.

I'll blend and no one will see me, she thought, until she remembered she hadn't dyed her hair back yet.

"Hallo, there, Max. What up?"

Of course the Brit-Boston Twit found me. The one time that green would've come in handy...

"Don't I look just ducky?" Carla asked, twirling in a canary chiffon dress with tan pumps and a matching floppy hat, plus a few strings of pearls. "This shit's wicked pissa."

Pick a region and stick to it, Max wanted to yell. Instead, she said politely, "Can I help you with something?"

Carla bit her lip, in what Max was sure was feigned concern. "Brooke is acting a bit off her trolley today," she confided. "I asked her what 'superhighway succubus' meant, and she looked like she was gonna choke like the BoSox." Carla cast Max a sly glance. "This latest entry *was* a little barmy."

"Some people are very different in writing," Max said, hoping that would be enough to stave off whatever Carla was percolating.

"And I heard she nailed this gig at least partially based on the blog," Carla said, her voice lowering conspiratorially. "Can you imagine if it turned out to be codswallop?"

"I'm sure Brooke is just overtired," Max said firmly.

"Right you are, darling, I'm sure," Carla said, gazing down at Max's notebook. "It'd be so friggin' wack if they had to recast Nancy," she added, unable to hide the note of hope in her ever-morphing voice.

So that's it. She thinks she can pounce.

Without even bothering to answer, Max clambered off the couch and started rooting around on the snack table. This called for beef jerky.

The photographer clapped his hands. "All cast to the set, please," he called out. "We are a go for the round table."

Max tucked herself into the shadows behind the Sparkletts water dispenser and watched. Carla was trying to chat brightly to Zander about Silversun Pickups, the band du jour on his shirt. Tad was pacing rings around the guys playing Carson Drew and one of the crackheads. And then Brady appeared, in a pin-striped waistcoat as gray as his eyes. Max's guts twisted and churned—seeing him hurt in a curiously satisfying way, like the first day you can scratch your skin again after having chicken pox. She resisted the urge to wave, instead shrinking back a bit farther into her place. He looked so dapper. So dashing. So...

"I'm here," Brooke said. "So sorry to keep you waiting."

So not into me.

Brooke strolled onstage looking more like a 1920s flapper than a '30s debutante, but Max wasn't about to quibble with *Vanity Fair.* Her hair had been ironed out and then crimped into one of those era-specific body waves and pinned by a headband; her sparkly silver dress was short and layered with intricate vintage necklaces that played off her black Mary Janes.

"Beautiful," Brick crowed, walking over to give Brooke a loving hug—*snap, snap, snap*, went a photographer's camera—before backing away again. Brooke smiled tentatively. She looked adorable, but a little frantic around the eyes. They seemed brighter than usual, as if they had recently been wet. Max knew her well enough at this point to see that the facade was close to cracking. Brooke took her place in one of the red plastic-and-metal chairs that had been placed in a circle just off set, and everyone filled in around her.

"Okay, first question," the reporter said, clicking on a tape recorder. "Brooke, were you nervous about stepping out of Brick's shadow and into your first leading role?"

Brooke smiled wide, as if she'd flipped a switch. "Not at all," she said. "My father does cast a very long shadow, but he also made sure I was raised to be strong and self-assured. I am my own person, and I know that, and he knows that, and he gave me the confidence to realize that eventually, everyone else will know that, too."

Brick nodded almost imperceptibly.

"Nice," Max said under her breath.

"And your blog seems to have been a great head start in that arena." The reporter smiled. "I was particularly intrigued by your *Catcher in the Rye* theory. Care to elaborate on that?"

Brooke's smile suddenly seemed a tiny bit stuck. "I think...it spoke for itself," she said.

"And how about that really intriguing piece that ran Monday, about technology?" the reporter continued.

Brooke waited. No other question came. "What about it?" she asked.

"It was just so impassioned."

"Well, you know, I was just...thinking...about connections," she said, running a finger up and down the length of one of her necklaces. "And how, like, we miss them. Or sometimes we make them. But. You know. What are they, *really?*"

Max began gnawing on a particularly nasty hangnail. *Shut up, Brooke.*

"For example, um, in *To Kill a Mockingbird*, Rumer—"

Brick frowned. Max screwed her eyes shut and channeled all her energies at Brooke. *Wrong Willis. Wrong Willis. Wrong Willis.*

"Um, I mean, Scout, how she, you know, sees the world differently, with innocence, and..." Brooke faltered.

Brick started tapping his feet uncomfortably, shifting his weight back and forth.

"Also, like...it's *computers*..."

Max felt queasy. She'd thought she'd enjoy seeing Brooke on the ropes, but under the hot studio lights, with everyone's eyes on Brooke's slow meltdown—Carla's were smug, Brick's confused, the producers' bugged out in horror—she just felt rotten. Max considered coming to Brooke's rescue, but she couldn't figure out how to run interference.

In the end, it was Brady who stepped in and saved Brooke. "I thought it was a very interesting rumination on whether the quality of relationships are improved or not by the instant access we have to people's thoughts," he said. "Judging by the time stamp on that entry, I think Brooke may have been up too late writing it, and she's fried."

"Care to comment on the YouTube video of the two of you?" the reporter asked.

"Nope," Brady said with a charming smile.

"Does viral video like that, really *personal* stuff, change or confirm your impression of the Internet as a 'super-highway succubus'?" the reporter pressed Brooke.

"It—" Brooke's hands were plucking her necklaces like guitar strings. Max was convinced she was going to break one of them. Her face sagged; she suddenly *did* look tired. "You know, Brady is right. I think I need a cup of coffee. My brain isn't working properly," Brooke said, her voice straining a bit. "Would you excuse me for a second, please?"

And Brooke turned tail and practically sprinted off the set, straight past Max's couch and out into the hall.

Don't follow her, Max's inner voice scolded. *She brought this on herself.*

But Max's feet apparently disagreed. She slipped out of the room just as Brick was saying, "Sorry about that, Janice—all work and no cardio, eh?"

Max assessed the hallway. The studio called Whitehaus

across the way was being used, and the other space a few paces down was locked, which just left the bathroom. Max gently pushed open the door. Brooke was standing in front of the mirror, trying to redo her makeup while surreptitiously wiping her eyes.

"Brooke?" she said, tentatively. "Brooke, I..."

But she fell silent, unsure of what to say.

"Oh, right, *now* you're at a loss for words," Brooke snapped, but her trembling voice lacked its usual bite.

What *could* Max say? She'd done it on purpose. She'd known. "It was just one entry, Brooke. I was just playing with—"

"Sure you were," Brooke spat, her voice dripping with sarcasm. "And it *never* occurred to you that publishing it might screw me over."

"I didn't mean—"

"Save it," Brooke said, holding up her hand. "I may not use the word *succubus* in everyday conversation, but I am not an idiot. I know what you're doing. You're trying to sabotage me." Her lip trembled. "After all I've done for you, you're ruining everything I've worked so hard for."

"Everything *you've*—" Max cut herself off and took a steadying breath, then started again. "I am grateful for the salary," she said. "I really am. Let's just calm down and—"

"Calm down?" Brooke said. "You were in there just now. I was terrible. This is a mess. And it's all your fault."

"Whoa," Max said. "Hold on here. None of this is *all* my fault."

"I never should have trusted you," Brooke continued, as if Max weren't even there. "All you ever did was sit in the corner and say rude things under your breath about me and my friends, and I should have seen this coming."

"Seen what coming, Brooke?" Max said. "That this whole giant lie might blow up in your face?"

"Let's cut the crap," Brooke said, glaring at Max in the mirror. "I know exactly what this is about. Or rather, who."

"Stop it, Brooke, I—"

Brooke unscrewed a mascara tube. "No. I want to hear you say it," she said, jabbing the wand in Max's direction like a sword. "You want Brady, and you're mad I got him."

"Brooke—"

"Say it."

"Fine!" Max threw up her hands. "Yes. I like him. And watching you two make out was horrible."

"I knew it!" Brooke said. "I asked you a million times if you wanted him, and you said no, and you helped me. I'm not a mind reader, Max."

"It didn't take a mind reader," Max said. "You and Molly figured it out before I even did." She ran her hands through her hair and tugged hard at the ends, letting out a frustrated breath. "Besides, what could I have done? If I'd said yes, you would have made fun of me and then tried to fake-date him anyway."

Brooke made an aggrieved face. "Okay, that is such a lame excuse. First of all, I am not *that* big of a bitch, and second of all, it's not my responsibility to make you suck it up and admit how you feel."

Max knew this particular comment held at least a grain of truth. She chose to ignore it.

Luckily, Brooke kept talking. "And for someone who claims to like Brady so much, I'm confused by why you don't believe that I could like him for real, too."

"Because, Brooke, *you* are the one who told me it was just for kicks. For PR. You told me it was *nothing*," Max pointed out. "And you told me you wouldn't hook up with him. But I guess that was all just a big lie to get me to go along with your insane little plan to snag him."

"I didn't lie. I said that I wouldn't lead him on, and I *didn't*," Brooke insisted. "I *like* him. He's awesome. He looks at me like he expects good things to happen when I talk. And obviously I'm used to that at school, but sometimes I think they're not really listening to *what* I'm saying—they just want to be around me when I say it, because I'm so charismatic."

"Right," Max said, infusing her voice with as much disbelief as she could.

"And since you're trying to call me a liar, I'd *love* to know how Jake would feel about this whole Brady thing," Brooke continued, curling her lip. "I think Brady and I saw *you* kissing someone that night, too."

So they did see. *He* saw.

"Jake and I are not meant to be," Max said. "I mean, we

didn't even leave together. He kissed me, and then he disappeared and spent half the night arguing with Jennifer."

"So you decided to torpedo my relationship, too?" Brooke said, knocking her purse off the ledge and inadvertently dumping its contents on the floor. A lip gloss rolled under one of the stall doors. "I can't help it that Brady likes me."

"Does he, though?" Max said. "Are you sure about that?"

Brooke touched her lips smugly. "Felt pretty definite to me."

"Really? Interesting. Because it seems to me all he can talk about is how cool your *blog* is, and how smart your *writing* is," Max said as Brooke visibly squirmed. "And we all know which one of us is responsible for *that*."

"Don't get pissed at me because people believed it," Brooke said. She angrily got down on her hands and knees and dug the gloss out from behind the toilet, wincing as if she'd just been asked to exfoliate with a porcupine. "And don't blame me for the fact that a great guy likes me. And *definitely* don't blame me for the fact that you're too much of a coward to stand up for what you want and live your own life instead of hiding in the shadows of somebody else's."

Max felt her spine crumple a little. "I knew I never should've gotten mixed up with someone like you," she whispered.

Brooke grabbed her purse and started throwing everything back into it. "I didn't realize this was such a *miserable* assignment," she said. "I thought you were actually having fun. I thought we were becoming friends, Max, I really did."

"Yeah, because it was so much fun letting you order me around just so I could write something that you took all the credit for," Max said. "You wouldn't even be here if it wasn't for me. But I let you do it." She shook her head. "I can't believe I let you. I know better."

Brooke picked up a crumpled envelope from the floor and thrust it at Max. "Well, if it's so horrible to be in the presence of such a grotesque human being, then why don't you just take your paycheck and quit," she said. "You can go back to being a bitter nobody, and we'll just see how much I need you."

Max took the envelope and rubbed it between her fingers. Her bank account was finally within spitting distance of the money she needed for NYU. She might be able to figure out the rest another way. Babysitting, maybe. Maybe she could even pick up a couple of shifts at Fu'd. Not too long ago that had seemed like the worst-case scenario, but after today, it looked like a party. Fu'd may have smelled awful, but at least it didn't *hurt*.

"Okay," Max said. "I quit."

She pocketed the check and quietly marched out of the bathroom. At the same moment, Carla Callahan burst out of the Playhaus.

"Max?" Carla called out. "Is Brooke coming back?"

"I don't care," Max said. "I'm done here." She stopped and gave Carla a sly look. "But for the record, someday maybe you'll make a *wonderful* Nancy."

Carla obviously remembered their earlier conversation, because a gleam of greedy understanding flashed in her eyes.

Have fun with that one, Brooke, Max thought savagely, turning on her heel and heading for her car.

OPENBR⬤⬤KE.COM

APRIL 25

My on-set tutors keep giving me tons of homework. On *top* of the homework I'm doing for my high school. Is that allowed? Aren't they just supposed to check my work? Or do it for me? Don't they know I'm getting up at the crack of dawn every day? What is the deal with that? I might call the union.

And why is it so cold on set all the time? I guess it's because the lights are hot. But I'm freezing when they're not on. This can't be good for my immune system. Power Bar needs to make an echinacea flavor. Why don't they? Maybe I'll buy a cardigan. Cardigans are so hot right now. Mr. Rogers was the man.

Yesterday I had makeup on my legs that made them look like I had hives. I tried to take a picture and upload it but it wasn't working. I looked gross. Movie makeup is really crazy!

Love,

B.

OPENBROOKE.COM

APRIL 27

Nancy has to wear leggings today. It's not my fault. I guess they think she sleuths better this way. Like *anyone* can be stealth with a panty line. But I don't get to decide, even though it's my panty line. Suddenly the word *panty* reads really weird to me. Panty. Panty. Panty. If you type it over and over it stops making sense. Panty. It looks like *party*, or *pantry*, but it's not. Panty. I hate it. I mean, I don't hate wearing them, I just hate typing *panty*. Why am I still doing it?

Also, nobody ever talks about how hard it is to memorize all these lines. I have a two-page speech that I have to learn by tomorrow, but I also have all this math homework to do. I can't remember words if all I'm thinking about is what X is. Can't some mysteries stay mysteries? Nancy Drew can't solve everything. It's true.

Love,

B.

APRIL 30

What no one tells you: Leggings chafe. Also, I'm really into sauces right now. Try it.

B.

twenty-one

"YO, FOZZIE BEAR," Chaz Kelly shouted across the cafeteria.

Max groaned inwardly. She wasn't sure what was worse: years of being called Kermit, or Chaz deciding her new dye job merited a new matching Muppet nickname. Technically, it was her own fault for wearing a polka-dot bandanna over her brown locks because she hadn't fallen asleep until 4 AM, then snored straight through her alarm and woke up with no time to wash her hair. Actually, it was even more her fault for not just dying it green again, but at first she'd been too preoccupied to think about her hair, and then she'd started to enjoy the change. After the first day of people staring at her, or in Mavis Moore's case asking if she was a new student, everybody seemed to have forgotten she existed. In her current mood, this was just fine by her.

"Dude, Foz, bring me a Coke," Chaz yelled. "For old times' sake. It's the least you can do for stomping on my buddy's heart like that."

A few heads turned. Max blew out air through her nose. It was hot, like she was blowing actual smoke instead of just imaginary plumes. She caught herself reaching for meatballs, then backtracked and grabbed a dish of mac and cheese (at CRAPS, this was made with whole-wheat macaroni, gorgonzola, and cruelty-free cream, whatever that meant). She headed in the direction of her usual table across the lawn—which of course meant passing straight through Chaz's lug-headed orbit.

"I liked you better when you were Kermit, bro," Chaz huffed as she stalked past him. "Somehow your new hair makes you *meaner*."

Max paused. With a beatific smile, she said, "Well, *your* new hair makes you look way smarter."

Chaz frowned. "I didn't change my hair."

"Ah. I spoke too soon." Max casually upended her mac and cheese bowl onto Chaz's stringy brown hair. "*Much* better."

As Chaz yelped and scraped pasta and béchamel off his head, Max stormed toward Molly and dropped her tray on the table with a bang.

"I hate everyone," she announced.

Molly cracked open her Diet Coke can and made a sympathetic face. "I would, too, if my lunch was a tray full of nothing. Guess you picked up a few more tips from Brooke than I thought."

"I picked up nothing from Brooke except frown lines," Max said. She sank her chin into her palm. "And apparently also a fear of frown lines."

"I thought quitting was supposed to make you feel better."

"It did," Max insisted. "It's like someone tried to drown me in the shallow end and then let me go right before I died. I feel great. I feel rejuvenated. I feel fan-freaking-tastic. Can't you tell? I'm annoyed all the time and I want to stab myself in the face with a fork. Back to my old self."

Molly laughed, then gazed thoughtfully at Max. "And I'm sure your return to gloomy form has *nothing* to do with Jake tweeting something about abandonment issues and then—what was it?—'a good woman made me a broken man.'"

"No!" Max all but shouted. Then she flushed. *Way to sound defensive, moron.* "Maybe a little," she said. "Chaz Kelly just basically called me a life-ruiner, and someone put a note in my locker calling me a 'dog-faced mold bucket.'"

Molly winced. "Yikes," she said. "That has to suck."

Max tapped her finger against the table. Honestly, it surprised her that she didn't feel worse. She was embarrassed, and a little uncomfortable—like she had accidentally seen someone naked—and, judging by Macaronigate, perhaps a little testy. But she wasn't *upset.*

"It's my own fault," she said, reaching over to snatch one of Molly's french fries. "I deserve it. I totally ditched Jake on Saturday. I should not be allowed in polite society, because obviously I don't know how to function in it."

"You two really should talk," Molly said, watching Jake cross the cafeteria and shoot them a mournful look.

Max stole another fry and laid her head down on the wooden tabletop. "He tried," she muttered. "He called. But I've had...other stuff going on. *And* I'm using my patented avoidance-and-denial strategy, which has been very effective."

She grabbed one of the toothpicks in Molly's club sandwich, one with a crinkly blue toupee, and started stabbing fries with it one by one. "What am I supposed to say, anyway?" she added through a mouthful of potato. "I can't be all, 'Hey, whoops, sorry I ran off and never came back, but when you kissed me in public I almost punched a hole in the floor just so I could crawl through it, and so it turns out I might not like you!'"

"Would it make you feel better to hear that I saw Jake and Jen sniffing around each other again?" Molly asked. "They were whispering by the lockers."

"Any canoodling?"

"I'd say maybe a half canoodle."

Max frowned. "In a way, that makes it worse," she said.

"It's like I drove him back to that hosebeast. But can you imagine if he tried to make out with *me* at the lockers? I might've accidentally had to break his face. It would've been like those stories where a kid gets pinned under a tire and the mother finds the superstrength to lift the car."

"Well, I'm sure the rest of the school would have enjoyed that." Molly plucked the toothpicks out of her sandwich. "But you can't avoid him for the rest of your life."

"I don't have to," Max said. "I only have to avoid him until we graduate next spring. Don't underestimate my skills."

"Very healthy. I've noticed you're practicing your craft with Brooke, too."

Max pierced a fry with especial zeal. "I don't want to talk about Brooke."

"Yeah, I'm going to have to overrule you on that one," Molly said, picking a slice of tomato off her sandwich. "What went down between the two of you? Brooke won't tell me why she's writing the blog herself now."

"I wouldn't exactly call it 'writing.'"

Molly just raised a brow.

"Sorry," Max mumbled. "We just…weren't working very well together."

Max could tell Molly was unsatisfied with this answer. But Max wasn't ready to say anything else. She'd always championed taking the high road, because of how gratifying it was to know you'd won the moral war, and how delicious said satisfactory smugness could taste. (Almost as good as bacon. Delicious, forbidden bacon.) And yet there she'd sat at her computer that night, digitally stabbing Brooke in the back—over a boy, no less; it was so irritatingly *Gossip Girl*—and then getting huffy when Brooke called her on it. That weakness of character nibbled at her, to the point that Max hadn't cashed her last check. She didn't think she'd done much to earn it this time.

"I'm sure Brooke will tell you everything," she told Molly. "And her version will be way more entertaining. If she tells you I came at her with a machete, though, please know it's not true. It was just a butter knife."

"Actually, Brooke isn't saying much to anyone these days," Molly said. "I don't think she's sleeping very well. She just told me you were having artistic differences. I figured it must have had something to do with that crazy piece you wrote the other day." Molly set down her sandwich. "What *was* that, Max?"

In that instant, Max remembered that Brooke Berlin wasn't just some expendable teen actress. She was also Molly's sister. *Great. Now I've alienated my best friend on top of everything else.*

"I don't know what happened. I guess...I kind of lost it." Max flinched. "You think I'm an asshole, don't you?"

Molly just raised an eyebrow. "I definitely don't think you're an asshole," she said. "But beyond that I don't really know *what* to think. Neither one of you will tell me what actually happened. I have a lot of theories, though, and all of them involve Brady Swift."

Max covered her eyes with her hands. She was saved from having to answer when Teddy slammed his own cafeteria tray on the table and sat down with a thump.

"I hate everyone," he announced.

"Not you, too," Molly groaned.

"We lost the contest," he said. "Bone just got the call from MTV."

Max uncovered her face. Teddy looked seriously bummed. "I'm sorry, Teddy."

"Me, too," Molly said, reaching out to thread her fingers through his.

Teddy shrugged. "I'm not really surprised. Everyone hated my song."

"Not me," Molly said loyally. There was a pause.

"Ow!" Max winced, grabbing at her ankle where Molly had kicked it. "I mean, I liked it, too." Teddy gave her a glare that said, *Sure, real convincing.*

"I did!" Max protested. "I was just"—at that moment, she spied Jake and Jennifer walking across the quad, deep in conversation—"distracted," she finished lamely. "I am sorry, Ted. That bites."

"It's okay. The Internet doesn't lie. I was a flop," Teddy said. "I can live with that, but I feel bad for Bone and the guys. I demanded to perform my song, and that's why we ended up losing. Apparently, MTV is not interested in being in business with an emo angst bag."

"You are not an emo angst bag," Molly said.

"At *most* you are a very small sachet of torment," Max contributed.

"Clever. You should start a blog," Teddy said pointedly.

"Touché," she admitted. "But come on—you've never demanded anything in your life. Except that Christmas that I tried to steal your Transformers and you ordered me to lock myself in the closet."

"And look how well *that* turned out. You should still be in there."

"I'm just saying, don't beat yourself up."

"I'll drink to that," Molly said, swigging her Diet Coke.

"And *you* are both biased," Teddy responded. "The song was totally wrong for the venue. I don't know what I was thinking. Basically, I torpedoed this for the rest of the band, all because I was totally hung up on thinking people were watching Brick Berlin's Daughter's Boyfriend instead of all of us as a group. I feel like such a loser."

Molly sighed. "No, you just got sucked into the Berlin family celebrity drama. Sometimes it's exciting, but once people start mentioning your name in the same breath as Brick's, or even Brooke's, it's easy to lose perspective. Even if you don't think that kind of thing has any effect on you." She squeezed his hand. "Trust me, I should know. The other day I spent ten minutes picking out my shoes because I didn't want to get it wrong. You know, just in case."

"Been there," Max agreed. "Besides, you were just trying to stand out. I don't think there's anything wrong with wanting to get some attention for your own work instead of always doing what somebody else wants you to do. I mean, God, she's not the boss of your whole life."

Oops. Both Molly and Teddy shot her very knowing looks.

"Sounds like this hits a little close to home," Teddy said.

"I'm just saying that you're allowed to get sick of being a cog in someone else's machine. That's all," Max replied airily.

"Okay, but I didn't even care about winning the contest in the first place," Teddy said. "Why didn't I just play along? No pun intended."

"But it's not like you just sprung this song on them as a surprise," Molly pointed out. "They signed off on you playing it for the contest, right?"

"Yeah," Teddy admitted. "Bone said he liked it."

"So there you go," Max said. "You made the decision as a group and it didn't pay off. You shouldn't feel guilty about that."

Unlike me. I totally earned my guilty feelings.

"Have you talked to the rest of the band?" Molly asked.

"No," Teddy said, picking at his spaghetti.

"Well," Molly said, looking sideways at Max, "I think you might feel better if you did. Bottling up this sort of thing isn't very helpful."

"Can I just wallow for a little bit, please?" Teddy asked, sounding a little crabby.

"Wallowing is highly underrated," Max agreed.

Molly looked from brother to sister and blew her over-grown bangs out of her eyes. "Tough week for the McCormack family," was all she said.

"It's not like the Berlins are that much better off," Teddy said, twirling some pasta around his fork.

"What do you mean?" Molly asked, furrowing her brow.

Teddy set down his fork and looked up at her. "Wait, didn't you hear?" He wrestled his cell from the front pocket of his jeans. "This is probably the first time in the history of the world that I've found out about something before you have. But everyone in my senior seminar was talking about it."

Teddy handed over his phone. Molly and Max put their heads together and looked at his browser. It was set to a blindingly pink-and-purple Tumblr called BabblingBrooke .com.

Max ripped the phone out of Molly's hand. The site was clearly anti-Brooke, with the tagline "Stupid is the new black" and entries pretending to be written by Brooke that parodied the new OpenBrooke.com. The top entry said simply, "Chewing is neat!"

Molly rubbed her forehead. "Well, I guess it was only a matter of time before the joke blogs started," she said, almost to herself. "I just hope it doesn't stress Brooke out *more*. Last night she ate an entire bag of Cheetos during *Lust for Life*."

"Maybe she'll be flattered," Max said, adopting her best

Brooke imitation to add, "After all, you're *nobody* until you've been parodied."

Molly laughed in spite of herself. "Not bad, and also, probably correct."

Teddy ran a hand through his unruly dark hair. He shook his head. "Can we get a do-over on this week, do you think?"

Unthinkingly, Max pulled over the untouched half of Molly's club sandwich and picked out a piece of crispy bacon. She popped it into her mouth. "Tell me about it."

"Excuse me, did you just eat a *pork product?*" Teddy asked. He looked stunned, then broke into a smile. "Doesn't that mean you owe me twenty bucks from, like, forever ago? What's the interest on that?"

Max groaned. "I *really* hate everyone," she repeated.

twenty-two

THE REST OF THE DAY passed in a blur. One or two more parodies went up on BabblingBrooke.com. Max considered texting Brooke about it, but it was none of her business, and besides, Brooke would definitely prefer talking it through with Molly. Strange to think that the long-lost half sister who had incited so much insecurity nine months ago was now the most soothing presence in Brooke's life. Then again, nine months ago Max probably would've started that site herself, and now she was stressing about how it might hurt Brooke's feelings. No doubt about it: The universe was screwing with her.

After the final bell rang, Max trudged down the hallway toward Mr. Kemp's classroom. She was late for yet another Spring Carnival planning meeting and toyed with the idea of ditching again—especially since Jake and Jennifer would be there.

"...that would be amazing, Emily. If we were *farmers*," a voice floated out of the classroom. It was Brie. Max stopped and peered through the open door. Brie was perched on top of Mr. Kemp's desk, one patent Louboutin hanging from a manicured toe as she swung a very tan leg back and forth. "Anyone else have any ideas? Correction: Any ideas that aren't totally *useless?*"

"What if we did organ-shaped cotton candy?" Magnus asked, staring straight at Mavis Moore.

"Ooh, or cheesecakes on—" Jen began.

Brie held up a warning palm. "Raise your hand," she said. "Respect the process."

Oh, hell, no, Max thought from her spot in the hallway, and bolted swiftly toward the exit. She'd much rather risk her mother's wrath than suffer through an hour of Baby Brooke.

Just as she got to the huge double doors at the front of the school, Max heard footsteps on the marble floor behind her. It was Jake, his popped pink polo collar bouncing in step with his feet.

"Wait up, Max," he called. "We should talk."

Awesome. First I ruin his Saturday, then he ruins my avoidance plan.

"Okay," she said unenthusiastically. Jake pushed open the doors and led her to one of the stone benches near the front of the school. On the quad, two freshman boys were tossing around a Frisbee. Never before had Max wished she were part of a Frisbee game rather than doing what she was actually doing.

"So," Jake began as they sat.

"I'm sorry," Max blurted.

Jake just looked at her for a long moment. Max tensed up and winced slightly, anticipating some kind of verbal slap. Instead, he said, "How long have you been into that guy?"

She blew out her cheeks. "What?"

"Bo Brady, or whatever his name was."

Max was confused. "Wait, aren't you going to yell at me?"

"That depends," Jake said. "Were you just using me to make him jealous?"

"No," Max said, but she could hear the lack of conviction in her own voice. "Maybe? I'm not sure."

Jake stared into the middle distance, as if something inspiring was happening in the parking lot—which was true, if you counted the two sophomores loosening the lug nuts on Shelby Kendall's tires. Which Max did. So would Brooke. Max made a mental note to tell her, then revised it to read, *Tell Molly to tell Brooke.*

"Did you *ever* like me?" Jake finally asked.

His face was so melancholy that Max burst out laughing. "Jake, you have *no idea*," she said. He crossed his arms and slumped against the back of the bench, irritated. "I'm sorry, I'm sorry," she apologized again. "I'm not making fun of you. It's just that... Seriously, I had a crush on you for years. *Years*. And so *of course* the first time you notice me back, it turns out to be too late."

"*Is* it too late?" he asked sadly. "I really liked you. I still do. You make me laugh, and you never once waved your finger in my face. I thought things were going okay, you know?"

Max patted his hand awkwardly. "I really liked you, too, and I still do," she said. "Just as a friend, though, it turns out."

Jake looked disappointed. "I could tell," he said. "You seemed kind of tense with me, but when you were talking to Tom Brady, or whatever, you seemed so relaxed and kind of..." He searched for a word. "*Happy*."

"Yeah, well, he's not an issue. I just think our timing was off," she said. "Besides, he's an actor, and I'm...me. It's totally platonic. I might as well be one of his guy friends."

Jake snorted. "That's not what I saw."

"You saw wrong," Max said firmly, even as her heart did a quick cartwheel. "He's dating Brooke. They were making out. It's..." She gulped. "It's why I ran off. Jake, I promise, I didn't know he was that important to me until I saw her all over him. I didn't know what to do."

"If he's actually into Brooke instead of you, then he's an idiot, and you are way out of his league," Jake said passionately. "Not that Brooke isn't great and all, but dude, I'm a *dude*. And if even a dude like me can see that you two kinda had something, then he's stupid for not seeing it himself. Because it's totally how I wanted it to be with us."

Max swallowed hard. "No," she said. "No, you are not allowed to do this. You are not allowed to be super cool when I acted like an asshat. Don't you want to swear at me, or tell me I look like a Muppet, or..." She took a chance. "I don't know, force me to watch your spring scrimmage or something?"

Jake's mouth twitched. "I *could* give you a lecture on how to read blitzes," he said. "No offense, but your poker face sucks. I knew you were faking it about the pistol offense."

"My poker face does *not* suck," she said. "I'll have you know that when I worked at Fu'd, I once saw Jennifer pick up a napkin that had been used by that bearded kid from *American Idol* and put it in her purse, and I didn't even crack a smile."

Jake laughed with her, the familiar old twinkle briefly returning to his blue eyes, then turned quiet. "She wants to get back together," he said, leaning forward and hanging his head slightly so that his blond locks hid part of his face. Despite knowing she was over him, Max still kind of wanted to reach over and brush them away, just to know what it felt like.

"Old habits," she murmured.

"Maybe. Probably," Jake said, not realizing her inner monologue was on another topic. "I really wanted it to work out with you, but it didn't, and...I don't know what it is about Jen, but it feels like we always have unfinished business or something."

"More like an unfinished argument," Max said. "You guys are kinda the Elizabeth Taylor and Richard Burton of our high school."

"Are they on *Glee*?" Jake asked.

"They're…never mind." Max turned to face him and inhaled deeply. "It's tough love time, from your Get-a-Grip Friend, which I hope you will let me be for a long time," she said. "Jake, you have turned out to be one of the nicest people I've ever met. And you deserve way more than being squawked at every ten seconds by someone who is so insecure about her own life that she's trying to control everything about yours."

"She *does* kind of do that," Jake said, chewing his lip. "I never thought of it that way."

"It's way easier to see what's going on in other people's lives than it is to see what's happening in your own."

"Maybe you just don't *want* to see what's happening in your own life," Jake said with unexpected wisdom. "Because that's when things get complicated. Take you and that Roman Brady kid. You like him, I think he likes you, he's going out with Brooke, and you know you should fight for him."

"I can't do that to Brooke." *I've done enough to her already.*

"But it's what you want. And since when are you guys even friends?" Jake asked. "Seriously?"

"It's complicated," Max said with an apologetic smile. "But as far as Brady is concerned, if I have to talk someone into liking me, then what's the point? Right?"

Jake slung an arm around her and hugged her. Max let him. It felt way more real than any embrace on their date had.

"I *do* like us as friends," he said. "It feels nice."

Behind them, the school's doors banged open. "Jake!" Jennifer squawked, barreling toward them.

Max stood up, then leaned down to Jake and whispered, "Friend to friend, if you get back together with her, promise me you'll make some changes. You deserve better."

He smiled. "I will get a grip."

Jennifer came to a halt next to their bench with a mighty pout. "You are missing the entire meeting!" she brayed. "What are you doing out here with Oscar the Grouch? And if you're coming to the meeting just to sit around and glare, Max, you can save it. No one cares what you think."

Jake opened his mouth as if to say something, but Max beat him to it.

"Chill out, Jen. I would rather eat toham than go in there with you," she said. "In fact, here's a thought: How about any time you have the urge to speak to me at all, *you* save it? Because I've never cared what you think, and I don't plan to start. And if you keep treating Jake like crap, I will make sure my old coworkers at Fu'd put meat juice in your tofu burger."

As Max stormed off toward the parking lot, she felt more than heard Jen's outraged gasp. Peeking over her shoulder, she saw Jake stand up and put his hands on his hips. "Jen, you can't talk to me or anyone else like that," he boomed. "Max is my friend, and she—"

With a private grin, Max wrestled open her car door. The engine noise drowned out the rest of Jake's lecture to Jen, but Max rode the high of having said exactly what she wanted, *when* she wanted to say it, all the way to her house. Slinging sarcasm was one thing; actually giving Jen a piece of her mind was another, and that was long overdue. After feeling so unmoored the past few days, Max reveled in the sudden surge of confidence that shot through her veins.

Max pulled into the driveway and braked so hard that the gravel was still making crackling noises when she got out of the car. She dashed up to her room and threw her backpack onto the window seat, where it assaulted her hardback of *The Eyre Affair* and an old careworn copy of Judith Krantz's *Scruples* that she'd purloined from her mother's stash three years ago (clearly, Max's own camp-loving heart beat beneath Eileen McCormack's sensibly shod exterior). Digging under her bed, Max pulled out several of her old black-and-white speckled notebooks. There was a poem she'd written about crayons in second grade, and a poem she'd written *with* crayons the year before, the beginnings of stories about a talking pig, and one about a planet full of blob people. It was all hideously embarrassing, and also deeply, deeply *her*, from a time when Max hadn't cared about what anyone thought because being creative made her happy. She'd been writing for *fun*.

Suddenly, words crowded her brain like people cramming toward the stage at a concert. Max woke up her sleeping computer, opened a new Word document, and began typing as quickly as possible, as if she were worried she wouldn't ever get this feeling back—this sensation that she had something to say. Something about herself. Something real. And, finally, the writing came easily, pouring out of Max like water from a garden hose. She called it "Diary of a Fake Teenage It Girl," and she had a complete rough draft in barely twenty minutes. She was proofreading her (hopefully) stirring conclusion when her cell phone rang.

Max didn't even look at the caller ID. "What?" she barked, wedging the phone between her ear and her shoulder as she tweaked the ending. She probably shouldn't have answered. It might kill her mojo.

"Max McCormack?"

"Yeah?"

"This is Elena, Kyle's assistant, from *Nancy Drew*," the woman said. Max remembered her as a perky blonde in her early twenties, way less severe than her voice now sounded. Suddenly, Max felt like she really *shouldn't* have answered.

"How can I help you, Elena?" she asked with a sinking feeling.

"You're needed at the studio," Elena said. "Brick Berlin

has requested your presence personally. He said to tell you . . . wait, I wrote it down . . . 'Stress commits brain murder.' Huh, that seems . . . Well, whatever—the point is, he thinks Brooke needs you on set to keep her calm."

"But I'm not . . ." *Speaking to Brooke anymore*, her mind finished for her. ". . . currently employed by the Berlins," she said instead.

"That's immaterial to him right now," Elena said. "How soon can you leave? Now?"

It didn't sound much like a question.

After they hung up, Max gave her blessedly finished essay one more glance before hitting Print. It was still warm from the printer when she clipped it to the NYU application and stuck it into her backpack. She could drop it off at school on the way back from the studio—someone would be at the main office until at least seven.

And yet, even though things were looking up—her writer's block was *finally* smashed—Max still felt a bit queasy. Not because of her essay, or even because she'd been summoned to help repair a psyche that she might've helped break. No, she was uncomfortable because she knew going to set meant seeing Brooke. And Brady.

twenty-three

BROOKE RUBBED BLEARILY at her eyes and glanced at the clock on her trailer's microwave: 4:04 PM. She bolted upright in her chair. Could that be right? Two hours ago, when she'd been handed the pink pages that signified last-minute script adjustments, she'd only meant to rest her eyes for a minute before studying her lines for the rewritten scenes. Now her call time was in half an hour, and she still had to touch up her hair and makeup. By Brooke's estimation, this gave her ten minutes to learn everything.

She felt a sticky wetness on her cheek. Apparently she had dozed off with her face resting on the table on top of the script, and then drooled on it. A visit to her bathroom mirror revealed a pinkish stain stubbornly clinging to her skin. Brooke rubbed it, to no avail, then scrubbed and scrubbed until her face turned red but the dye was gone. She rechecked the clock. Great. *Five* minutes to learn everything.

Brooke smacked her cheeks and shook her head, willing her brain to work. She tried to focus on Brady, and the kiss so epic that it made one of the inside pages of *OK!* magazine, but the warmth she'd felt in her extremities that night had faded over time. Now she just felt uneasy around him. Brooke had thought he was considering asking her out again after their date, but once Max quit, Brooke had found herself spread so thin that they'd barely spoken—and when they did, Brady always seemed sort of concerned, even confused. Brooke suspected this was because of her blog.

That stupid, stupid blog.

It had been a rough week. Her fight with Max last Wednesday had left Brooke feeling prickly yet optimistic. The blog was already in full swing, so she'd figured keeping it up would be easy: Max had found it simple enough to pose as Brooke Berlin; surely Brooke would have an edge due to actually *being* Brooke Berlin. But panic had set in when she wrapped shooting at exactly midnight— God bless child labor laws—and slumped through her bedroom door, dying for sleep but feeling obligated to post something before she crashed. She'd spent the next three hours pacing in front of her picture window, chewing on Twizzlers she'd stashed under her mattress, and watching infomercials (the one where Jennifer Parker posed as a Yoga Booty Ballet pupil was running on the CBS affiliate at 2:30 AM; delirious by that point, Brooke decided sitting through it made her a better friend). In the end she'd banged out something she wasn't even sure made sense, hit Publish, and passed out on top of her comforter.

This kicked off a chain reaction of late nights, flubbed lines, inability to focus on her work *or* her blog, paranoia, stress-induced insomnia, and finally outright exhaustion. After yet another bout of writer's block—it turned out Brooke had slipped into Max's shoes as easily as Max had slipped into hers—Brooke determined, with the help of WebMD, that she was probably about to start losing her hair, and also that she most likely had leukemia. This meant that not only were her looks *and* her career threatened, but she might kick it before she could star in her own Lifetime movie. Even Brick had noticed something was awry; last night he'd come up to her room and asked very seriously if she needed her Chaka Khans realigned, which led to a very strange ten minutes in which Brooke snacked on the vegan flaxseed brownie he'd brought her (a recipe he'd found on GOOP) while Brick called his meditation specialist and clarified that, in fact, Chaka Khan was fine, and it was Brooke's *chakras* that were in doubt.

And now there was that stupid Tumblr, cracking on her best efforts—well, okay, they weren't her best efforts, but they were *efforts*—and implying she was a fraud.

(Which was only even *partly* true.) Molly had sent her five text messages about it, trying to be cool but clearly panicked that the site would send Brooke into some kind of fugue state. Brooke appreciated her worry, but the truth was, she was too numb to feel much of anything. She was too tired. So tired.

At 4:13 PM, Brooke heaved herself out of her seat, grabbed the new pages, and shuffled out of her trailer with a monstrous yawn. She'd study while the makeup people fixed her sleep-creased face.

"Brooke!" squealed Carla Callahan the second Brooke hit daylight. Brooke squinted against the May sun and regained her sight just as Carla hugged the crook of her arm. "That Tumblr blogger is a wicked chowderhead."

"You're nobody until you've been parodied," Brooke chirped, giving Carla as blasé a wave as she could before disentangling herself and speeding ahead toward hair and makeup. But all of Brooke's internal organs seemed to be trading places, her stomach down in her toes and her liver somewhere up in her throat. Theoretically, the Tumblr was just another silly site poking fun at a famous person. Today, however, after the horrors of what she knew were some truly terrible performances on her part this week, it was the last straw. Anyone with third-grade reading comprehension knew the Open Brooke entries from three weeks ago were superior to the new ones; so far, probably because of her obvious stress, nobody had mentioned it. Now that dumb blog might give them an excuse to start.

And then what? Could she get away with claiming she'd simply cracked her head on the floor underneath Nancy's garbage-bag bed?

Snap out of it. You are Brick Berlin's daughter, and you have wiggled your way out of way worse messes than this one. This was just some random jealous jerkface ragging on a star, and the best way to stick it to him or her was to get her act together and nail it on set that afternoon. Her Oscar wasn't going to win itself. Brooke's mind drifted to one of her favorite fantasies, where she was giving a stirring acceptance speech while her husband, Channing Tatum, wept lovingly in the front row of the Kodak Theatre.

But first she had to make it through her scenes. Gazing down at her pages, which were littered with lines totally foreign to her, Brooke prayed her luck hadn't just run out.

✦ ✦ ✦

Max waited until the red light went off over the door to Stage 32, signifying that the cameras were no longer rolling. Then she tapped on the door and whispered a greeting at Mario, the security guard who answered it. He waved her through into the dark space, putting a finger to his lips and pointing to the set.

Rough day, he mouthed.

Max tiptoed toward the action. Brooke and Brady, plus

a couple of secondary actors and about twelve extras, were standing in a makeshift police station. Tad, the director, was crouched down next to Brooke, intently instructing her on something while she picked at a button on her costume, a simple khaki Old Navy dress and crimson cardigan (this job had to be Brooke's first time wearing anything that cost less than sixty dollars). Brady was next to her, tugging uncomfortably at the collar of his dress shirt. The cameramen were giving one another concerned glances, and a hush had fallen despite the fact that no filming was happening. Max spied Brick looking tense, tapping his right foot on the ground, tearing into an orange like it was the skin of his worst enemy and dropping the peels onto an already-sizable hill of them beneath him on the craft services table. How apt that Brick would be the world's first person to cope with stress by bingeing on *fruit*.

Clearly, something was going down. And Brooke was at the center of it.

Tad headed back to his chair and hoisted himself into it. "Okay everyone let's do it right everyone find your marks okay action!" he shouted in his typical punctuation-free way.

"What do *you* know?" rasped the actor playing the cop. "You're just a kid. A kid with no home address."

"Homeless people aren't stupid," Brooke said, trying to make her lip tremble. It looked like a facial tic.

"Cut cut stop everyone cut!" Tad shouted in a mad rush.

"Brooke once again the line is 'Homeless people aren't less because they have no home' so let's focus and get it right and take a deep breath and slow down."

Director, heal thyself, Max thought.

"Right, right," Brooke said, rubbing her forehead.

"And try putting your hands on the desk remember you're really letting him have it and this time let's nail it okay thanks," Tad boomed.

"Right," Brooke echoed. "Got it. Yeah."

"Okay action!"

The cop repeated his line. Brooke woodenly planted her hands on the table and said, "Homeless people are less. *Dammit*."

"Cuuuut!" Tad wailed. He put his head in his hands. "God okay reset go again."

Carla Callahan was over near a wardrobe rack readjusting one of George's cockeyed baseball caps in the mirror. Max swallowed her loathing—and a remaining stubborn sprinkling of guilt—and inched over to Carla's side.

"What's going on?" Max whispered.

"Brooke's a right mess," Carla said, savoring each word like a 3 Musketeers bar. "All's I know is, she's flubbing lines, standing in people's light, blocking camera angles... totally tanking."

Carla was barely concealing her amusement. Max felt sick knowing that her old self, from not too long ago, would've rubbed her hands together just like Carla and settled in to watch this catastrophe unfold with the same morbid glee people deploy while watching the MTV Movie Awards. Max abruptly walked away.

"Action!" Tad yelled.

"Homeless people aren't homeless," Brooke said. Then she buried her face in her hands. "Cut," she moaned.

Max craned her head to the left and saw Zander and Kyle whispering furiously in a corner. Tad shook his head at them, and they glanced at each other and hastily adjourned toward a cubbyhole along one of the side walls, which they used as their makeshift headquarters when they didn't feel like walking back to the production office. Or whenever something was urgent.

This is not good.

They pulled the door closed, but it popped open a crack and hung there, a tantalizing invitation to eavesdrop. Max stole along the side of the set, mentally congratulating herself for being too lazy to dye her hair green again, because the brown was so much easier for skulking. She perched on a stray sofa next to the production office, pretending to rummage in her bag for something, and trained her ears on the sound of their voices.

"This blows, man," Zander said. "What is wrong with her?"

"I don't know what her g.d. problem is, but I'm f'ing majorly rethinking being in the Brooke Berlin business," Kyle said. "She hasn't remembered a g.d. line all day."

Zander let out a grunt. "What the hell happened? We are screwed if she doesn't pull this together."

"I think Tad is going to kill her," Kyle added. "He just motherf'ing told her where to stand and she's f'ing acting like she doesn't speak English."

Max didn't dare breathe. She summoned her strongest poker face, but it wouldn't come. This was *really* not good.

"So do we pull the trigger?" Zander asked.

"Well, half the reason we hired her was because of that g.d. blog, and all of a sudden, it's f'ing awful, just like her acting yesterday. Her latest entries are, like, a hellstorm of suck."

"Booting her would be expensive."

"A month of f'ing pricey reshoots is better than a lousy f'ing movie. Tad said it was the worst motherf'ing week of his life. Let's just jump ship and buy another ship before we sink this ship." He paused. "That was a shizzy f'ing metaphor."

"Ky, *shizzy* is the dumbest version of *shitty* that I have ever heard. Snap the rubber band."

"No! I didn't f'ing swear!" Kyle protested.

As they argued, Max crept away from her perch and spun behind a set wall, letting out the breath she'd been holding.

Holy crap. Brooke was about to get fired.

Remind me again why you care? She's a jerkwad who's made the last few weeks of your life a major pain.

But this wasn't run-of-the-mill high school melodrama; this was someone's career. Obviously, Max's stupidly ornate entry about social media, which had seemed so hilarious at the time, was as much a catalyst for Brooke's downturn as anything else. So the part of Max that had known Brooke's financial generosity might enable Max to change the trajectory of her *own* life—the same part that had come to like (or at least not hate) Brooke Berlin—could not sit by and watch her go down in flames.

Not to mention, Brooke wasn't technically a jerkwad at all. Max had spent eons believing that people like Brooke were rich with cash but bankrupt when it came to humanity. But now she knew that Brooke had insecurities and feelings that were unexpectedly similar to her own. They both just wanted to be recognized as something *more*. More than what people saw in them at first glance. More than what they were right now.

I can't let them fire her. But how do I stop them? It's not like I can just pop out of the shadows and warn Brooke. She's standing in front of fifty other people, getting reamed out for not learning her lines.

Zander and Kyle came out of their room. They headed straight for Brick.

Come on. Think fast.

Defying her first instinct, Max popped out of the shadows.

"Max!" Brady grabbed her arm and pulled her aside. "Where have you been? I haven't seen you in forever."

"Hey! Um, this is a *really* bad time...."

315

Zander and Kyle were talking quietly to Brick, as Zander tugged uncomfortably at his snug Coachella music festival T-shirt.

"I need to talk to you," Brady insisted. "Brooke is acting really strange. She's running hot and cold, and she's totally whiffing her lines all of a sudden, and it's like the awesome blogger part of her just evaporated."

"Great, Skippy," Max said absently, as Brick—looking uncharacteristically downtrodden—beckoned to Brooke. If Max was going to do anything to stop the impending firing, she had to act fast.

"It's so different, and *she's* so different, and…look, Max, I need to ask—"

"I so wish I could help you, Brady, but seriously, this is *so* not a good time," she said. Then she grabbed his arms. "Listen, do you like her blog, or do you like *her*? If it's the latter, then the rest of it shouldn't matter."

With that, Max bodily moved him aside and marched up to the producers, who were in the act of escorting Brooke off the set.

"No, wait, don't—you can't be mad at Brooke," Max blurted. "You just can't."

"Not now, Max," Brick said sadly.

"But you need to hear this. Brooke is a mess because of me—it's all my fault." Max took a deep breath. "Brooke didn't write those entries. I did."

twenty-four

ON TELEVISION, big, revealing statements always elicit loud gasps, and then a lot of background whispering with hands clapped to open mouths, while the truth-teller stands by looking refreshingly liberated. But TV is a dirty, dirty liar. Because there were no dramatic sound effects for Max's confession, no slow clap, nor a handy background-music swell to let everyone know she'd just done something courageous. There was just silence. And then, fury.

"Wha-aaaaaaaaaat?" Brick boomed. "Explain this outrageous tomfoolery!"

"I think you'd better tell us exactly what the goddamn shit you're talking about," Kyle said. *Snap-snap* went his wristband.

"When this happened on *Dirk Venom 3*, we did

interrogation through yoga," Brick boomed. "It was crane pose that broke the bastard. But I think all this will take is one downward dog."

Max knew this meant he was truly angry. Insulting someone's physical fitness was the nuclear option as far as Brick Berlin was concerned—his version of throwing a drink in her face. Max tried not to flinch. Everyone looked so very, very mad at her right now. Maybe she could move somewhere chill like Seattle and become a roadie for Pearl Jam's AARP tour or something. Surely they needed able-bodied youths at this point in their lives and would at least spring for coffee.

But then her eyes fell on Brooke, who was simply staring at the floor, wan and dazed. Max shook off her nerves and stood her ground. She'd come this far. *Finish it.*

"I'm just trying to tell you…I know you're, um, concerned about the quality of Brooke's blog and how distracted she is, and so I'm telling you it's my fault, that's all," Max began. "I wrote the last couple entries of Brooke's blog. The, um…" *How to say this delicately?* "…strange ones."

"Ruthless trickery!" Brick bellowed. "Impersonating Brooke online for fun and profit! Making a mockery of her sensitive brain! I do pilates with Anderson Cooper, and he will not let this stand!"

"This is some major goddamn fucking bullshit," Kyle roared, plucking his rubber band with abandon.

"I *knew* she was bonkers," Carla piped up.

"Get me the lawyers!" Zander said, pushing his hipster glasses up his nose so vigorously that Max was worried he might end up with a bruise. "All of them. Any of them. Right now!"

"Also! I'm beginning to think there *is* no Maxschtagen cheese!" Brick hollered.

Max felt Brady's eyes on her but refused to look at him, focusing instead on how hollow Brooke looked—Max wondered briefly if she'd fallen asleep with her eyes open, but then she started rubbing vacantly at a spot on her cheek—and how disgusted everyone sounded. This was a whopper of a lie she was telling, but at this point, what was one more? It was for a good cause.

"I didn't do it for malicious reasons," Max insisted. "Brooke has been really stressed, with her schoolwork and wanting to do well on this movie *and* her blog. It was too much. So I told her I'd take care of the blog so she could concentrate on her part. And I wrote a few entries, but she didn't get to see them until... recently... and then she was so upset with me that I think she stopped sleeping."

"Oh," Zander said. Then he looked at Kyle. "*Oh!*"

"I did think that lately the blog was missing Brooke's usual joie de vivre," Brick said thoughtfully, tapping his index finger against the cleft in his chin. "But I assumed she was just iron-deficient."

"So," Zander said brightly, "what you're saying is, she *didn't* turn stupid?"

Behind him, Max saw Brooke flinch. She recovered in

time to present a calm face to Kyle, who actually did a dorky little dance before throwing his arms in the air. "Man, Brooke, you had us fucking scared," he said. *Snap.* "Those posts were so *bad.*"

Brick turned to Max. "Young lady, I have not seen such wanton commotion since Jamba Juice had a two-for-one sale on wheatgrass," he said sternly. "Do you have anything to say for yourself?"

With nearly everyone's eyes on her, from the camera guys to the makeup girls to the security officers, who may have been about to carry her out in handcuffs—everyone, in fact, but Brooke, who was again looking at her feet—Max had never wanted to disappear more than she did at that moment. What *did* she have to say for herself?

"I'm...sorry?" she ventured. "I didn't mean for this to get so out of hand. I just wanted to help."

At least that was true.

"I was trying to be a friend," she added, looking at Brooke.

Also true, to Max's everlasting surprise.

Brooke slowly lifted her head and looked at Max, expressionless. Max felt a strange, silent conversation unfold between them. Her actions stood as her apology, and Brooke's eyes held a mixture of bewilderment, gratitude, and...was that regret?

Brick broke the bond by enfolding Brooke in a beefy hug. The set sprang to life around them, everyone talking and gossiping about what had just happened, what to do, what it all meant. It was the period at the end of whatever silent sentence she and Brooke had been trying to write. That was it. Their tenuous association, whatever might have come of it, was broken. *Nancy Drew* would move on without Max, but not without its star, and that was as it should be.

Max couldn't help feeling a pang of sadness. She hated endings. Maybe that was why she always made a mess of beginnings—both in her writing and in her life. If you start something, its destiny is to conclude. If you start nothing, *feel* nothing, you're free. Max's tear ducts constricted inconveniently. She turned away from the set... and banged straight into Brady. He looked down at her with a cryptic expression. Max knew he'd have questions. He probably wanted to ask why she ever believed her idiocy could pass as Brooke's intellectual sparkle.

I can't take this. Not from him. Not now.

"Max—"

And I will not let him see me cry.

"I can't." She shook her head. "I've said enough today. And I don't need to hear how disgusted you are with me. Please, Brady, just leave me alone."

Max's feet handled the rest, which was good, because knowing she likely wouldn't see him again after all this drama made it awfully hard to tear herself away.

And Brady let her go. Of course. In the romantic comedy of her life, Brady would ignore the obvious lie she'd just told him and chase after her, or she'd turn around and he'd be staring at her back, unwilling to let her go so easily. Of course, in the romantic comedy of her life, she would also have thick, curly locks and three more inches to her height, and Brady wouldn't have been macking on Brooke.

Max stopped by the door and pretended to look for something in her bag. She stole a peek. Brady had vanished. *I told him to leave me alone. What did I expect?* But her heart sank anyway, and a tear squeaked out of her left eye.

See? she told herself. *Beginnings aren't worth it.*

Her hand closed on her printed NYU essay, clipped to her application. Max pulled it out and gave one last glance up to the set. Everyone had swarmed Brooke like worker bees to their monarch, with Max just a faint memory, an unpleasant speed bump on the road to the festival circuit. A tear slipped down Max's cheek, and then another. They left ugly splashes on the printed pages in her hand. What had she been thinking? She couldn't turn the essay in, certainly not now. So much for being herself. Abruptly Max crumpled up the application, dropped it in the trash, and left, swatting at her streaming eyes with the sleeve of her hoodie.

✦   ✦   ✦

Brooke wriggled so that her nose was no longer buried in her father's armpit. She was trying to piece together what had just happened, and if she wasn't mistaken, it went like this: She had been stinking up the joint on set, and then Max appeared out of nowhere and said exactly the right thing to get everyone to stop giving Brooke a hard time and start trying to cuddle her into mental wellness. Ergo, just as Brooke was about to be hoisted on her own petard, Max had thrown herself onto it.

She felt a swell of joy. Max had saved her. It was the perfect white lie—nobody got hurt.

Except for Max.

This all reminded Brooke very keenly of what had gone down last fall, when Brooke's inadvertent betrayal of Molly had been revealed right before the curtain went up on the opening night of *My Fair Lady*. Brooke had a visceral memory of being paralyzed by deciding between running after her sister to set things right or going onstage and claiming Brick's long-sought undivided attention. A timely shove from Jennifer Parker had made the choice for her, but Brooke had kept on making it, over and over, with every subsequent entrance and exit. She'd picked fame over family, and when it was all said and done, she had felt rotten about it. She couldn't make that mistake again. Could she?

She's not Molly, her inner voice argued. *It's not the same thing.*

Shifting until she found a small pocket of air to use as a window, Brooke saw Max running away from a distraught-looking Brady. Something else was nagging at her. Where had Max come from, and why? What had she known? It felt like a giant piece of this puzzle was still missing, which was only okay on *Lust for Life*, where that piece was Pip's now *un*recapitated head.

"Well I don't know about you guys but I feel about a thousand times better," said Tad, popping two Red Bull cans in one hand. "After this week I was starting to think maybe y'all were drunk when you cast this one."

"We were all wondering what the f' we were thinking," Kyle agreed. "Okay, so, we have an f'load to do here. Tad, figure out when we can redo those scenes Brooke totally f'ing blew the other day. Elena can jigger the schedule so Brooke gets a little time to rest up, take a break from the blog, get some sleep. F'ing rejuvenate, girl."

"Have Elena cancel the casting session, too," Zander added. "Man, this is going to be so much cheaper than redoing everything with a different girl."

"Right?" Kyle crowed. "Thank f'ing god!"

Rewind. A different girl?

Brooke looked up and searched Brick's face. But she couldn't find any trace of anything except...well, there it was: relief.

"Daddy," she whispered, "were they going to fire me?"

Brick looked down at her fondly. "It is a moot point, Sunshine. The truth is out there now. Let's cheat on our diets and get some ice cream on the way home."

Brooke slowly pulled away from her father. Not even

illicit dairy could distract her. "Just like that? They weren't even going to talk to me about it?"

"Well, Sunshine…" Brick looked uncomfortable.

Suddenly Brooke wanted to cry so badly, it felt like her whole face was going to implode. She gazed around at the set and saw people celebrating, essentially, that she was not secretly a worthless waste of space. People who, somehow, thought her blog represented the sum of who she was, which—unbeknownst to them—meant that they actually thought the real Brooke Berlin truly *was* worthless. And that felt rotten. It was not okay for them to think it about her, and it was doubly not okay to sit back and let them think it about Max.

"If I could interrupt your revelry for a second," Brooke said coldly. "This won't take long."

Kyle paused in the midst of high-fiving one of the gaffers. Zander put down his iPad, and Tad almost spat out the mouthful of energy drink he'd been chugging.

"Brookie, I don't think—" Brick began.

"Don't worry, Daddy, I know what I'm doing," she said, steeling herself as much as she could so that her voice didn't tremble. "It's just that I'm watching you all basically celebrate that I was simply burned out, and not a total dumbass, and I'd like to address a couple points about that."

"Oh, um, okay," Kyle said, caught off guard. "Sure."

"Point one is that you apparently were never going to sit

down with me and *ask* what was wrong," Brooke said, tossing back her hair in what she hoped was a supremely confident gesture. "Frankly, it is inhumane to just fire your lead actress without talking to her about what might be going on in her life. You're supposed to have my back, but instead you were going to sweep me under the rug and pretend I never happened. I am disgusted."

That felt good—even better when she saw Zander's eyes bug out so hard they nearly popped the lenses out of his thick-framed glasses. Everyone was hooked on her every word. It was glorious. So glorious. Like *My Fair Lady* all over again, except no pressure to fake an accent.

"Point two is that you are placing an insane amount of importance on this blog," she continued, starting to pace as she warmed up to her speech. "If I'm not mistaken, you hired me to act, not write. If you wanted a glorified typist to play Nancy, you could've hired someone from a temp pool for a lot cheaper."

"This is seriously ballsy," Kyle said under his breath.

Brooke inhaled deeply and surveyed the room. As she processed the group's rapt, shocked faces, she realized anew that she didn't want to be associated with any of these people if they thought Brooke Berlin, the *real* Brooke Berlin, was so freaking inferior.

"Point three, pursuant to point two, is that you're assuming that if I can't write a blog, I can't act," she concluded. "And yet, I've been acting since before the blog existed, I auditioned for you when it *barely* existed, and I've been awesome for most of this shoot and, in fact, my whole life. All despite the fact that I never wrote a word of that blog myself."

Everyone gasped like they were in a courtroom scene on *Lust for Life*. Max would've loved it, a fact that made Brooke miss her a little bit. But she didn't dwell on it, because her audience was still hungry. And Brooke knew exactly what to feed them.

"That's right," she said triumphantly. "Max didn't write the recent entries. She wrote the *other* ones—the ones you were drooling over, the ones you said made me seem so *unexpectedly* smart." She poured a little extra venom into her voice for that one, and it worked. Everyone, including Brick, winced. Brooke felt more in her element than she had in weeks.

Now, a little humble pie...

"Max was using her talents to be an incredible friend. Then she took a bullet for me today, and I owe her for that. But I couldn't let her leave you thinking she's less than she is. It's not right." Brooke dropped her gaze to the floor. "When Max and I had a falling out, the blog was one ball too many for me to juggle, and in the end I dropped them all."

Brick's expression was one of pride. *Of course. Because that sounded just like him.*

Zander leaned against a desk, ostensibly wobbly at the knees. Tad was doing that dumb director thing where he held up his hands to frame her face. Carla Callahan, that suck-up, looked gobsmacked. Suddenly, Brooke wondered why she hadn't done this sooner. It felt really good to be honest, finally—mostly about Max, after she'd watched Max lie for her like that, but also because for the first time in a while Brooke had this room in the palm of her hand. And there was nothing she loved more than an audience.

"I admit, it was a deception, and I'm sorry for that. But the popularity of the lie took over my life," Brooke said softly, sensing it was time to take things down a notch. She allowed her eyes to moisten. "You all were so shocked that someone like me could have something worthwhile to say. It made me feel like the real Brooke Berlin had nothing to offer. That I was...expendable. And apparently, I was."

She let out a calculatedly shaky breath and wiped the deliciously punctual tear that trickled out of her eye. "But one thing I am *not* is worthless," Brooke insisted, strengthening her tone. "And I only struggled when I tried to become someone else, to please masters who, as it turned out, never had faith in me to begin with."

One of the makeup ladies let out a sob. Brooke took a moment to bless the gods of genetics for giving her Brick's penchant for melodrama, and for having a best friend like Arugula who handed out multisyllabic words like breath mints.

"If you want to fire me, that's your prerogative," she finished. "But you cast me because I can act, not because I can blog. Some of us are lyrical on paper, and others, like me, deal in the power of emotive speech. And your pro-prose bias punishes those of us who still believe that the ability to move others by baring our feelings without hiding behind a computer is our most powerful tool as a people. If you judge me for being more gifted at that than I am at typing, then I am not your Nancy Drew, and I never was."

Brooke realized she had, unconsciously, moved to the center of the room and was all but raising her fist aloft, as if calling her comrades to arms. If she'd had the national anthem on her iPhone, she'd have cued it up right then and there.

Instead, silence.

"Well, I feel like an f'ing f'head," Kyle eventually said.

"That was better than half of what's in the script," Tad mused. "*That* is my Nancy."

"Stirring!" Brick clapped. "A tour de force!"

"You got me, Brooke," Zander said apologetically. "I don't like being lied to, but, yeah. We could have handled this better. And you're right. You were our pick, and you earned it in your audition, not on the Internet." He ran a hand through his hair, which fluffed it out to John Mayer levels. "We're gonna get you those days off, and then we'll all come back in here and shoot this week's stuff over again. Fresh start."

He hopped off the desk and walked over to Brooke to extend his hand. Brooke took a second to collect herself— her roiling emotions, most of them jubilant, were somewhat

at war with the ones she had just unleashed on the room—
and then shook it firmly.

"I will not let you down," she said.

Brick let out a shout of glee and hugged her and Zander,
bemusing the latter so thoroughly that his glasses actually
dropped to the ground.

"Oh, and, uh, Brooke," Zander said through Brick's
biceps. "Listen, you don't have to, but if you want to have
Max...I mean, she could keep...if you want."

Brooke was tempted. Continuing as they had begun,
with the rest of the world none the wiser, seemed like the
easiest Band-Aid. But then she thought of the toll the situation had taken on Max, and of all the people on that set
who knew the truth. Lies were like zits: They always
exploded eventually, and concealer never worked.

"No," Brooke said. "Fresh start, right? If I keep blogging,
it'll be me doing me. But better. No pressure to copy the
way it used to be."

Zander nodded. "Fair enough," he said. "God, I really
need a latte right now. With a shot of whiskey in it."

Brick clapped him on the back. "I'm buying," he said.
But first, he turned to Brooke and placed his hands on her
shoulders. "Sunshine, I'm proud of you for being honest.
You didn't have to be, but you did the right thing. And
that, to me, says more about your heart and soul and mind
than any blog ever could."

Brick stretched and slung an arm around Zander's bony

shoulders. "Zander, buddy, we need to talk about your deltoids," he said. "Have you ever used a climbing wall?"

As Brick launched into a sales pitch for his Berlin Wall idea to a nonplussed Zander, Brooke sat down in one of the cold metal chairs on the police-station set. The crew killed the lights and everyone dispersed, some stopping to squeeze Brooke's arm supportively, others merely whispering to one another about the brouhaha. Brooke tried to stay cheerful, but she shivered. Maybe people hadn't liked that entry, but it was accurate. It was always freezing once the spotlights went off—a metaphor if Brooke had ever heard one. She'd have to remember that one for her blog. Her new, *real* blog.

A lean shadow fell across her feet. Brooke knew who it was without looking.

"Hi, Brady," she said.

"Hi," he said, dropping into the chair opposite her. "So, that happened."

"It did," Brooke said, forcing herself to make eye contact with him. "And so did a lot of other stuff, which I guess we should talk about."

"Probably," he said. "Come on, let's bust out of here and get some In-N-Out. We've earned it today, and also, I just found out I can order my fries animal-style, which blew my mind. You in?"

Brooke let out a happy sigh. "Yes, *please*," she said, taking his outstretched hand as he helped her out of her seat. His was warm, which, weirdly, made her shiver again.

"It's going to be okay, Brooke," he said, interpreting her tremor as jitters.

Looking into his kind eyes, which were refreshingly devoid of judgment or disappointment, Brooke felt hope rise up in her chest like a balloon. Maybe none of this mattered to him. Maybe Brady had seen enough of the real Brooke that he didn't care how much of the other stuff was true. Maybe her fresh start could be with *everyone*.

twenty-five

THE MORNING DAWNED unbearably stuffy in Max's room, which had not contained fresh air since she'd stormed home from the studio Wednesday night.

"Eileen, I told you, I used the immersion blender to fix the sprinklers!" her dad boomed somewhere in the vicinity of the kitchen.

Max cracked an eye.

"I thought that was the SaladShooter!" her mother replied, exasperated.

Max's open eye rolled.

"No, that went toward trying to make a new immersion blender," her father said, sounding as though he were trying to explain math to a fifth grader.

What day is it, even? Max wondered. It felt like two

weeks had passed, but her phone said it was the first Saturday of May, so it had really only been three days since she'd bolted from the set of *Nancy Drew*. She'd driven home that night feeling more upset than she could really explain, even to herself. At the studio, the decision not to apply to NYU had felt right: Max was sick of caring about things that were obviously beyond her reach. But in the car that night she'd been unable to convince her tear ducts of that.

Luckily, no one had been home when she arrived. So Max took her red, splotchy face to bed, and then begged off school the next day, claiming cramps and a demi-migraine. Her mother had just eyeballed her for a moment and then nodded, which is how Max knew she must have looked as miserable as she felt.

And then she had mostly just...lain there and tried not to think about anything. One day stretched into two, and now into this morning. She slept occasionally, she stared at the wall, she stared at a different wall, she counted cracks in the ceiling. She was beginning to understand how people became shut-ins. It was so much easier than dealing with other people, and all their *feelings* and *reactions*. Molly had called her five times, and Teddy twice (even though he lived upstairs). Even Brooke phoned, and Jake texted, but Max ignored them all. She didn't feel up to talking to anyone. She barely felt like talking to herself.

There was a knock at the door. "Are you alive?" Teddy called.

"Debatable," Max muttered.

"Can I come in?"

Max ignored him. Teddy pushed her door open with his guitar case and stuck a concerned head into the room. He sniffed the air.

"Debatable is right," he said. "It smells like a corpse in here."

"I don't recall inviting you in," Max said, trying to pull the sheet over her face. But it got stuck around her stomach.

"So," Teddy said, sitting on the corner of her bed and untwisting the sheet. Max promptly burrowed underneath it. "What's going on?"

"Nothing," Max said, the bedding muffling her voice.

"Liar. I heard what happened on the set."

"What happened on the set?"

Teddy pulled down the corner of the sheet covering her eyes. "That was really solid of you to do that for Brooke. Most people would've let her fry."

"Where'd you hear this?" Max asked, trying to sound disinterested.

"I guess you've been watching your wallpaper curl for so long you forgot that I have an in at the Berlin household."

"Oh, right," Max said. "Well, hooray. A happy ending."

"Except for you, apparently."

"I don't want to talk about it."

"I gathered that. This is taking antisocial to new levels, even for you."

"What do you want, Teddy?"

He looked thoughtful for a moment, then shook his head as if trying to knock an impulse out of it. "Should we carpool to the carnival?" he asked instead.

"Can't you tell everyone I have Brain Fever and can't come?"

"Sure," Teddy said, "but I don't think Mom's tolerance of your fake illness will extend much further." He nodded at the floor, where Max noticed for the first time that he'd laid down his guitar case. "And you'll miss the big Mental Hygienist show."

"At the carnival? Since when?"

"We're a last-minute addition," Teddy explained. "While you were off at the studio throwing yourself on a sword for Brooke Berlin, Bone was on the phone with this rep from Chop Shop."

"Chop Shop *Records*?"

Teddy grinned. "That's the one," he said. "I guess he was at the House of Blues concert and he loved Bone's stuff. They want to sign us."

"Shut up!" Max said, sitting up so fast to punch him in the shoulder that her head spun. She lay back down again.

Teddy nodded. "Crazy, right? Brie said we had to play a set at the carnival to celebrate." He frowned. "Actually, I think she said that having a band with a record deal on the bill would improve the carnival's Q rating. But anyway. There you have it."

"And how do you feel about this?" Max asked. "Weren't you going to quit the band or something?"

"I was embarrassed," he admitted. "And I figured they'd want me out after everyone hated my stuff. But Molly kinda made me sack up and go talk to them, and it turned out no one was mad at me about it."

"I told you!" Max crowed.

"No, you didn't," Teddy said. "You sat next to Molly while she told me that."

"Same thing. I'm moral-support-*adjacent*."

"Of course," Teddy said. "Anyway, Bone said that there isn't a group in the world that hasn't had something like this happen, and he thinks we can all make each other better." He blew out his cheeks. "I never thought a person named Bone—much less *this* person named Bone—would be the voice of reason."

"So you're sticking with it?"

"For now," Teddy said, leaning over to retie the shoelace on his left Converse. "I mean, graduation is in six weeks. And then I start UCLA in the fall, and who knows what will happen then. But for now, why not see where it takes me? I obviously have a lot to learn about songwriting."

Max leaned back against her headboard. "Ew. That's so mature."

"Just returning the favor," he said. "I recall you giving me some pretty sage advice, too."

"Definitely a fluke," Max said. "I think when it comes right down to it, I am actually really stupid."

"Okay, drama queen. Either spill it or get over it and rejoin the world," Teddy said. "Or would you prefer if I had Mom come up and carry you downstairs?"

"So we should probably leave soon if we're going to make the carnival in time, right?" Max responded brightly.

"I knew you'd see reason," Teddy said. "I'll meet you downstairs. If you don't shower first, you're going to asphyxiate everyone before we even get onstage."

✦ ✦ ✦

The carnival took place every year off-campus at the historic Rose Bowl stadium, nestled in the mountains in Pasadena. Underneath the stadium's famous red cursive logo hung the biggest and most garish banner Max had ever seen, which read in part COLBY-RANDALL PREPARATORY SCHOOL SPRING CARNIVAL and noted that the proceeds were going to a women's shelter in downtown Los Angeles. Under that—in substantially larger script—it screamed, BROUGHT TO YOU BY DIET COKE, BAKED TOSTITOS, AND OUR GRACIOUS COMMITTEE CHAIR, BROOKE BERLIN.

I am never going to escape that girl.

Max and Brooke had parted on decent terms, or so it seemed from their silent exchange before Max fled the set, but in the car on the way over, Max realized what she dreaded most was what came next. How were they supposed to act now? It was like breaking up with someone and then trying to stay friends: It never truly worked, and tended to involve minimal contact and awkward sentence fragments. This was a compelling reason Max preferred to avoid these kinds of entanglements. Aftermaths were not her thing. But Max was thankful she'd have more time to figure it out—Brooke would be away filming for at least another month, and by then...well, by then, instead of being at NYU, Max would probably be very busy taking drive-thru orders at McDonald's.

"Maxine! Theodore!" screeched a blonde banshee from just to the left of the stadium entrance.

Wait, Brooke is here? Max panicked.

But as they drew closer to the registration table, Max saw that this was Brie, her hair an even blonder and fuller mass of curls than before, and her skin at least two shades tanner. She waved Teddy through but motioned for Max to stop at the table.

"Thanks for joining us, Maxine," she said, rummaging around in a cardboard box on the ground. "One never can tell with you. Aha!"

Brie withdrew a large Hefty bag from the box and handed it to Max. Confused, Max gave it an exploratory poke—it was awfully squashy—and looked quizzically at Brie.

"Your costume," Brie prompted her.

"My *what*?"

"You were missing in action—again—when everyone signed up for a booth," Brie said sunnily. "So we had to assign you to something."

Max set the bag on the ground and opened it. A pile of brightly colored velvets peered back at her. On top sat a gold lamé turban, topped with an emerald-green ostrich feather.

"The fortune-telling booth?" she gasped. "You are not serious."

"These are the consequences of shirking your extracurricular commitments," Brie said. Then she waved her hand in the air dismissively, a very Brooke-like gesture. "It'll be entertaining. Think of all the downer fortunes you can make up for people."

Max opened her mouth to point out that it was probably well on its way to being a hundred degrees out, and that she would likely die of heat prostration under her turban. But then she thought better of it. The prospect of an afternoon telling some schmo from her chemistry class that the Spirits claimed he was going to set his pants on fire next Tuesday fit her mood perfectly.

"Fine," she said. "Where is my tent?"

They set off, past the fame-themed first attraction—a step-and-repeat emblazoned with their sponsor logos (and Brooke's signature, in pink) behind a stretch of bubble-gum-colored carpet, where a couple of students dressed as paparazzi were setting up cameras—and then deep into the heart of the stadium. In spite of the planning committee's endless discussions, it looked exactly like every other carnival Max had ever seen: a Ferris wheel, a Skee-Ball station, some game where you could knock over pictures of all the teachers with water guns (a touch Max rather appreciated, since shooting her mother was worth the most points), cotton-candy and caramel-corn stands, several games involving balls, and a rickety teacups ride that actually had buckets marked FOR VOMIT lined up near the exit. There was a carnival jail—Anna Fury had obviously won that argument; it was five bucks per arrest, and either an hour of captivity or another five bucks for bail—followed by a bunch of stalls where local merchants and some of Max's classmates were selling crafts and jewelry. Between that area and the giant stage, where Mental Hygienist would be playing, sat a tiny purple-draped tent with a sign reading MADAME ESMERELDA: WHERE A FORTUNE WON'T COST ONE. The jar outside indicated the fee for entrance was a buck.

Max walked inside. The "walls" had been clumsily adorned with glow-in-the-dark stars and swirls and other allegedly mystical nonsense. There was a red velvet–covered table, and two ancient folding chairs that promised to numb her butt within about fifteen minutes. Max dumped out her robes with an aggrieved sigh.

"I want it on the record that I am only consenting to this because Bucky wore a turban at his wedding to Klaus on *Lust for Life*," she said. Then she noticed her irritation had been wasted on Brie, who was gazing into space, cradling the prop crystal ball and tapping her toe.

"Why so antsy?" Max asked, pulling on the robes. They weighed approximately a thousand pounds. This boded ill for the turban. How did Bucky do it?

Brie flushed. "I'm fine." She cleared her throat. "Um, what time is Brooke coming today?"

Max shivered involuntarily. "You'd know better than I would."

"I haven't talked to her much lately," Brie said, twirling a blonde curl around her finger in an agitated way.

Max studied Brie curiously. The girl did look more and more like Brooke every time Max saw her, right down to the clothes: Somehow, Brie had hooked herself a Pucci mini and sparkly Manolos. Her teeth were unnaturally white, and she also had a necklace with a script *B* around her neck that reminded Max of the logo that hung off Brooke's doorknob. They were one meat hook away from a horror movie that ended very badly for Brooke.

"Madame Esmerelda senses that you're nervous about running into Brooke," Max said, plopping the turban on her head and waggling her finger to try to lighten the mood.

"It was just really fun to step into her shoes," Brie confessed, tapping the crystal ball with her flawless greige manicure (also a Brooke Berlin favorite). "And so I kind of...*really* stepped into her shoes. All of a sudden I'm taking yoga with Ari."

"Madame Esmerelda sees why you might worry," Max said. "You have sort of turned into Brooke's clone."

Brie smoothed her hair. "I just feel more in *charge* this way. But Brooke does *not* like people horning in on her territory."

"Tell me about it." Max snorted.

Brie checked her watch. "Okay, the doors are opening right now," she said. "I should go check on everyone else."

She pulled open the velvet curtain and came face-to-face with Brooke, whose folksy outfit for the day made her look like the world's most impossibly chic country bumpkin (apparently in her mind, carnivals were the chief export of America's farmlands).

"Oh...my God," Brie squeaked.

"Good, Anna told me you'd be here," Brooke said. She glanced around the room, her eyes flickering over Max briefly, dismissively.

So that's how it's going to be. I should have known.

"Is everything...okay?" Brie asked. She began gnawing on a hangnail that Max knew she didn't actually have.

Brooke looked Brie up and down, then walked around her slowly, in an appraising circle.

"Brie," she began, "when I put you in charge of the carnival, this is the last thing I expected."

"I'm sorry," Brie said, her shoulders slumping with disappointment.

"Why? I am seriously *so impressed* with you right now."

"Really?" Brie squeaked.

"You have shown initiative *and* excellence in personal grooming," Brooke said. "I have to say, after a year of you never even so much as bookmarking Shopbop.com, I had assumed this day would never come."

"I just wanted to make you proud," Brie said hopefully.

"You are everything I had hoped for when I plucked you from freshman obscurity," Brooke said proudly. "I mean, there are some rough spots—I would never have worn those shoes with that skirt—but we are making such progress. It's reassuring to know that I have a mini-me who can represent my interests at school while I am busy with my craft on set."

Brie was as red as the cloth under Max's crystal ball. Max stifled a yawn. She was happy for the kid, but *Single White Female* was way more entertaining on a Saturday morning than what was effectively an episode of *A Makeover Story*.

"How's it looking out there?" Brie asked, more confidently. She threw open the curtain again. The grounds of the Rose Bowl were already packed, and Mental Hygienist was doing its sound check on the main stage. Mavis Moore was manning the cotton-candy stand across the way, having artfully shaped all her sugary swirls to look like animals. Magnus Mitchell had been roped into selling his mother's wooden bracelets nearby, but he kept gazing at Mavis and her edible zoo as if she were Brett Favre. A huge group of chattering students swarmed the area, obscuring the rest of their view.

"It's a hit and it only just started," Brooke said. "I am a genius."

"Oh, yes, well, whenever I was stumped, I just thought, *What would Brooke Berlin do?*" Brie trilled, delighted.

Brooke nodded sagely. "Exactly," she said. "In fact, you're officially in charge of my birthday-party planning this year. It's less than two weeks away, so it's a huge responsibility. I'm not sure how you're going to get the elephants on such short notice."

"*Details,*" Brie said, waving her hand. "I know someone at the zoo."

"Of course you do." Brooke beamed. "Now, I'm looking for Max. Have you seen her?"

Brie looked puzzled. "Well, yeah." She jerked a thumb in Max's direction.

Brooke peered at Max intently. "Well, well," she said, thoughtfully. "Nice turban. It's very directional." She turned to Brie. "Could you give us a moment, please?"

Brie fought through the heavy curtains to get outside. As soon as she disappeared, Max yanked off the robes. "I draw the line at caftans," she muttered.

"Right? Maxi dresses are bad enough. Nicole Richie needs to stop giving people bad ideas," Brooke said, sliding into the seat opposite Max. "So, fortune-teller, what do you see in my future?"

"Fame and fortune," Max replied flatly.

"Duh. And what do you see in yours?"

"Why are we doing this?"

"Well, for one thing, because you didn't answer any of my calls," Brooke said, leaning back in her chair. "I need to return some of your stuff."

She reached into her Victoria Beckham tote and fished out a handful of paper, which she dropped on the table next to the crystal ball. It was Max's discarded NYU application. There was a coffee stain on the left corner, and it smelled faintly of bananas.

"It's good, Max," Brooke said. "It's really good."

"You *read* it?"

"Don't act so shocked. It's not like I snuck into your bedroom and read your diary," Brooke said, offended. "You practically threw it in my face."

"It was in the garbage."

"At my *workplace*," Brooke said pointedly. "And you're welcome for me rescuing it. I especially liked the part where you basically compared me dating Brady to Heidi Montag becoming a neurosurgeon."

Max willed her turban to drop over her face again. It complied. "Artistic license," she mumbled.

Brooke plucked the turban off Max's head. "I laughed," she said. "Seriously. You are even better at writing as yourself than you are at writing as me."

"Thank you," Max said, fixating on one cloudy spot on the crystal ball.

Brooke stabbed at Max's NYU application with a red-painted nail. "I can't believe you're not turning this in. That's a winning application if I ever saw one. And," she said, brandishing a long rectangle of paper, "Brick wrote you a letter of recommendation that I don't think the selection committee can ignore."

Max unfolded the letter. The first line read, *This totally anonymous writer is nothing less than a preeminent Amer-*

ican hero of our century. Turns out Brick loved hyperbole as much as he loved protein powder.

Brooke smiled. "He's really impressed with what you did for me. So am I, Max."

Max wanted to crawl under the table. She never knew how to take compliments. Mostly because she rarely got them. "I couldn't let you get fired," she said to the crystal ball. "You wouldn't have even been in that position if I hadn't written that ridiculous entry about social media."

"And you wouldn't have written that entry if I hadn't swooped in on Brady."

"That's my fault, too," Max pointed out.

Brooke shrugged. "It's hard to be truthful about matters of the heart," she said. "I learned that during the *Lust for Life* episode where Veronica goes mute after falling in love with Hedge von Henson while they're trapped in the mine shaft."

"Yes. This is very much like that."

"Don't be sarcastic," Brooke scolded. "I'm trying to have a heart-to-heart here." She cleared her throat and the imperious tone disappeared. "I liked how it felt when people acted like I was smart. I mean, I *am* smart, but not in the same way you are, and I liked the way the blog made people treat me. Like the producers, and Daddy, and... and Brady." Her voice cracked. "No boy ever made me feel brainy before. Hot, yes, but not brainy. So I kind of got carried away, and I'm...sorry about that. I thought you liked him even when you denied it, but it was easier for me to decide you were telling the truth because...well."

"It's okay. It's my bad." Max tapped the turban. "Madame Esmerelda can't expect *everyone* to be psychic."

"The thing is, a huge part of what he liked about me wasn't really me. It was you," Brooke said. "Your writing did that. So it's super lame of you to give up on NYU."

"Look, it's fine. It doesn't really matter anymore anyway," Max said. "The application deadline is Monday. I'll never write something new between now and then."

Brooke crinkled up her nose. "And why would you do something dumb like that? I just told you, this is good," she said. "And everyone knows the truth now, so what's the problem?"

"Wait, *what*?"

"The truth about the blog. I told it. After you left," Brooke said impatiently. "Didn't Teddy tell you?"

"No!" Max gasped, wanting simultaneously to hug Brooke and throttle her brother. "He must've wanted to make me hear it from you."

"Well. That was bossy of him," Brooke said. "Well played, Teddy."

Max straightened up in her chair. "But everything was going to be fine! Why did you do that? You'll get annihilated on the Internet!"

"Well, we're going to say that the whole blog thing was illustrative of the undue pressure the Internet puts on Young Hollywood to be one hundred percent accessible to the world," Brooke said, as if reciting a press release (which she probably was). She scratched at a sticky spot on the velvet tablecloth. "But the real answer is, because you made yourself look totally crazy to help me out, and you didn't have to. I don't think I would have done that for me, if I were you."

Max snorted. "Apparently, all that green hair dye didn't blitz my conscience like I had hoped."

"Well, I think I got a taste of how you felt all this time," Brooke said. "Everyone was screaming about how *happy* they were that Brooke Berlin really did have a brain, and I just thought, *I do have one, and it's perfectly fine the way it is.* It must have sucked having everyone treat you like you weren't important when actually everything they liked came from you. So I couldn't let everyone think you were a nutball." She paused. "Well, not for *those* reasons, anyway."

"Thanks?"

"So I reamed them in this seriously inspired speech," Brooke said dreamily.

Max chuckled. "I can't believe I missed it. I hope someone was taping it for YouTube."

"Maybe Carla Callahan was," Brooke said mischievously. "They found out she was writing that pathetic parody blog, and Zander was *not* happy."

Max straightened. "Did she get fired?"

Brooke's lip twitched. "George is going to die in the latest rewrite, and then they're going to leak that they killed

349

her off for performance reasons. Kyle said that would be more satisfying. But he used different words. There was a rubber-band snap involved."

The girls exchanged smiles. Max reached out her hand.

"Thanks, Brooke," she said. "For...well, all of it, really. It was good for me." She gulped. "When I went back to *not* having something to care about, I kind of missed it."

Brooke shook her hand. "So would you say I changed your life?"

"Yes," Max deadpanned. "Because of you, I once wore boots with an actual heel."

"Excellent!" Brooke chirped. "I wonder if I can fit 'life-changing spiritual force' onto my résumé." She turned to leave.

"Brooke," Max blurted. "Congratulations. I'm glad you got everything you wanted."

Brooke paused and smiled. "Well, not everything," she said. "But I'm working on it." She clapped her hands. "Okay, get to your customers," she said. "It won't do to keep people from their futures."

Max lightly touched the application on the table. It *wouldn't* do, and for the first time in a long time, there wasn't anything keeping her from her own.

twenty-six

AFTER FOUR HOURS manning the fortune-telling booth, Max was almost tempted to write *Lust for Life* an angry letter: Bucky made wearing a turban look hilarious and fun, but on Max, the stupid thing would not stay put, and it was so heavy that it was giving her a head- *and* neck ache. She ended up pulling it off and sitting on it to give her chair some much-needed extra padding.

Turban woes aside, after Brooke's visit, Max felt light. She was touched that Brooke had told the truth, especially knowing what that could have cost her. (Although, being Brooke, she seemed to have emerged unscathed *again*. The girl was Teflon.) Max's ensuing good mood allowed her to sit back and make the best of her afternoon, which actually ended up being pretty fun. People seemed to enjoy her dramatic made-up fortunes—like Anna Fury, who seemed weirdly pleased when Max predicted she'd become a pro on *Dancing with the Stars* and get paired with one of the Winklevoss twins, and the girl in her English class who was delighted to hear that Jennifer Parker was doubtless going to burn off her lips in a tragic hair-straightening accident. Max would rather eat toham than tell her mother this, but...maybe Eileen McCormack had been right. Doing high school stuff wasn't *always* a drag.

"Knock knock, Madame Kermit-relda," said Chaz Kelly, heaving open the curtains as if he had heard Max's last thought and was determined to make her regret it. Chaz was dressed in a too-tight police uniform, with an avalanche of doughnut crumbs down his front that suggested he felt *very* strongly about realism. He hooked his thumbs through his belt loops and wriggled his hips in their polyester sheath.

"You're not a strip-o-gram, are you?" Max asked warily.

"You wish, bro," Chaz said, grinning and smacking his belly. Max actually laughed. "No, Kermit, dude, you are officially under arrest."

"Cute," Max said. "But I have customers."

"The laws of the carnival cannot be ignored, and I have here a warrant," Chaz intoned.

"You have got to be kidding me."

"You're being cited for...wait, let me see here...'unlawful disrespect of the mighty turban,'" Chaz said, waving at the crushed lump of satin on Max's empty chair. "And your penance is wearing it in jail."

"You're mental. And how did—"

"I have informants," Chaz intoned. "Come with me, please, dude."

He snatched the turban and forcibly plopped it onto Max's head as she wracked her brain for who could have done this and, therefore, whom she would be shunning for the foreseeable future. There seemed to be only one person who would delight in teasing her this much.

"I am going to kill my brother," Max fumed.

Chaz frowned. "Why would you do that? Dude's a nice guy, even if he is an emo angst bag."

Chaz grabbed her arm and dragged her from the tent. They looked like members of a Village People cover band as conjured by the court of King Arthur.

Chaz deposited her inside a rectangular area about the size of three parking spots, marked off by wooden posts joined by just enough chicken wire to prevent climbing. "Soon you will face your accuser," Chaz droned as he padlocked the door. "*Sayonara*, scumsucker!" Then he winked. "Nothing personal, Kermit," he whispered. "I'm totally not mad about that macaroni thing. It turned out to be really delicious."

Max wrinkled her nose and looked around at the makeshift prison. It was full of freshman boys who had been imprisoned by their female classmates as part of some asinine mating ritual, a couple of humorless-looking mothers (including, Max could swear, Jennifer Parker's) who may have had it coming, and one very drunk Magnus Mitchell, who was leering at one very quiet Mavis Moore.

"What are you in for?" Max asked.

"Magnus had me arrested for public displays of hotness," Mavis said. "Then he had himself thrown in here for public drunkenness so he could ask me about my intestine."

"I love that thing," Magnus slurred, gazing adoringly at Mavis. "I want to wrap myself in it. So *cozy*."

Max blinked. "I don't understand today," she said, reaching her hands up to remove her turban.

"I wouldn't do that if I were you," said a familiar male voice. "It specifically says in your citation that you have to keep it on."

Max whirled around and looked right into a pair of warm gray eyes. *No, that's not right. He doesn't go here*, her mind said stupidly.

"Keep…the turban?" her voice said, equally stupidly. Her entire vocabulary seemed to have abandoned her, along with, it felt like, most of her internal organs. *Maybe Mavis could knit me a couple*. But Mavis was too busy patting Magnus's head as he rested it in her lap and sang a very sloppy and lyrically suspect version of "Dancing Queen."

I cannot believe Brady Swift is watching me sweat buckets in a turban.

"I'm just kidding. You can take it off, if you want," Brady said. His grin was wide.

"What are you . . . okay, I *really* don't understand today."

His smile got wider. "Brooke totally called it. She said you'd be confused."

"Wait, Brooke *knew* you were having me arrested?" Max shook her head, as if trying to eject the cobwebs. "Can't you guys go on a date that doesn't involve me?"

"You think I'm so lame that my idea of a date involves chicken wire?" Brady said, feigning offense. "I'm not here with Brooke. I want to talk to you, but I heard a rumor you aren't answering your phone. So, drastic measures." He made a sweeping arm gesture at the prison.

Okay, it's beyond not understanding—today is officially speaking freaking Swahili. Max fleetingly wished her costume included a mask, so she could process this without also trying to maintain a calm facial expression.

Brady dropped his hand and fiddled with the top button on his shirt. "Shoot. I'm better when I memorize lines. But let's start with, why didn't you just tell me you were writing Brooke's blog?"

Max looked down at the grass. "I'm sorry I lied. But it wasn't only my truth to tell."

"You are the Knitting Queen, young and sweet, only seventeen," Magnus crooned.

Mavis nodded thoughtfully. "True," she said.

"I kind of can't believe I didn't figure it out myself," Brady mused, ignoring them. "I was having the hardest time reconciling Brooke in person with the girl who was so funny and smart on her blog. I mean, not that Brooke

355

isn't funny or smart, but...well, you know her. It was like..." Brady chuckled ruefully. "I was about to say, 'two different people.'"

"Because she was," Max finished for him. "I guess we both were."

"I really *liked* the girl who was writing that blog," he continued. "And I really liked you—the real you, the one I hung out with in person. I wish I'd known it was the same girl."

"See that giiiirl, watch that *spleen*, dig it, the Knitting Queen," Magnus continued, dissolving into a cackle.

Brady cocked a skeptical brow. "This is not as romantic as Brooke suggested."

"Romantic?" Max's airway felt constricted.

"Yeah, the jail part was actually Brooke's idea," Brady said. "So was making you wear the turban. She seemed to think it would feel more soapy. Something about someone named Bucky." He shoved his glasses back into place. "But now that we're standing here separated by chicken wire, I can't remember why I listened to her."

"Wait, she thought it would make *what* feel more soapy?" Max asked, not caring anymore if she sounded dense.

Brady wrapped his fingers around the wire. "Me asking for a second chance," he said. "Or a first chance. Whichever."

Max felt faint. "Madame Esmerelda thinks she needs to take five," she said, yanking off the turban. "I can't have this conversation dressed as Merlin's mother."

"But you *do* want to have this conversation."

Max could barely look at him. "I do."

"Okay, good," Brady said, exhaling with relief. "I was afraid I'd have to arrest you more than once. I would have felt like a dumbass having that cop chase you all day."

"Well. You *are* kind of a dumbass," Max said.

Brady looked surprised, then chagrined. "That's fair. I kind of am. But come on, you were dating Mr. High School Jock, and he was all over you, and..."

Max heard the jealousy in his voice and let out a bleat of laughter. "Oh, that is so over," she said. "It never even really began."

"Oh, good," he said, looking relieved. "I didn't want to have to fight him for you. That guy is ripped."

Max took a deep breath. "I don't know, though, Brady," she said ruefully. "This seems a little nuts to me. Like, if I'm so great, why were you after Brooke in the first place? I mean, I know she's Brooke, so she's, like, a goddess, and I'm just sort of a runt, but—"

"No way," Brady interrupted. "You're just as beautiful as Brooke is. Although I miss the green hair, so I hope that's negotiable."

Max felt light-headed. She didn't think it was the heat this time.

He rested his head against the wire and gazed at her. "You have to understand, it just didn't occur to me not to take the blog at face value. I was attracted to the point of view. Actually, I was attracted to *you,* but you seemed more into being friends, and then Brooke fell into my lap...kind of literally, actually, at times," he said, laughing. Then he cleared his throat. "I do wish I had asked a few more questions, but by the time things really stopped adding up, you were gone."

"Avoidance is my trademark," Max mumbled.

"Well, hopefully dating girls who are in prison isn't mine," he quipped, tapping the fence. "Can we maybe start over? If there's anything I've learned from being an actor, it's that the second take is generally superior to the first."

Max tilted her head and stared at him until he blushed a bit. She nodded. "Okay. Take two."

"Excellent," he said, visibly relieved, and shoved his hand through a hole someone had torn in the wire earlier in the day. "Hi. I'm...Taylor," he said. "Taylor Swift."

"It's a loooove stooooory, baby, won't you say yeeeeeees," sang Magnus, who was now somehow wearing Max's turban.

Max let out a genuine laugh. Suddenly, she felt freer than she had in her whole life. Even if she was standing in a prison.

"Pleased to meet you, Taylor," she said, beaming, shaking his hand and letting her grip linger. "I'm Maxine."

Suddenly, something caught her eye in the distance, over Brady's shoulder. It was a watchful Brooke, beaming out from under the brim of an enormous pink cowboy hat. In that moment Max understood what Brooke had meant by *I'm working on it*. Max had never even asked what happened between her and Brady. She'd just assumed any guy worth his Y chromosome would choose Brooke. But she'd never bothered to wonder what any girl worth her X chromosome would do.

As she looked back and forth from Brady to Brooke, Max silently thanked the universe for shaking her out of the tiny, cynical confines of her paisley-papered bedroom and into a world where she did more than just snark from the sidelines—one where, somehow, impossibly, magically, she got a boy *and* a Brooke. Not just a Brooke, but... God, it sounded so damn sappy, Max wanted to smack herself for even thinking it: a *friend*. Max had spent a lot of time around movie sets in the last month, but she never thought the drama in her own life would have this kind of happy ending. It couldn't have worked out better if she'd written it herself.

Although, technically, maybe she had.

Acknowledgments

WE BARELY CAUGHT OUR BREATH from *Spoiled* before we dove into *Messy*, and we owe so many people eternal gratitude for keeping us sane (and on deadline). As always, our family and friends gave us peerless support, especially Alan and Kathleen Cocks; Kevin, Dylan, and Liam Mock; Alison, Mike, Leah, Lauren, and Maddie Hamilton; Julie, Colin, and Nicholas O'Sullivan; Maria Huezo; Jim and Susan Morgan; and Elizabeth Morgan. We'd be remiss if we didn't thank our delightful agent, Scott Hoffman; publicist Lindsley Lowell; and lawyer Ed Labowitz; and, of course, our wonderful, encouraging, and wise editors, Elizabeth Bewley and Cindy Eagan, who always know how to save us from ourselves. Additional thanks to the Poppy team, including Pam Gruber, Sara Zick, Ames O'Neill, Mara Lander, and the genius Liz Casal, whose cover designs gave our babies a face so pretty it puts Brooke Berlin's to shame. Extra heartfelt gratitude goes to Jen Pray for her bean-wrangling skills; Gretchen McNeil, for knowing how to get us off a variety of emotional ledges; to Joe Zee and Megan McCafferty, whose early love for *Spoiled* renewed our energy to write *Messy*; and to J. K. Rowling, whom we have never met, but who came like fiction's guardian angel to remind kids and adults alike that reading is not just cool, but rewarding. Finally, a huge Intern George–sized hug to Fug Nation, the most intelligent, generous, loyal, and supportive readers a website could ever have. Without you, we'd just be two girls who type a lot.

WELCOME to THE HAMPTONS,
where beautiful people come to play.

When Rory McShane left her rural home in New Jersey to go work for the wealthy Rule family in the Hamptons of New York, she could never have prepared herself for what was to come—a summer of friendship, secrets, and wild romance.